Classics

JOHN COOPER.

Cover illustration by
John Cooper

IVANHOE

SIR WALTER SCOTT

Published by Priory Books, Bridlington.
A Peter Haddock Limited imprint.
© B. W. (Leicester) Limited.

CHAPTER 1

IN THAT pleasant district of merry England which is watered by the river Don, there extended in ancient times a large forest, covering the greater part of the beautiful hills and valleys which lie between Sheffield and the pleasant town of Doncaster. The remains of this extensive wood are still to be seen at the noble seats of Wentworth, of Warncliffe Park, and around Rotherham. Here haunted of yore the fabulous Dragon of Wantley; here were fought many of the most desperate battles during the Civil Wars of the Roses; and here also flourished in ancient times those bands of gallant outlaws, whose deeds have been rendered so popular in English song.

Such being our chief scene, the date of our story refers to a period towards the end of the reign of Richard I., when his return from his long captivity had become an event rather wished than hoped for by his despairing subjects, who were in the meantime subjected to every species of subordinate oppression. The nobles, whose power had become exorbitant during the reign of Stephen, and whom the prudence of Henry the Second had scarce reduced to some degree of subjection to the crown, had now resumed their ancient license in its utmost extent; despising the feeble interference of the English Council of State, fortifying their castles, increasing the number of their dependants, reducing all around them to a state of vassalage, and striving by every means in their power to place themselves each at the head of such forces as might enable him to make a figure in the national convulsions which appeared to be impending.

The situation of the inferior gentry, or Franklins, as they were called, who, by the law and spirit of the English constitution, were entitled to hold themselves independent of feudal tyranny, became now unusually precarious. If, as was most generally the case, they placed themselves under the protection of any of the petty kings in their vicinity, accepted of feudal offices in his household, or bound themselves by mutual treaties of alliance and protection to support him in his enterprises, they might indeed purchase temporary repose; but it must be with the sacrifice of that independence which was so dear to every English bosom, and at the certain hazard of being involved as a party in whatever rash expedition the ambition of their protector might lead him to undertake. On the other hand, such and so multiplied were the means of vexation and oppression possessed by the great Barons, that they never wanted the pretext, and seldom the will, to harass and pursue, even to the very edge of destruction, any of their less powerful neighbours who attempted to separate themselves from their authority, and to trust for their protection, during the dangers of the times, to their own inoffensive conduct, and to the laws of the land.

A circumstance which greatly tended to enhance the tyranny of the nobility, and the sufferings of the inferior classes, arose from the consequences of the Conquest by Duke William of Normandy. Four generations had not sufficed to blend the hostile blood of the Normans and Anglo-Saxons, or to unite, by common language and mutual interests, two hostile races, one of which still felt the elation of triumph, while the other groaned under all the consequences of defeat. The power had been completely placed in the hands of the Norman nobility, by the extent of the battle of Hastings; and it had been used, as our histories assure us, with no moderate hand. The whole race of Saxon princes and nobles had been extirpated or disinherited, with few or no exceptions; nor were the numbers great who possessed land in the country of their fathers, even as proprietors of the second, or of yet inferior classes. All the monarchs of the Norman race had shown the most marked predilection for their Norman subjects; the laws of the chase, and many others equally unknown to the milder and more free spirit of the Saxon constitution, had been fixed upon the necks of the subjugated inhabitants, to add weight, as it were, to the feudal chains with which they were loaded. At court, and in the castles of the great nobles, where the pomp and state of a court was emulated, Norman-French was the only language employed; in courts of law, the pleadings and judgments were delivered in the same tongue. In short, French was the language of honour, of chivalry, and even of justice; while the far more manly and expressive Anglo-Saxon was abandoned to the use of rustics and hinds, who knew no other. Still, however, the necessary intercourse between the lords of the soil, and those oppressed inferior beings by whom that soil was cultivated, occasioned the gradual formation of a dialect, compounded betwixt the French and the Anglo-Saxon, in which they could render themselves mutually intelligible to each other; and from this necessity arose by degrees the structure of our present English language, in which the speech of the victors and the vanquished have been so happily blended together, and which has since been so richly improved by importations from the classical languages, and from those spoken by the southern nations of Europe.

The sun was setting upon one of the rich grassy glades of that forest which we have mentioned in the beginning of the chapter. Hundreds of broad-headed, short-stemmed, wide-branched oaks, which had witnessed perhaps the stately march of the Roman soldiery, flung their gnarled arms over a thick carpet of the most delicious green sward. A considerable open space, in the midst of this glade, seemed formerly to have been dedicated to the rites of Druidical superstition; for, on the summit of a hillock, so regular as to seem artificial, there still remained part of a circle of rough unhewn stones of large dimensions. Seven stood upright; the rest had been dislodged from their places, probably by the zeal of some convert to Christianity, and lay, some prostrate near their former site, and others on the side of the hill. One large stone only had found its way to the bottom, and in stopping the course of a small brook, which glided smoothly round the foot of the eminence, gave, by its opposition, a feeble voice of murmur to the placid and elsewhere silent streamlet.

The human figures which completed this landscape were in number two, partaking, in their dress and appearance, of that wild and rustic character which belonged to the woodlands of the West-Riding of Yorkshire at that early period. The eldest of these men had a stern, savage, and wild aspect. His garment was of the simplest form imaginable, being a close jacket with sleeves, composed of the tanned skin of some animal, on which the hair had been originally left, but which had been worn off in so many places that it would have been difficult to distinguish, from the patches that remained, to what creature the fur had belonged. This primeval vestment reached from the throat to the knees, and served at once all the usual purposes of body-clothing. Sandals, bound with thongs made of boar's hide, protected the feet; and a roll of thin leather was twined artificially round the legs, and, ascending above the calf, left the knees bare, like those of a Scottish Highlander. To make the jacket sit yet more close to the body, it was gathered at the middle by a broad leathern belt secured by a brass buckle; to one side of which was attached a sort of scrip, and to the other a ram's horn, accoutred with a mouthpiece for the purpose of blowing. In the same belt was struck one of those long, broad, sharp-pointed, and two-edged knives, with a buck's-horn handle, which were fabricated in the neighbourhood, and bore even at this early period the name of a Sheffield whittle. The man had no covering upon his head, which was only defended by his own thick hair, matted and twisted together, and scorched by the influence of the sun into a rusty dark-red colour, forming a contrast with the overgrown beard upon his cheeks, which was rather of a yellow or amber hue. One part of his dress only remains, but it is too remarkable to be suppressed: it was a brass ring, resembling a dog's collar, but without any opening, and soldered fast round his neck, so loose as to form no impediment to his breathing, yet so tight as to be incapable of being removed, excepting by the use of the file. On this singular gorget was engraved, in Saxon characters, an inscription of the following purport: —"Gurth, the son of Beowulph, is the born thrall of Cedric of Rotherwood."

Beside the swineherd, for such was Gurth's occupation, was seated, upon one of the fallen Druidical monuments, a person about ten years younger in appearance, and whose dress, though resembling his companion's in form, was of better materials, and of a more fantastic description. His jacket had been stained of a bright purple hue, upon which there had been some attempt to paint grotesque ornaments in different colours. To the jacket he added a short cloak, which scarcely reached half-way down his thigh. It was of crimson cloth, though a good deal soiled, lined with bright yellow; and as he could transfer it from one shoulder to the other, or at his pleasure draw it all around him, its width, contrasted with its want of longitude, formed a fantastic piece of drapery. He had thin silver bracelets upon his arms, and on his neck a collar of the same metal, bearing the inscription, "Wamba, the son of Witless, is the thrall of Cedric of Rotherwood." This personage had the same sort of sandals with his companion; but instead of the roll of leather thong, his legs were cased in a sort of gaiters, of which one was red and the other yellow. He was provided also with a cap, having around it more than one bell, about the size of those attached to hawks, which jingled as he turned his head to one side or other; and as he seldom remained a minute in the same posture, the sound might be considered as incessant. Around the edge of this cap was a stiff bandeau of leather, cut at the top into open work, resembling a coronet; while a prolonged bag arose from within it, and fell down on one shoulder like an old-fashioned nightcap, or a jelly-bag, or the head-gear of a modern hussar. It was to this part of the cap that the bells were attached; which circumstance, as well as the shape of his head-dress, and his own half-crazed, half-cunning expression of countenance, sufficiently pointed him out as belonging to the race of domestic clowns or jesters, maintained in the houses of the wealthy to help away the tedium of those lingering hours which they were obliged to spend within doors. He bore, like his companion, a scrip, attached to his belt; but had neither horn nor knife, being probably considered as belonging to a class whom it is esteemed dangerous to entrust with edge-tools. In place of these, he was equipped with a sword of lath, resembling that with which Harlequin operates his wonders upon the modern stage.

"The curse of St. Withold upon these infernal porkers!" said the swineherd, after blowing his horn obstreperously, to collect together the scattered herd of swine, which, answering his call with notes equally melodious, made, however, no haste to remove themselves from the luxurious banquet of beech-mast and acorns on which they had fattened, or to forsake the marshy banks of the rivulet, where several of them, half-plunged in mud, lay stretched at their ease, altogether regardless of the voice of their keeper. "Here, Fangs! Fangs!" he ejaculated at the top of his voice to a ragged wolfish-looking dog, a sort of lurcher, half-mastiff, half-greyhound, which ran limping about as if with the purpose of seconding his master in collecting the refractory grunters; but which, in fact, only drove them hither and thither, and increased the evil which he seemed to design to remedy. "Wamba, up and help me, an thou beest a man. Take a turn round the back o'the hill to gain the wind on them; and when thou'st got the weather-gauge, thou mayst drive them before thee as gently as so many innocent lambs."

"Truly," said Wamba, without stirring from the spot. "I have consulted my legs upon this matter, and they are altogether of opinion that to carry my gay garments through these sloughs, would be an act of unfriendship to my sovereign person and royal wardrobe. Wherefore, Gurth, I advise thee to call off Fangs, and leave the herd to their destiny, which, whether they meet with bands of travelling soldiers, or of outlaws, or of wandering pilgrims, can be little else than to be converted into Normans before morning, to thy no small ease and comfort."

"The swine turned Normans to my comfort!" quoth Gurth: "expound that to me, Wamba, for my brain is too dull and my mind too vexed to read riddles."

"Why, how call you those grunting brutes running about on their four legs?" demanded Wamba.

"Swine, fool, swine," said the herd; "every fool knows that."

"And swine is good Saxon," said the Jester. "But how call you the sow when she is flayed, and drawn, and quartered, and hung up by the heels, like a traitor?"

"Pork," anwered the swineherd.

"I am very glad every fool knows that too," said Wamba; "and pork, I think, is good Norman-French. And so, when the brute lives, and is in the charge of a Saxon slave, she goes by her Saxon name; but becomes a Norman, and is called pork, when she is carried to the Castlehall to feast among the nobles. What dost thou think of this, friend Gurth, ha?"

"By St. Dunstan," answered Gurth, "thou speakest but sad truths; little is left to us but the air we breathe, and that appears to have been reserved with much hesitation, solely for the purpose of enabling us to endure the tasks they lay upon our shoulders. The finest and the fattest is for their board; the loveliest is for their couch; the best and bravest supply their foreign masters with soldiers, and whiten distant lands with their bones, leaving few here who have either will or the power to protect the unfortunate Saxon. God's blessing on our master Cedric, he hath done the work of a man in standing in the gap; but Reginald Front-de-Bœuf is coming down to this country in person, and we shall soon see how little Cedric's trouble will avail him. –Here, here," he exclaimed again, raising his voice, "so ho! so ho! well done, Fangs! thou hast them all before thee now, and bring'st them on bravely, lad."

"Gurth," said the Jester, "I know thou thinkest me a fool, or thou wouldst not be so rash in putting thy head into my mouth. One word to Reginald Front-de-Bœuf, or Philip de Malvoisin, that thou hast spoken treason against the Norman, and thou art but a castaway swineherd; thou wouldst waver on one of these trees as a terror to all evil-speakers against dignities."

"Dog, thou wouldst not betray me," said Gurth, "after having led me on to speak so much at disadvantage?"

"Betray thee!" answered the Jester. "No, that were the trick of a wise man; a fool cannot half so well help himself. – But soft, whom have we here?" he said, listening to the trampling of several horses which became then audible.

"Never mind whom," answered Gurth, who had now got his herd before him, and, with the aid of Fangs, was driving them down one of the long dim vistas which we have endeavoured to describe.

"Nay, but I must see the riders," answered Wamba; "perhaps they are come from Fairyland with a message from King Oberon."

"A murrain take thee," rejoined the swineherd; "wilt thou talk of such things, while a terrible storm of thunder and lightning is ranging within a few miles of us? Hark, how the thunder rumbles! and for summer rain I never saw such broad downright flat drops fall out of the clouds. The oaks, too, notwithstanding the calm weather, sob and creak with their great boughs as if announcing a tempest. Thou canst play the rational if thou wilt; credit me for once, and let us home ere the storm begins to rage, for the night will be fearful."

Wamba seemed to feel the force of this appeal, and accompanied his companion, who began his journey after catching up a long quarterstaff which lay upon the grass beside him. This second Eumæus strode hastily down the forest glade, driving before him, with the assistance of Fangs, the whole herd of his inharmonious charge.

CHAPTER 2

NOTWITHSTANDING the occasional exhortation and chiding of his companion, the noise of the horsemen's feet continued to approach.

Their numbers amounted to ten men, of whom the two who rode foremost seemed to be persons of considerable importance, and the others their attendants. It was not difficult to ascertain the condition and character of one of these personages. He was obviously an ecclesiastic of high rank; his dress was that of a Cistercian Monk, but composed of materials much finer than those which the rule of that order admitted.

His mantle and hood were of the best Flanders cloth, and fell in ample and not ungraceful folds around a handsome though somewhat corpulent person. His countenance bore as little the marks of self-denial, as his habit indicated contempt of worldly splendour. His features might have been called good, had there not lurked under the pent-house of his eye that sly epicurean twinkle which indicates the cautious voluptuary. In defiance of conventional rules, and the edicts of popes and councils, the sleeves of this dignitary were lined and turned up with rich furs, his mantle secured at the throat with a golden clasp.

This worthy churchman rode upon a well-fed ambling mule, whose furniture was highly decorated, and whose bridle, according to the fashion of the day, was ornamented with silver bells. In his seat he had nothing of the awkwardness of the convent, but displayed the easy and habitual grace of a well-trained horseman. Indeed, it seemed that so humble a conveyance as a mule, in however good case, and however well broken to a pleasant and accommodating amble, was only used by the gallant monk for travelling on the road. A lay brother, one of those who followed in the train, had, for his use on other occasions, one of the most handsome Spanish jennets ever bred in Andalusia, which merchants used at that time to import, with great trouble and risk, for the use of persons of wealth and distinction. The saddle and housings of this superb palfrey were covered by a long footcloth, which reached nearly to the ground, and on which were richly embroidered mitres, crosses, and other ecclesiastical emblems. Another lay brother led a sumpter mule, loaded probably with his superior's baggage; and two monks of his own order, of inferior station rode together in the rear, laughing and conversing with each other, without taking much notice of the other members of the cavalcade.

The companion of the church dignitary was a man past forty, thin, strong, tall, and muscular; an athletic figure, which long fatigue and constant exercise seemed to have left none of the softer part of the human form, having reduced the whole to brawn, bones, and sinews, which had sustained a thousand toils, and were ready to dare a thousand more. His head was covered with a scarlet cap faced with fur—of that kind which the French call *mortier*, from its resemblance to the shape of an inverted mortar. High features, naturally strong and powerfully expressive, had been burnt almost into Negro blackness by constant exposure to the tropical sun, and might, in their ordinary state, be said to slumber after the storm of passion had passed away; but the projection of the veins of the forehead, the readiness with which the upper lip and its thick black moustaches quivered upon the slightest emotion, plainly intimated that the tempest might be again and easily awakened.

The upper dress of this personage resembled that of his companion in shape, being a long monastic mantle; but the colour, being scarlet, showed that he did not belong to any of the four regular orders of monks. On the right shoulder of the mantle there was cut, in white cloth, a cross of a peculiar form. The upper robe concealed what at first view seemed rather inconsistent with its form—a shirt, namely, of linked mail, with sleeves and gloves of the same, curiously plaited and interwoven, as flexible to the body as those which are now wrought in the stocking-loom out of less obdurate materials. The fore-part of his thighs, where the folds of his mantle permitted them to be seen, were also covered with linked mail; the knees and feet were defended by splints, or thin plates of steel, ingeniously jointed upon each other; and mail hose, reaching from the ankle to the knee, effectually protected the legs, and completed the rider's defensive armour. In his girdle he wore a long and double-edged dagger, which was the only offensive weapon about his person.

He rode, not a mule, like his companion, but a strong hackney for the road, to save his gallant war-horse, which a squire led behind, fully accoutred for battle, with a chamfron or plaited headpiece upon his head, having a short spike projecting from the front. On one side of the saddle hung a short battle-axe, richly inlaid with Damascene carving; on the other the rider's plumed headpiece and hood of mail, with a long two-handed sword, used by the chivalry of the period. A second squire held aloft his master's lance, from the extremity of which fluttered a small banderole, or streamer, bearing a cross of the same form with that embroidered upon his cloak. He also carried his small triangular shield, broad enough at the top to protect the breast, and from thence diminishing to a point. It was covered with a scarlet cloth, which prevented the device from being seen.

These two squires were followed by two attendants, whose dark visages, white turbans, and the Oriental form of their garments, showed them to be natives of some distant Eastern country. The whole appearance of this warrior and his retinue was wild and outlandish. The dress of his squires was gorgeous; and his Eastern attendants wore silver collars round their throats, and bracelets of the same metal upon their swarthy arms and legs, of which the former were naked from the elbow, and the latter from midleg to ankle. Silk and embroidery distinguished their dresses, and marked the wealth and importance of their master; forming, at the same time, a striking contrast with the martial simplicity of his own attire. They were armed with crooked sabres, having the hilt and baldric inlaid with gold, and matched with Turkish daggers of yet more costly workmanship. Each of them bore at his saddle-bow a bundle of darts or javelins, about four feet in length, having sharp steel heads, a weapon much in use among the Saracens, and of which the memory is yet preserved in the martial exercise called *El Jerrid*, still practised in the Eastern countries.

The steeds of these attendants were in appearance as foreign as their riders. They were of Saracen origin, and consequently of Arabian descent.

The singular appearance of this cavalcade not only attracted the curiosity of Wamba, but excited even that of his less volatile companion. The monk he instantly knew to be the Prior of Jorvaulx Abbey, well known for many miles around as a lover of the chase, of the banquet, and of other worldly pleasures still more inconsistent with his monastic vows.

Yet so loose were the ideas of the times respecting the conduct of the clergy, whether secular or regular, that the Prior Aymer maintained a fair character in the neighbourhood of his abbey. His free and jovial temper, and the readiness with which he granted absolution from all ordinary delinquencies, rendered him a favourite among the nobility and principal gentry, to several of whom he was allied by birth, being of a distinguished Norman family. The ladies, in particular, were not disposed to scan too nicely the morals of a man who was a professed admirer of their sex, and who possessed many means of dispelling the ennui which was too apt to intrude upon the halls and bowers of an ancient feudal castle.

But the singular appearance of his companion and his attendants arrested their attention and excited their wonder, and they could scarcely attend to the Prior of Jorvaulx' question, when he demanded if they knew of any place of harbourage in the vicinity; so much were they surprised at the half-monastic, half-military appearance of the swarthy stranger, and at the uncouth dress and arms of his Eastern attendants. It is probable, too, that the language in which the benediction was conferred, and the information asked, sounded ungracious, though not probably unintelligible, in the ears of the Saxon peasants.

"I asked you, my children," said the Prior, raising his voice, and using the Lingua Franca, or mixed language, in which the Norman and Saxon races conversed with each other, "if there be in this neighbourhood any good man, who, for the love of God, and devotion to Mother Church, will give two of her humblest servants, with their train, a night's hospitality and refreshment?"

"The reverend fathers could turn to the hermitage of Copmanhurst," replied Wamba.

The armed rider broke in. "Tell us, if thou canst, the road to — How called you your Franklin, Prior Aymer?"

"Cedric," answered the Prior; "Cedric the Saxon. — Tell me, good fellow, are we near his dwelling, and can you show us the road?"

"The road will be uneasy to find," answered Gurth, who broke silence for the first time, "and the family of Cedric retire early to rest."

"Tush, tell not me, fellow," said the military rider; "'tis easy for them to arise and supply the wants of travellers such as we are, who will not stoop to beg the hospitality which we have a right to command."

"I know not," said Gurth sullenly, "if I should show the way to my master's house, to those who demand as a right the shelter which most are fain to ask as a favour."

"Do you dispute with me, slave!" said the soldier; and, setting spurs to his horse, he caused him to make a demivolte across the path, raising at the same time the riding rod which he held in his hand, with a purpose of chastising what he considered as the insolence of the peasant.

Gurth darted at him a savage and revengeful scowl, and with a fierce yet hesitating motion laid his hand on the haft of his knife; but the interference of Prior Aymer, who pushed his mule betwixt his companion and the swineherd, prevented the meditated violence.

"Nay, by St. Mary, brother Brian, you must not think you are now in Palestine, predominating over heathen Turks and infidel Saracens. We islanders love not blows, save those of holy Church, who chasteneth whom she loveth. –Tell me, good fellow," said he to Wamba, and seconded his speech by a small piece of silver coin, "the way to Cedric the Saxon's. You cannot be ignorant of it, and it is your duty to direct the wanderer even when his character is less sanctified than ours."

"Well, then," answered Wamba, "your reverences must hold on this path till you come to a sunken cross, of which scarce a cubit's length remains above ground; then take the path to the left, for there are four which meet at Sunken Cross, and I trust your reverences will obtain shelter before the storm comes on."

The Abbot thanked his sage adviser, and the cavalcade rode on. As their horses' hoofs died away, Gurth said to his companion, "If they follow thy wise direction, they will hardly reach Rotherwood this night."

"No," said the Jester, grinning, "but they may reach Sheffield if they have good luck, and that is as fit a place for them. I am not so bad a woodsman as to show the dog where the deer lies, if I have no mind he should chase him."

"Thou art right," said Gurth. "It were ill that Aymer saw the Lady Rowena; and it were worse, it may be, for Cedric to quarrel, as is most likely he would, with this military monk. But, like good servants, let us hear and see, and say nothing."

The riders had soon left the bondsmen far behind them.

"What mean these fellows by their capricious insolence?" said the Templar to the Cistercian, "and why did you prevent me from chastising it?"

"Every land has its own manners and fashions," answered Prior Aymer; "and, beating this fellow could procure us no information respecting the road of Cedric's house. This wealthy Franklin is proud, fierce, jealous, and irritable; a withstander of the nobility, and even of his neighbours, Reginald Front-de-Bœuf and Philip Malvoisin, who are no babes to strive with. He stands up so sternly for the privileges of his race, and is so proud of his uninterrupted descent from Hereward, a renowned champion of the Heptarchy, that he is universally called Cedric the Saxon; and makes a boast of his belonging to a people from whom many others endeavour to hide their descent, lest they should encounter a share of the *vae victis*, or severities imposed upon the vanquished."

"Prior Aymer," said the Templar, "you are a man of gallantry, learned in the study of beauty, and as expert as a troubadour in all matters concerning the arrets of love; but I shall expect much beauty in this celebrated Rowena, to counterbalance the self-denial and forbearance which I must exert, if I am to court the favour of such a seditious churl as you have described her father Cedric."

"Cedric is not her father," replied the Prior, "and is but of remote relation; she is descended from higher blood than even he pretends to, and is but distantly connected with him by birth. Her guardian, however, he is, self-constituted as I believe; but his ward is as dear to him as if she were his own child. Of her beauty you shall soon be judge; and if the purity of her complexion, and the majestic yet soft expression of a mild blue eye, do not chase from your memory the black-tressed girls of Palestine, ay, or the houris of old Mahound's paradise, I am an infidel, and no true son of the church."

"Should your boasted beauty," said the Templar, "be weighed in the balance and found wanting, you know our wager?"

"My gold collar," answered the Prior, "against ten butts of Chian wine. They are mine as securely as if they were already in the convent vaults under the key of old Dennis the cellarer."

"And I am myself to be judge," said the Templar, "and I am only to be convicted on my own admission, that I have seen no maiden so beautiful since Pentecost was a twelve-month. Ran it not so?—Prior, your collar is in danger; I will wear it over my gorget in the lists of Ashby-de-la-Zouche."

"Win it fairly," said the Prior, "and wear it as ye will; I will trust your giving true response, on your word as a knight and as a churchman. Yet, brother, take my advice, and file your tongue to a little more courtesy than your habits of pre-dominating over infidel captives and Eastern bondsmen have accustomed you. Cedric the Saxon, if offended—and he is no way slack in taking offence—is a man who, without respect to your knighthood, my high office, or the sanctity of either, would clear his house of us, and send us to lodge with the larks, though the hour were midnight. And be careful how you look on Rowena, whom he cherishes with the most jealous care; an he take the least alarm in that quarter, we are but lost men. It is said he banished his only son from his family for lifting his eyes in the way of affection towards this beauty, who may be worshipped, it seems, at a distance, but is not to be approached with other thoughts than such as we bring to the shrine of the Blessed Virgin."

"Well, you have said enough," answered the Templar. "I will for a night put on the needful restraint, and deport me as meekly as a maiden; but as for the fear of his expelling us by violence, myself and squires, with Hamet and Abdalla, will warrant you against that disgrace. Doubt not that we shall be strong enough to make good our quarters."

"We must not let it come so far," answered the Prior. "But here is the clown's sunken cross, and the night is so dark that we can hardly see which of the roads we are to follow. He bid us turn, I think, to the left."

"To the right," said Brian, "to the best of my remembrance."

"To the left, certainly, the left; I remember his pointing with his wooden sword."

"Ay, but he held his sword in his left hand, and so pointed across his body with it," said the Templar.

Each maintained his opinion with sufficient obstinacy, as is usual in all such cases. The attendants were appealed to, but they had not been near enough to hear Wamba's directions. At length Brian remarked what had at first escaped him in the twilight. "Here is some one either asleep or lying dead at the foot of this cross.—Huga, stir him with the butt-end of thy lance."

This was no sooner done than the figure arose, exclaiming in good French, "Whosoever thou art, it is discourteous in you to disturb my thoughts."

"We did but wish to ask you," said the Prior, "the road to Rotherwood, the abode of Cedric the Saxon."

"I myself am bound thither," replied the stranger; "and if I had a horse, I would be your guide, for the way is somewhat intricate, though perfectly well known to me."

"Thou shalt have both thanks and reward, my friend," said the Prior, "if thou wilt bring us to Cedric's in safety."

And he caused one of his attendants to mount his own led horse, and give that upon which he had hitherto ridden to the stranger, who was to serve for a guide.

Their conductor pursued an opposite road from that which Wamba had recommended for the purpose of misleading them. The path soon led deeper into the woodland, and crossed more than one brook, the approach to which was rendered perilous by the marshes through which it flowed; but the stranger seemed to know, as if by instinct, the soundest ground and the safest points of passage, and by dint of caution and attention brought the party safely into a wider avenue than any they had yet seen; and pointing to a large, low, irregular building at the upper extremity, he said to the

Prior, "Yonder is Rotherwood, the dwelling of Cedric the Saxon."

This was a joyful intimation to Aymer, whose nerves were none of the strongest, and who had suffered such agitation and alarm in the course of passing through the dangerous bogs, that he had not yet had the curiosity to ask his guide a single question. Finding himself now at his ease and near shelter, his curiosity began to awake, and he demanded of the guide who and what he was.

"A Palmer, just returned from the Holy Land," was the answer. "I was born a native of these parts," and as he made the reply they stood before the mansion of Cedric –a low, irregular building, containing several courtyards or enclosures, extending over a considerable space of ground, and which, though its size argued the inhabitant to be a person of wealth, differed entirely from the tall, turreted, and castellated buildings in which the Norman nobility resided, and which has become the universal style of architecture throughout England.

Rotherwood was not, however, without defences; no habitation, in that disturbed period, could have been so, without the risk of being plundered and burnt before the next morning. A deep fosse, or ditch, was drawn round the whole building, and filled with water from a neighbouring stream. A double stockade, or palisade, composed of pointed beams, which the adjacent forest supplied, defenced the outer and inner bank of the trench. There was an entrance from the west through the outer stockade, which communicated by a drawbridge with a similar opening in the interior defences. Some precautions had been taken to place those entrances under the protection of projecting angles, by which they might be flanked in case of need by archers or slingers.

Before this entrance the Templar wound his horn loudly; for the rain, which had long threatened, began now to descend with great violence.

CHAPTER 3

IN A hall, the height of which was greatly disproportioned to its extreme length and width, a long oaken table, formed of planks rough-hewn from the forest, and which had scarcely received any polish, stood ready prepared for the evening meal of Cedric the Saxon. The roof, composed of beams and rafters, had nothing to divide the apartment from the sky excepting the planking and thatch. There was a huge fireplace at either end of the hall; but as the chimneys were constructed in a very clumsy manner, at least as much of the smoke found its way into the apartment as escaped by the proper vent. The constant vapour which this occasioned had polished the rafters and beams of the low-browed hall, by encrusting them with a black varnish of soot. On the sides of the appartment hung implements of war and of the chase; and there were at each corner folding doors, which gave access to other parts of the extensive building.

The other appointments of the mansion partook of the rude simplicity of the Saxon period, which Cedric piqued himself upon maintaining. The floor was composed of earth mixed with lime, trodden into a hard substance, such as is often employed in flooring our modern barns. For about one quarter of the length of the apartment the floor was raised by a step, and this place, which was called the dais, was occupied only by the principal members of the family, and visitors of distinction. For this purpose, a table richly covered with scarlet cloth was placed transversely across the platform, from the middle of which ran the longer and lower board, at which the domestics and inferior persons fed, down towards the bottom of the hall. The whole resembled the form of the letter T, or some of those ancient dinner-tables, which, arranged on the same principles, may be still seen in the antique Colleges of Oxford or Cambridge.

The walls of this upper end of the hall, as far as the dais extended, were covered with hangings or curtains, and upon the floor there was a carpet, both of which were adorned with some attempts at tapestry, or embroidery, executed with brilliant or rather gaudy colouring. Over the lower range of table, the roof, as we have noticed, had no covering; the rough plastered walls were left bare, and the rude earthen floor was uncarpeted; the board was uncovered by a cloth, and rude massive benches supplied the place of chairs.

In the centre of the upper table were placed two chairs more elevated than the rest, for the master and mistress of the family, who presided over the scene of hospitality, and from doing so derived their Saxon title of honour, which signifies "the Dividers of Bread."

To each of these chairs was added a footstool, curiously carved and inlaid with ivory, which mark of distinction was peculiar to them. One of these seats was at present occupied by Cedric the Saxon, who, though but in rank a thane, or, as the Normans called him, a Franklin, felt, at the delay of his evening meal, an irritable impatience which might have become an alderman, whether of ancient or of modern times.

It appeared, indeed, from the countenance of this proprietor, that he was of a frank but hasty and choleric temper. He was not above the middle stature, but broad-shouldered, long-armed, and powerfully made, like one accustomed to endure the fatigue of war or of the chase; his face was broad, with large blue eyes, open and frank features, fine teeth, and a well-formed head, altogether expressive of that sort of good-humour which often lodges with a sudden and hasty temper. Pride and jealousy there was in his eye, for his life had been spent in asserting rights which were constantly liable to invasion; and the prompt, fiery, and resolute disposition of the man had been kept constantly upon the alert by the circumstances of his situation. His long yellow hair was equally divided on the top of his head and upon his brow, and combed down on each side to the length of his shoulders; it had but little tendency to grey, although Cedric was approaching his sixtieth year.

Two or three servants of a superior order stood behind their master upon the dais; the rest occupied the lower part of the hall. Other attendants there were of a different description: two or three large and shaggy greyhounds, such as were then employed in hunting the stag and wolf; as many slowhounds of a large bony breed, with thick necks, large heads, and long ears; and one or two of the smaller dogs, now called terriers, which waited with impatience the arrival of the supper, but, with the sagacious knowledge of physiognomy peculiar to their race, forbore to intrude upon the moody silence of their master, apprehensive probably of a small white truncheon which lay by Cedric's trencher, for the purpose of repelling the advances of his four-legged dependants. One grisly old wolf-dog alone, with the liberty of an indulged favourite, had planted himself close by the chair of state, and occasionally ventured to solicit notice by putting his large hairy head upon his master's knee, or pushing his nose into his hand. Even he was repelled by the stern command, "Down, Balder, down! I am not in the humour for foolery."

In fact, Cedric, as we have observed, was in no very placid state of mind. The Lady Rowena, who had been absent to attend an evening mass at a distant church, had but just returned, and was changing her garments, which had been wetted by the storm. There were as yet no tidings of Gurth and his charge, which should long since have been driven home from the forest; and such was the insecurity of the period, as to render it probable that the delay might be explained by some depredation of the outlaws, with whom the adjacent forest abounded, or by the violence of some neighbouring baron, whose consciousness of strength made him equally negligent of the laws of property. The matter was of consequence, for great part of the domestic wealth of the Saxon proprietors consisted in numerous herds of swine, especially in forest-land, where those animals easily found their food.

From his musing, Cedric was suddenly awakened by the blast of a horn, which was replied to by the clamorous yells and barking of all the dogs in the hall, and some twenty or thirty which were quartered in other parts of the building. It cost some exercise of the white truncheon, well seconded by the exertions of the domestics, to silence this canine clamour.

"To the gate, knaves!" said the Saxon hastily, as soon as the tumult was so much appeased that the dependants could hear his voice.

Returning in less than three minutes, a warder announced, "that the Prior Aymer of Jorvaulx, and the good knight Brian de Bois-Guilbert, commander of the valiant and venerable order of Knights Templars, with a small retinue, requested hospitality and lodging for the night, being on their way to a tournament which was to be held not far from Ashby-de-la-Zouche, on the second day from the present."

"Aymer? the Prior Aymer? Brian de Bois-Guilbert?" muttered Cedric; "Normans both. But Norman or Saxon, the hospitality of Rotherwood must not be impeached; they are welcome, since they have chosen to halt—more welcome would they have been to have ridden farther on their way. –Go, Hundebert," he added, to a sort of major-domo who stood behind him with a white wand; "take six of the attendants, and introduce the strangers to the guests' lodging. Look after their horses and mules, and see their train lack nothing. Let them have change of vestments if they require it, and fire, and water to wash, and wine and ale; and bid the cooks add what they hastily can to our evening meal; and let it be put on the board when those strangers are ready to share it. Say to them, Hundebert, that Cedric would himself bid them welcome, but he is under a vow never to step more than three steps from the dais of his own hall to meet any who shares not the blood of Saxon royalty. Begone! see them carefully tended; let them not say in their pride, the Saxon churl has shown at once his poverty and his avarice."

The major-domo departed with several attendants to execute his master's commands. "The Prior Aymer?" repeated Cedric, looking to Oswald the cupbearer, "the brother, if I mistake not, of Giles de Maleverer, now lord of Middleham?"

Oswald made a respectful sign of assent. "His brother sits in the seat and usurps the patrimony of a better race, the race of Ulfgar of Middleham; but what Norman lord doth not the same? This Prior is, they say, a free and jovial priest, who loves the wine-cup and the buglehorn better than bell and book. Good; let him come, he shall be welcome. How named ye the Templar?"

"Brian de Bois-Guilbert."

"Bois-Guilbert?" said Cedric, still in the musing, half-arguing tone, which the habit of living among dependants had accustomed him to employ, and which resembled a man who talks to himself rather than to those around him – "Bois-Guilbert? that name has been spread wide both for good and evil. They say he is valiant as the bravest of his order; but stained with their usual vices—pride, arrogance, cruelty, and voluptuousness; a hard-hearted man, who knows neither fear of earth nor awe of Heaven. So say the few warriors who have returned from Palestine. – Well; it is but for one night; he shall be welcome too. – Oswald, broach the oldest wine-cask; place the best mead, the mightiest ale, the richest morat, the most sparkling cider, the most odoriferous pigments, upon the board; fill the largest horns – Templars and Abbots love good wines and good measure. – Elgitha, let thy Lady Rowena know we shall not this night expect her in the hall, unless such be her especial pleasure."

"But it will be her especial pleasure," answered Elgitha, with great readiness, "for she is ever desirous to hear the latest news from Palestine."

Cedric darted at the forward damsel a glance of hasty resentment; but Rowena, and whatever belonged to her, were privileged and secure from his anger. He only replied, "Silence, maiden; thy tongue outruns thy discretion. Say my message to thy mistress, and let her do her pleasure. Here, at least, the descendant of Alfred still reigns a princess." Elgitha left the apartment.

The Saxon knit his brows, and fixed his eyes for an instant on the ground. As he raised them, the folding doors at the bottom of the hall were cast wide, and, preceded by the major-domo with his wand, and four domestics bearing blazing torches, the guests of the evening entered the apartment.

CHAPTER 4

THE Prior Aymer had taken the opportunity afforded him of changing his riding robe for one of yet more costly materials, over which he wore a cope curiously embroidered. Besides the massive golden signet ring which marked his ecclesiastical dignity, his fingers, though contrary to the canon, were loaded with precious gems; his sandals were of the finest leather which was imported from Spain; his beard trimmed to as small dimensions as his order would possibly permit, and his shaven crown concealed by a scarlet cap richly embroidered.

The appearance of the Knight Templar was also changed; and, though less studiously bedecked with ornament, his dress was as rich, and his appearance far more commanding, than that of his companion. He had exchanged his shirt of mail for an under tunic of dark purple silk, garnished with furs, over which flowed his long robe of spotless white in ample folds. The eight-pointed cross of his order was cut on the shoulder of his mantle in black velvet. The high cap no longer invested his brows, which were only shaded by short and thick curled hair of a raven blackness, corresponding to this unusually swart complexion. Nothing could be more gracefully majestic than his step and manner had they not been marked by a predominant air of haughtiness, easily acquired by the exercise of unresisted authority.

These two dignified persons were followed by their respective attendants, and at a more humble distance by their guide, whose figure had nothing more remarkable than it derived from the usual weeds of a pilgrim. A cloak or mantle of coarse black serge enveloped his whole body. It was in shape something like the cloak of a modern hussar, having similar flaps for covering the arms, and was called a *Sclaveyn* or *Sclavonian*. Coarse sandals, bound with thongs, on his bare feet; a broad and shadowy hat, with cockleshells stitched on its brim; and a long staff shod with iron, to the upper end of which was attached a branch of palm, completed the palmer's attire. He followed modestly the last of the train which entered the hall, and, observing that the lower table scarce afforded room sufficient for the domestics of Cedric and the retinue of his guests, he withdrew to a settle placed beside and almost under one of the large chimneys, and seemed to employ himself in drying his garments, until the retreat of some one should make room at the board, or the hospitality of the steward should supply him with refreshments in the place he had chosen apart.

Cedric rose to receive his guests with an air of dignified hospitality, and, descending from the dais, or elevated part of his hall, made three steps towards them, and then awaited their approach.

"I grieve," he said, "reverend Prior, that my vows bind me to advance no farther upon this floor of my fathers, even to receive such guests as you, and this valiant Knight of the Holy Temple. But my steward has expounded to you the cause of my seeming discourtesy. Let me also pray that you will excuse my speaking to you in my native language, and that you will reply in the same if your knowledge of it permits; if not, I sufficiently understand Norman to follow your meaning."

"Vows," said the Abbot, "must be unloosed, worthy Franklin, or permit me rather to say, worthy Thane, though the title is antiquated. Vows are the knots which tie us to Heaven –they are the cords which bind the sacrifice to the horn of the altar – and are therefore, as I said before, to be unloosened and discharged, unless our holy Mother Church shall pronounce the contrary. And respecting language, I willingly hold communication in that spoken by my respected grandmother, Hilda of Middleham, who died in odour of sanctity, little short, if we may presume to say so, of her glorious namesake, the blessed Saint Hilda of Whitby, God be gracious to her soul!"

When the Prior had ceased what he meant as a conciliatory harangue, his companion said briefly and emphatically, "I speak ever French, the language of King Richard and his nobles; but I understand English sufficiently to communicate with the natives of the country."

Cedric darted at the speaker one of those hasty and impatient glances, which comparisons between the two rival nations seldom failed to call forth; but, recollecting the duties of hospitality, he suppressed further show of resentment, and motioning with his hand, caused his guests to assume two seats a little lower than his own, but placed close beside him, and gave a signal that the evening meal should be placed upon the board.

While the attendants hastened to obey Cedric's commands, his eye distinguished Gurth the swineherd, who, with his companion Wamba, had just entered the hall. "Send these loitering knaves up hither," said the Saxon impatiently. And when the culprits came before the dais, —"How comes it, villains! that you have loitered abroad so late as this? Hast thou brought home thy charge, sirrah Gurth, or hast thou left them to robbers and marauders?"

"The herd is safe, so please ye," said Gurth.

"But it does not please me, thou knave," said Cedric, "that I should be made to suppose otherwise for two hours, and sit here devising vengeance against my neighbours for wrongs they have not done me. I tell thee, shackles and the prison-house shall punish the next offence of this kind."

Gurth, knowing his master's irritable temper, attempted no exculpation; but the Jester, who could presume upon Cedric's tolerance, by virtue of his privileges as a fool, replied for them both: "In troth, uncle Cedric, you are neither wise nor reasonable to-night."

"How, sir?" said his master; "you shall to the porter's lodge, and taste of the discipline there, if you give your foolery such license."

"First let your wisdom tell me," said Wamba, "is it just and reasonable to punish one person for the fault of another?"

"Certainly not, fool," answered Cedric.

"Then why should you shackle poor Gurth, uncle, for the fault of his dog Fangs? for I dare be sworn we lost not a minute by the way, when we had got our herd together, which Fangs did not manage until we heard the vesper-bell."

"Then hang up Fangs," said Cedric, turning hastily towards the swineherd, "if the fault is his, and get thee another dog."

"Under favour, uncle," said the Jester, "that were still somewhat on the bow-hand of fair justice; for it was no fault of Fangs that he was lame and could not gather the herd, but the fault of those that struck off two of his fore-claws, an operation for which, if the poor fellow had been consulted, he would scarce have given his voice."

"And who dared to lame an animal which belonged to my bondsman?" said the Saxon, kindling in wrath.

"Marry, that did old Hubert," said Wamba, "Sir Philip de Malvoisin's keeper of the chase. He caught Fangs strolling in the forest, and said he chased the deer contrary to his master's right, as warden of the walk."

"The foul fiend take Malvoisin," answered the Saxon, "and his keeper both! I will teach them that the wood was disforested in terms of the great Forest Charter. But enough of this. Go to, knave, go to thy place—And thou, Gurth, get thee another dog, and should the keeper dare to touch it, I will mar his archery; the curse of a coward on my head, if I strike not off the forefinger of his right hand?—he shall draw bowstring no more.—I crave your pardon, my worthy guests. I am beset here with neighbours that match your infidels, Sir Knight, in Holy Land. But your homely fare is before you; feed, and let welcome make amends for hard fare."

The feast, however, which was spread upon the board needed no apologies from the lord of the mansion. Swine's flesh, dressed in several modes, appeared on the lower part of the board, as also that of fowls, deer, goats, and hares, and various kinds of fish, together with huge loaves and cakes of bread, and sundry confections made of fruits and honey. The smaller sorts of wild-fowl, of which there was abundance, were not served up in platters, but brought in upon small wooden spits or broaches, and offered, by the pages and domestics who bore them, to each guest in succession, who cut from them such a portion as he pleased. Beside each person of rank was placed a goblet of silver; the lower board was accommodated with large drinking horns.

When the repast was about to commence, the major-domo, or steward, suddenly raising his wand, said aloud, "Forbear!— Place for the Lady Rowena." A side-door at the upper end of the hall now opened behind the banquet table, and Rowena, followed by four female attendants, entered the apartment. Cedric, though surprised, and perhaps not altogether agreeably so, at his ward appearing in public on this occasion, hastened to meet her, and to conduct her, with respectful ceremony, to the elevated seat at his own right hand, appropriated to the lady of the mansion. All stood up to receive her; and, replying to their courtesy by a mute gesture of salutation she moved gracefully forward to assume her place at the board. Ere she had time to do so, the Templar whispered to the Prior, "I shall wear no collar of gold of yours at the tournament. The Chian wine is your own."

"Said I not so?" answered the Prior; "but check your raptures, the Franklin observes you."

Formed in the best proportions of her sex, Rowena was tall in stature, yet not so much so as to attract observation on account of superior height. Her complexion was exquisitely fair. Her profuse hair was braided with gems, and, being worn at full length, intimated the noble birth and freeborn condition of the maiden. A golden chain, to which was attached a small reliquary of the same metal, hung round her neck. She wore bracelets on her arms, which were bare. Her dress was an under-gown and kirtle of pale sea-green silk, over which hung a long loose robe, which reached to the ground, having very wide sleeves, which came down, however, very little below the elbow. This robe was crimson, and manufactured out of the very finest wool. A veil of silk, interwoven with gold, was attached to the upper part of it, which could be, at the wearer's pleasure, either drawn over the face and bosom after the Spanish fashion, or disposed as a sort of drapery round the shoulders.

When Rowena perceived the Knight Templar's eyes bent on her with an ardour that, compared with the dark caverns under which they moved, gave them the effect of lighted charcoal, she drew with dignity the veil around her face, as an intimation that the determined freedom of his glance was disagreeable. Cedric saw the motion and its cause. "Sir Templar," said he, "the cheeks of our Saxon maidens have seen too little of the sun to enable them to bear the fixed glance of a crusader."

"If I have offended," replied Sir Brian, "I crave your pardon—that is, I crave the Lady Rowena's pardon, for my humility will carry me no lower."

"The Lady Rowena," said the Prior, "has punished us all, in chastising the boldness of my friend. Let me hope she will be less cruel to the splendid train which are to meet at the tournament."

"Our going thither," said Cedric, "is uncertain. I love not these vanities, which were unknown to my fathers when England was free."

"Let us hope, nevertheless," said the Prior, "our company may determine you to travel thitherward; when the roads are so unsafe, the escort of Sir Brian de Bois-Guilbert is not to be despised."

"Sir Prior," answered the Saxon, "wheresoever I have travelled in this and faithful followers, in no respect needful of other aid. At present, if we indeed journey to Ashby-de-la-Zouche, we do so with my noble neighbour and countryman, Athelstane of Coningsburgh, and with such a train as would set outlaws and feudal enemies at defiance. I drink to you, Sir Prior, in this cup of wine, which I trust your taste will approve, and I thank you for your courtesy. Should you be so rigid in adhering to monastic rule," he added, "as to prefer your acid preparation of milk, I hope you will not strain courtesy to do me reason."

"Nay," said the Priest, laughing, "it is only in our abbey that we confine ourselves to the *lac dulce* or the *lac acidum* either. Conversing with the world, we use the world's fashions, and therefore I answer your pledge in this honest wine, and leave the weaker liquor to my laybrother."

"And I," said the Templar, filling his goblet, "drink wassail to the fair Rowena; for since her namesake introduced the word into England, has land, I have hitherto found myself, with the assistance of my good sword never been one more worthy of such a tribute. By my faith, I could pardon the unhappy Vortigern, had he half the cause that we now witness, for making shipwreck of his honour and his kingdom."

"I will spare your courtesy, Sir Knight," said Rowena with dignity, and without unveiling herself; "or rather I will tax it so far as to require of you the latest news from Palestine, a theme more agreeable to our English ears than the compliments which your French breeding teaches."

"I have little of importance to say, lady," answered Sir Brian de Bois-Guilbert, "excepting the confirmed tidings of a truce with Saladin."

Conversation was here interrupted by the entrance of the porter's page, who announced that there was a stranger at the gate, imploring admittance and hospitality.

"Admit him," said Cedric, "be he who or what he may;— a night like that which roars without compels even wild animals to herd with tame, and to seek the protection of man, their mortal foe, rather than perish by the elements. Let his wants be ministered to with all care—look to it, Oswald."

And the steward left the banqueting hall to see the commands of his patron obeyed.

CHAPTER 5

OSWALD, returning, whispered into the ear of his master, "It is a Jew, who calls himself Isaac of York. Is it fit I should marshal him into the hall?"

"Let Gurth do thine office, Oswald," said Wamba, with his usual effrontery; "the swineherd will be a fit usher to the Jew."

"St. Mary," said the Abbot, crossing himself, "an unbelieving Jew, and admitted into this presence!"

Introduced with little ceremony, and advancing with fear and hesitation, and many a bow of deep humility, a tall thin old man, who, however, had lost by the habit of stooping much of his actual height, approached the lower end of the board.

The reception of this person in the hall of Cedric the Saxon was such as might have satisfied the most prejudiced enemy of the tribes of Israel. Cedric himself coldly nodded in answer to the Jew's repeated salutations, and signed to him to take place at the lower end of the table, where, however, no one offered to make room for him.

"Pledge me a cup of wine, Sir Templar," said Cedric, "and fill another to the Abbot, while I look back some thirty years to tell you another tale. As Cedric the Saxon then was, his plain English tale needed no garnish from French troubadours, when it was told in the ear of beauty; and the field of North-allerton, upon the day of the Holy Standard, could tell whether the Saxon war-cry was not heard as far within the ranks of the Scottish host as the *cri de guerre* of the boldest Norman baron. To the memory of the brave who fought there! Pledge me, my guests." He drank deep, and went on with increasing warmth. "Ay, that was a day of cleaving of shields, when a hundred banners were bent forward over the heads of the valiant, and blood flowed round like water, and death was held better than flight.—Cupbearer! knave, fill the goblets.—To the strong in arms, Sir Templar, be their race or language what it will, who now bear them best in Palestine among the champions of the Cross!"

"It becomes not one wearing this badge to answer," said Sir Brian de Bois-Guilbert; "yet to whom, besides the sworn

Champions of the Holy Sepulchre, can the palm be assigned among the champions of the Cross?"

"To the Knights Hospitallers," said the Abbot; "I have a brother of their order."

"I impeach not their fame," said the Templar; "nevertheless—"

"I think, friend Cedric," said Wamba, interfering, "that had Richard of the Lion's Heart been wise enough to have taken a fool's advice, he might have stayed at home with his merry Englishmen, and left the recovery of Jerusalem to those same Knights who had most to do with the loss of it."

"Were there, then, none in the English army," said the Lady Rowena, "whose names are worthy to be mentioned with the Knights of the Temple and of St. John?"

"Forgive me, lady," replied De Bois-Guilbert; "the English monarch did, indeed, bring to Palestine a host of gallant warriors, second only to those whose breasts have been the unceasing bulwark of that blessed land."

"Second to NONE," said the Pilgrim, who had stood near enough to hear, and had listened to this conversation with marked impatience. All turned toward the spot from whence this unexpected asseveration was heard. "I say," repeated the Pilgrim, in a firm and strong voice, "that the English chivalry were second to NONE who ever drew sword in defence of the Holy Land. I say besides, for I saw it, that King Richard himself, and five of his knights, held a tournament after the taking of St. John-de-Acre, as challengers against all comers. I say that, on that day, each knight ran three courses, and cast to the ground three antagonists. I add, that seven of these assailants were Knights of the Temple—and Sir Brian de Bois-Guilbert well knows the truth of what I tell you."

Cedric, whose feelings were all of a right onward and simple kind, and were seldom occupied by more than one object at once, omitted, in the joyous glee with which he heard of the glory of his countrymen, to remark the angry confusion of his guest; "I would give thee this golden bracelet, Pilgrim," he said, "couldst thou tell me the names of those knights who upheld so gallantly the renown of merry England."

"The first in honour as in arms, in renown as in place," said the Pilgrim, "was the brave Richard, King of England."

"I forgive him," said Cedric –"I forgive him his descent from the tyrant Duke William."

"The Earl of Leicester was the second," continued the Pilgrim; "Sir Thomas Multon of Gilsland was the third."

"Of Saxon descent he at least," said Cedric, with exultation.

"Sir Foulk Doilly the fourth," proceeded the Pilgrim.

"Saxon also, at least by the mother's side," continued Cedric, who listened with the utmost eagerness, and forgot, in part at least, his hatred to the Normans, in the common triumph of the King of England and his islanders. "And who was the fifth?" he demanded.

"The fifth was Sir Edwin Turneham."

"Genuine Saxon, by the soul of Hengist!" shouted Cedric. – "And the sixth?" he continued with eagerness –"how name you the sixth?"

"The sixth," said the Palmer, after a pause, in which he seemed to recollect himself, "was a young knight of lesser renown and lower rank, assumed into that honourable company, less to aid their enterprise than to make up their number; his name dwells not in my memory."

"Sir Palmer," said Sir Brian de Bois-Guilbert scornfully, "this assumed fortgetfulness, after so much has been remembered, comes too late to serve your purpose. I will myself tell the name of the knight before whose lance fortune and my horse's fault occasioned my falling –it was the Knight of Ivanhoe; nor was there one of the six that, for his years, had more renown in arms. Yet this I will say, and loudly, that were he in England, and durst repeat, in this week's tournament, the challenge of St. John-de-Acre, I, mounted and armed as I now am, would give him every advantage of weapons, and abide the result."

"Your challenge would be soon answered," replied the Palmer, "were your antagonist near you. As the matter is, disturb not the peaceful hall with vaunts of the issue of a conflict which you well know cannot take place. If Ivanhoe ever returns from Palestine, I will be his surety that he meets you."

"A goodly security!" said the Knight Templar; "and what do you proffer as a pledge?"

"This reliquary," said the Palmer, taking a small ivory box from his bosom, and crossing himself, "containing a portion of the true cross, brought from the Monastery of Mount Carmel."

The Prior of Jorvaulx crossed himself and repeated a Paternoster, in which all devoutly joined, excepting the Jew, the Mahomedans, and the Templar; the latter of whom, without vailing his bonnet, or testifying any reverence for the alleged sanctity of the relic, took from his neck a gold chain, which he flung on the board, saying, "Let Prior Aymer hold my pledge and that of this nameless vagrant, in token that when the Knight of Ivanhoe comes within the four seas of Britain, he underlies the challenge of Brian de Bois-Guilbert, which, if he answer not, I will proclaim him as a coward on the walls of every Temple Court in Europe."

"It will not need," said the Lady Rowena, breaking silence, "My voice shall be heard, if no other in this hall is raised in behalf of the absent Ivanhoe. I affirm he will meet fairly every honourable challenge. Could my weak warrant add security to the inestimable pledge of this holy pilgrim, I would pledge name and fame that Ivanhoe gives this proud knight the meeting he desires."

"Lady," said Cedric, "this beseems not. Were further pledge necessary, I myself, offended, and justly offended, as I am, would yet gage my honour for the honour of Ivanhoe. But the wager of battle is complete, even according to the fantastic fashions of Norman chivalry. –Is it not, Father Aymer?"

"It is," replied the Prior; "and the blessed relic and rich chain will I bestow safely in the treasury of our convent, until the decision of this warlike challenge."

He delivered the reliquary to Brother Ambrose, his attendant monk, while he himself swept up with less ceremony, but perhaps with no less internal satisfaction, the golden chain, and bestowed it in a pouch lined with perfumed leather, which opened under his arm. "And now, Sir Cedric," he said, "my ears are chiming vespers with the strength of your good wine. Permit us another pledge to the welfare of the Lady Rowena, and indulge us with liberty to pass to our repose."

The grace-cup was accordingly served round, and the guests, after making deep obeisance to their landlord and to the Lady Rowena, arose and mingled in the hall, while the heads of the family, by separate doors, retired with their attendants.

The Templar and Prior were shortly after marshalled to their sleeping apartments by the steward and the cupbearer, each attended by two torch-bearers and two servants carrying refreshments; while servants of inferior condition indicated to their retinue and to the other guests their respective places of repose.

CHAPTER 6

AS THE Palmer was about to retire, he was met by the waiting-maid of Rowena, who said in a tone of authority that her mistress desired to speak with him.

A short passage, and an ascent of seven steps, each of which was composed of a solid beam of oak, led him to the apartment of the Lady Rowena, the rude magnificence of which corres-

ponded to the respect which was paid to her by the lord of
the mansion. The walls were covered with embroidered hangings, on which different-coloured silks, interwoven with gold
and silver threads, had been employed, with all the art of
which the age was capable to represent the sports of hunting
and hawking. The bed was adorned with the same rich tapestry,
and surrounded with curtains dyed with purple. The seats
had also their stained coverings, and one, which was higher
than the rest, was accommodated with a footstool of ivory,
curiously carved.

The Lady Rowena, with three of her attendants standing
at her back, and arranging her hair ere she lay down to
rest, was seated on the sort of throne already mentioned,
and looked as if born to exact general homage. The Pilgrim
acknowledged her claim to it by a low genuflection.

"Rise, Palmer," said she graciously. "The defender of the
absent has a right to a favourable reception from all who
value truth and honour manhood." She then said to her train,
"Retire, excepting only Elgitha; I would speak with this holy
Pilgrim."

"Pilgrim," said the lady, after a moment's pause, during
which she seemed uncertain how to address him, "you this
night mentioned a name –I mean," she said, with a degree
of effort, "the name of Ivanhoe, in the halls where by nature
and kindred it should have sounded most acceptably; and yet,
such is the perverse course of fate, that of many whose hearts
must have throbbed at the sound, I only dare ask you where,
and in what condition, you left him of whom you spoke? We
heard that, having remained in Palestine, on account of his
impaired health, after the departure of the English army, he
had experienced the persecution of the French faction, to
whom the Templars are known to be attached."

"I know little of the Knight of Ivanhoe," answered the
Palmer, with a troubled voice. "I would I knew him better,

since you, lady, are interested in his fate. He hath, I believe, surmounted the persecution of his enemies in Palestine, and is on the eve of returning to England, where you, lady, must know better than I what is his chance of happiness."

The Lady Rowena sighed deeply, and asked more particularly when the Knight of Ivanhoe might be expected in his native country, and whether he wolud not be exposed to great dangers by the road. On the first point, the Palmer professed ignorance; on the second, he said that the voyage might be safely made by the way of Venice and Genoa, and from thence through France to England. "Ivanhoe," he said, "was so well acquainted with the language and manners of the French, that there was no fear of his incurring any hazard during that part of his travels."

"Would to God," said the Lady Rowena, "he were here safely arrived, and able to bear arms in the approaching tournay, in which the chivalry of this land are expected to display their address and valour. Should Athelstane of Coningsburgh obtain the prize, Ivanhoe is like to hear evil tidings when he reaches England. –How looked he, stranger, when you last saw him? Had disease laid her hand heavy upon his strength and comeliness?"

"He was darker," said the Palmer, "and thinner, than when he came from Cyprus in the train of Cœur-de-Lion, and care seemed to sit heavy on his brow; but I approached not his presence, because he is unknown to me."

"He will," said the lady, "I fear, find little of his native land to clear those clouds from his countenance. Thanks, good Pilgrim, for your information concerning the companion of my childhood. –Maidens," she said, "draw near; offer the sleeping-cup to this holy man, whom I will no longer detain from repose."

One of the maidens presented a silver cup containing a rich mixture of wine and spice, which Rowena barely put to her lips. It was then offered to the Palmer, who, after a low obeisance, tasted a few drops.

"Accept this alms, friend," continued the lady, offering a piece of gold, "in acknowledgment of thy painful travail, and of the shrines thou hast visited."

The Palmer received the boon with another low reverence, and followed Elgitha out of the apartment.

In the anteroom he found his attendant Anwold, who, taking the torch from the hand of the waiting-maid, conducted him with more haste than ceremony to an exterior and ignoble part of the building, where a number of small apartments, or rather cells, served for sleeping places to the lower order of domestics and to strangers of mean degree.

"In which of these sleeps the Jew!" said the Pilgrim.

"The unbelieving dog," answered Anwold, "kennels in the cell next your holiness. –St. Dunstan, how it must be scraped and cleansed ere it be again fit for a Christian!"

"And where sleeps Gurth the swineherd?" said the stranger.

"Gurth," replied the bondsman, "sleeps in the cell on your right, as the Jew in that to your left; you serve to keep the child of circumcision separate from the abomination of his tribe. You might have occupied a more honourable place had you accepted of Oswald's invitation."

"It is as well as it is," said the Palmer; "the company, even of a Jew, can hardly spread contamination through an oaken partition."

So saying, he entered the cabin allotted to him, and taking the torch from the domestic's hand, thanked him, and wished him good-night. Having shut the door of his cell, he placed the torch in a candlestick made of wood, and looked around his sleeping apartment, the furniture of which was of the most simple kind. It consisted of a rude wooden stool, and still ruder hutch or bed-frame, stuffed with clean straw, and accommodated with two or three sheepskins by way of bed-clhothes.

The Palmer, having extinguished his torch, threw himself, without taking off any part of his clothes, on this rude couch, and slept, or at least retained his recumbent posture, till the earliest sunbeams found their way through the little grated window which served at once to admit both air and light to his uncomfortable cell. He then started up, and after repeating his matins and adjusting his dress, he left it and entered that of Isaac the Jew, lifting the latch as gently as he could.

"Fear nothing from me, Isaac," said the Palmer; "I come as your friend."

"The God of Israel requite you," said the Jew, greatly relieved; "I dreamed – but Father Abraham be praised, it was but a dream." Then collecting himself, he added in his usual tone, "And what may it be your pleasure to want at so early an hour with the poor Jew?"

"It is to tell you," said the Palmer, "that if you leave not this mansion instantly, and travel not with some haste, your journey may prove a dangerous one."

"Holy father!" said the Jew, "whom could it interest to endanger so poor a wretch as I am?"

"The purpose you can best guess," said the Pilgrim; "but rely on this, that when the Templar crossed the hall yesternight, he spoke to his Mussulman slaves in the Saracen language, which I well understand, and charged them this morning to watch the journey of the Jew, to seize upon him when at a convenient distance from the mansion, and to conduct him to the castle of Philip de Malvoisin, or to that of Reginald Front-de-Bœuf."

The extremity of terror which seized upon the Jew at this information, seemed to overpower his faculties. His arms fell down to his sides, his knees bent under his weight, and he sunk at the foot of the Palmer like a man borne down by the pressure of some invisible force.

"Holy God of Abraham!" was his first exclamation, folding and elevating his wrinkled hands, but without raising his grey head from the pavement: "O holy Moses! O blessed Aaron! the dream is not dreamed for nought, and the vision cometh not in vain! I feel their irons already tear my sinews! I feel the rack pass over my body like the saws, and harrows, and axes of iron over the men of Rabbah, and of the cities of the children of Ammon!"

"Stand up, Isaac, and hearken to me," said the Palmer, who viewed the extremity of his distress with a compassion in which contempt was largely mingled; stand up, I say, and I will point out to you the means of escape. Leave this mansion instantly, while its inmates sleep sound after the last night's revel. I will guide you by the secret paths of the forest, known as well to me as to any forester that ranges it, and I will not leave you till you are under safe-conduct of some chief or baron going to the tournament, whose good-will you have probably the means of securing."

He led the way to the adjoining cell, which was occupied by Gurth the swineherd. "Arise, Gurth," said the Pilgrim, "arise quickly. Undo the postern gate, and let out the Jew and me."

Gurth was offended at the familiar and commanding tone assumed by the Palmer. "The Jew leaving Rotherwood," said he, raising himself on his elbow, "and travelling in company with the Palmer to boot—"

"I should as soon have dreamt," said Wamba, who entered the apartment at the instant, "of his stealing away with a gammon of bacon."

"Nevertheless," said Gurth, again laying down his head on the wooden log which served him for a pillow, "both Jew and Gentile must be content to abide the opening of the great gate; we suffer no visitors to depart by stealth at these unseasonable hours."

"Nevertheless," said the Pilgrim, in a commanding tone, "you will not, I think, refuse me that favour."

So saying, he stooped over the bed of the recumbent swineherd and whispered something in his ear in Saxon. Gurth started up as if electrified. The Pilgrim, raising his finger in an attitude as if to express caution, added, "Gurth, beware; thou art wont to be prudent. I say, undo the postern; thou shalt know more anon."

With hasty alacrity Gurth obeyed him, while Wamba and the Jew followed, both wondering at the sudden change in the swineherd's demeanour.

"Fetch him his mule," said the Pilgrim; "and, hearest thou, let me have another, that I may bear him company till he is beyond these parts. I will return it safely to some of Cedric's train at Ashby. And do thou" –he whispered the rest in Gurth's ear.

"Willingly, most willingly shall it be done," said Gurth, and instantly departed to execute the commission.

"I wish I knew," said Wamba, when his comrade's back was turned, "what you Palmers learn in the Holy Land."

"To say our orisons, fool," answered the Pilgrim, "to repent our sins, and to mortify ourselves with fastings, vigils, and long prayers."

"Something more potent than that," answered the Jester; "for when would repentance or prayer make Gurth do a courtesy, or fasting or vigil persuade him to lend you a mule? I trow you might as well have told his favourite black boar of thy vigils and penance, and wouldst have gotten as civil an answer."

At this moment Gurth appeared on the opposite side of the moat with the mules. The travellers crossed the ditch upon a drawbridge of only two planks breadth, the narrowness of which was matched with the straitness of the postern, and with a little wicket in the exterior palisade which gave access to the forest. No sooner had they reached the mules, than the

Jew, with hasty and trembling hands, secured behind the saddle a small bag of blue buckram, which he took from under his cloak, containing, as he muttered, "a change of raiment—only a change of raiment." Then getting upon the animal with more alacrity and haste than could have been anticipated from his years, he lost no time in so disposing of the skirts of his gaberdine as to conceal completely from observation the burden which he had thus deposited *en croupe*.

The Pilgrim mounted with more deliberation, reaching, as he departed, his hand to Gurth, who kissed it with the utmost possible veneration.

When the travellers had pushed on at a rapid rate through many devious paths, the Palmer at length broke silence. Said he: "We are now not far from the town of Sheffield, where thou mayest easily find many of thy tribe with whom to take refuge."

"The blessing of Jacob be upon thee, good youth!" said the Jew; "in Sheffield I can harbour with my kinsman Zareth, and find some means of travelling forth with safety."

"Be it so," said the Palmer; "at Sheffield then we part, and half an hour's riding will bring us in sight of that town."

The half hour was spent in perfect silence on both parts; the Pilgrim perhaps disdaining to address the Jew, except in case of absolute necessity, and the Jew not presuming to force a conversation with a person whose journey to the Holy Sepulchre gave a sort of sanctity to his character. They paused on the top of a gently rising bank, and the Pilgrim, pointing to the town of Sheffield, which lay beneath them, repeated the words, "Here, then, we part."

"Stay, stay," said the Jew, laying hold of his garment; "something would I do more than this—something for thyself. God knows the Jew is poor—but forgive me should I guess what thou lackest at this moment. Thy wish even now is for a horse and armour."

The Palmer started, and turned suddenly towards the Jew. "What fiend prompted that guess?" said he, hastily.

"No matter," said the Jew, smiling, "so that it be a true one; and, as I can guess thy want, so I can supply it."

"But consider," said the Palmer, "my character, my dress, my vow."

"I know you Christians," replied the Jew, "and that the noblest of you will take the staff and sandal in superstitious penance, and walk afoot to visit the graves of dead men."

"Blaspheme not, Jew," said the Pilgrim sternly.

"Forgive me," said the Jew; "But there dropped words from you last night and this morning that, like sparks from flint, showed the metal within; and in the bosom of that Palmer's gown is hidden a knight's chain and spurs of gold."

The Pilgrim could not forbear smiling. "Were thy garments searched by as curious an eye, Isaac," said he, "what discoveries might not be made!"

Drawing forth his writing materials in haste, the Jew began to write upon a piece of paper, which he supported on the top of his yellow cap without dismounting from his mule. When he had finished, he delivered the scroll, which was in the Hebrew character, to the Pilgrim, saying, "In the town of Leicester all men know the rich Jew, Kirjath Jairam of Lombardy. Give him this scroll. He hath on sale six Milan harnesses, the worst would suit a crowned head; ten goodly steeds, the worst might mount a king, were he to do battle for his throne. Of these he will give thee thy choice, with everything else that can furnish thee forth for the tournament. When it is over, thou wilt return them safely—unless thou shouldst have wherewith to pay their value to the owner."

"But, Isaac," said the Pilgrim, smiling, "dost thou know that in these sports the arms and steed of the knight who is unhorsed are forfeit to his victor? Now I may be unfortunate, and so lose what I cannot replace or repay."

The Jew looked somewhat astounded at this possibility; but collecting his courage, he replied hastily, "No—no—no, it is impossible; I will not think so. The blessing of our Father will be upon thee. Thy lance will be powerful as the rod of Moses."

So saying, he was turning his mule's head away, when the Palmer, in his turn, took hold of his gaberdine. "Nay, but, Isaac, thou knowest not all the risk. The steed may be slain, the armour injured—for I will spare neither horse nor man. Besides, those of thy tribe give nothing for nothing; something there must be paid for their use."

The Jew twisted himself in the saddle, like a man in a fit of the colic; but his better feelings predominated over those which were most familiar to him. "I care not," he said, "I care not; let me go. If there is damage, it will cost you nothing; if there is usage money, Kirjath Jairam will forgive it for the sake of his kinsman Isaac. Fare thee well!"

They parted, and took different roads for the town of Sheffield.

CHAPTER 7

THE condition of the English nation was at this time sufficiently miserable. King Richard was absent, a prisoner and in the power of the perfidious and cruel Duke of Austria. Even the very place of his captivity was uncertain, and his fate but very imperfectly known to the generality of his subjects, who were, in the meantime, a prey to every species of subaltern oppression.

Prince John, in league with Philip of France, Cœur-de-Lion's mortal enemy, was using every species of influence with the Duke of Austria to prolong the captivity of his brother Richard, to whom he stood indebted for so many favours. In the meantime, he was strengthening his own faction in the kingdom, of which he proposed to dispute the succession, in case of the King's death, with the legitimate heir, Arthur, Duke of Brittany, son of Geoffrey Plantagenet, the elder brother of John. This usurpation, it is well known, he afterwards effected. His own character being light, profligate, and perfidious, John easily attached to his person and faction, not only all who had reason to dread the resentment of Richard for criminal proceeding during his absence, but also the numerous class of "lawless resolutes" whom the crusades had turned back on their country.

Yet amid these distresses, neither duty nor infirmity could keep youth or age from a tournament, which was the grand spectacle of that age.

The Passage of Arms, as it was called, which was to take place at Ashby, in the county of Leicester, as champions of the first renown were to take the field in the presence of Prince John himself, who was expected to grace the lists, had attracted universal attention, and an immense confluence of persons of all ranks hastened upon the appointed morning to the place of combat.

The scene was singularly romantic. On the verge of a wood, which approached to within a mile of the town of Ashby, was an extensive meadow, of the finest and most beautiful green turf, surrounded on one side by the forest, and fringed on the other by straggling oak-trees, some of which had grown to an immense size. The ground, as if fashioned on purpose for the martial display which was intended, sloped gradually down on all sides to a level bottom, which was enclosed for the lists with strong palisades, forming a space of a quarter of a mile in length, and about half as broad. The form of the enclosure was an oblong square, save that the corners were considerably rounded off, in order to afford more convenience for the spectators. The openings for the entry of the combatants were at the northern and southern extremities of the lists, accessible by strong wooden gates, each wide enough to admit two horsemen riding abreast. At each of these portals were stationed two heralds, attended by six trumpets, as many pursuivants, and a strong body of men-at-arms for maintaining order, and ascertaining the quality of the knights who proposed to engage in this martial game.

On a platform beyond the southern entrance, formed by a natural elevation of the ground, were pitched five magnificent pavilions, adorned with pennons of russet and black, the chosen colours of the five knights challengers. The central pavilion, as the place of honour, had been assigned to Brian de Bois-Guilbert, whose renown in all games of chivalry, no less than his connections with the knights who had undertaken this Passage of Arms, had occasioned him to be eagerly received into the company of the challengers, and even adopted as their chief and leader, though he had so recently joined them. On one side of his tent were pitched those of Reginald Front-de-Bœuf and Richard de Malvoisin, and on the other was the pavilion of Hugh de Grandmesnil, a noble baron in the vicinity, whose ancestor had been Lord High Steward of England in the time of the Conqueror, and his son William Rufus. Ralph de Vipont, a knight of St. John of Jerusalem, who had some ancient possessions at a place called Heather, near Ashby-de-la-Zouche, occupied the fifth pavilion.

The exterior of the lists was in part occupied by temporary galleries, spread with tapestry and carpets, and accommodated with cushions for the convenience of those ladies and nobles who were expected to attend the tournament. A narrow space, betwixt these galleries and the lists, gave accommodation for yeomanry and spectators of a better degree than mere vulgar, and might be compared to the pit of a theatre. The promiscuous multitude arranged themselves upon large banks of turf prepared for the purpose, which, aided by the natural elevation of the ground, enabled them to overlook the galleries, and obtain a fair view into the lists. Besides the accommodation

which these stations afforded, many hundreds had perched themselves on the branches of the trees which surrounded the
meadow; and even the steeple of a country church, at some
distance, was crowded with spectators.

One gallery in the very centre of the eastern side of the lists,
and consequently exactly opposite to the spot where the shock
of the combat was to take place, was raised higher than the
others, more richly decorated, and graced by a sort of throne
and canopy, on which the royal arms were emblazoned.
Squires, pages, and yeomen in rich liveries waited around this
place of honour, which was designed for Prince John and his
attendants. Opposite to this royal gallery was another, elevated to the same height, on the western side of the lists, and
more gaily, if less sumptuously decorated, than that destined for the Prince himself. A train of pages and of young maidens, the most beautiful who could be selected, gaily dressed
in fancy habits of green and pink, surrounded a throne decorated in the same colours. Among pennons and flags bearing
wounded hearts, burning hearts, bleeding hearts, bows and
quivers, and all the commonplace emblems of the triumph of
Cupid, a blazoned inscription informed the spectators that
this seat of honour was designed for *La Royne de la Beaulté
et des Amours*. But who was to represent the Queen of Beauty
and of Love on the present occasion no one was prepared to
guess.

Meanwhile, spectators of every description thronged forward
to occupy their respective stations, and not without many
quarrels concerning those which they were entitled to hold.
Some of these were settled by the men-at-arms with brief ceremony; the shafts of their battle-axes, and pommels of their
swords, being readily employed as arguments to convince the
more refractory. Others, which involved the rival claims of
more elevated persons, were determined by the heralds, or by
the two marshals of the field, William de Wyvil and Stephan

de Martival, who, armed at all points, rode up and down the lists to enforce and preserve good order among the spectators.

Gradually the galleries became filled with knights and nobles, in their robes of peace, whose long and rich-tinted mantles were contrasted with the gayer and more splendid habits of the ladies, who, in a greater proportion than even the men themselves, thronged to witness a sport, which one would have thought too bloody and dangerous to afford their sex much pleasure. The lower and interior space was soon filled by substantial yeomen and burghers, and such of the lesser gentry as, from modesty, poverty, or dubious title, durst not assume any higher place. It was, of course, amongst these that the most frequent disputes for precedence occurred.

"Dog of an unbeliever," said an old man, whose threadbare tunic bore witness to his poverty, as his sword, and dagger, and golden chain intimated his pretensions to rank, — "whelp of a she-wolf! darest thou press upon a Christian, and a Norman gentleman of the blood of Montdidier?"

This rough expostulation was addressed to no other than our acquaintance Isaac, who, richly and even magnificently dressed in a gaberdine ornamented with lace and lined with fur, was endeavouring to make place in the foremost row beneath the gallery for his daughter, the beautiful Rebecca, who had joined him at Ashby, and who was now hanging on her father's arm, not a little terrified by the popular displeasure which seemed generally excited by her parent's presumption. But Isaac, though we have seen him sufficiently timid on other occasions, knew well that at present he had nothing to fear. It was not in places of general resort, or where their equals were assembled, that any avaricious or malevolent noble durst offer him injury. At such meetings the Jews were under the protection of the general law; and if that proved a weak assurance, it usually happened that there were among the persons assembled some barons, who, for their own interested motives, were ready to act as their protectors. On the present occasion, Isaac felt more than usually confident, being aware that Prince John was even then in the very act of negotiating a large loan from the Jews of York, to be secured upon certain jewels and lands. Isaac's own share in this transaction was considerable, and he well knew that the Prince's eager desire to bring it to a conclusion would ensure him his protection in the dilemma in which he stood.

Splendidly dressed in crimson and in gold, bearing upon his hand a falcon, and having his head covered by a rich fur bonnet adorned with a circle of precious stones, from which his long curled hair escaped and overspread his shoulders, Prince John, upon a grey and high-mettled palfrey, caracoled within the lists at the head of his jovial party, laughing loud with his train, and eyeing with all the boldness of royal criticism the beauties who adorned the lofty galleries.

In his joyous caracole round the lists, the attention of the Prince was called by the commotion, not yet subsided, which had attended the ambitious movement of Isaac toward the higher places of the assembly. The quick eye of Prince John instantly recognized the Jew, but was much more agreeably attracted by the beautiful daughter of Zion, who clung close to the arm of her aged father.

"What is she, Isaac?" asked the Prince. "Thy wife or thy daughter, that Eastern houri that thou lockest under thy arm as thou wouldst thy treasure-casket?"

"My daughter Rebecca, so please your Grace," answered Isaac, with a low congee.

"The wiser man thou," said John, with a peal of laughter, in which his gay followers obsequiously joined. "But, daughter or wife, she should be preferred according to her beauty and thy merits. — Who sits above there?" he continued, bending his eye on the gallery. "Saxon churls, lolling at their lazy length! Out upon them! — let them sit close, and make room for my prince of usurers and his lovely daughter. I'll make the hinds know they must share the high places of the synagogue with those whom the synagogue properly belongs to."

Those who occupied the gallery to whom this injurious and unpolite speech was addressed, were the family of Cedric the Saxon, with that of his ally and kinsman, Athelstane of Conings-burgh, a personage, who, on account of his descent from the last Saxon monarchs of England, was held in the highest respect by all the Saxon natives of the north of England.

It was to Athelstane that the Prince addressed his imperious command to make place for Isaac and Rebecca. Athelstane, utterly confounded at an order which the manners and feelings of the times rendered so injuriously insulting, unwilling to obey, yet undetermined how to resist, opposed only the *vis inertiae* to the will of John, and, without stirring or making any motion whatever of obedience, opened his large grey eyes, and stared at the Prince with an astonishment which had in it something extremely ludicrous. But the impatient John regarded it in no such light.

"The Saxon porker," he said, "is either asleep or minds me not. — Prick him with your lance, De Bracy," speaking to a knight who rode near him, the leader of a band of Free Companions, or Condottieri — that is, of mercenaries belonging to no particular nation, but attached for the time to any prince by whom they were paid. There was a murmur even among the attendants of Prince John; but De Bracy, whose profession freed him from all scruples, extended his long lance over the space which separated the gallery from the lists, and would have executed the commands of the Prince before Athelstane the Unready had recovered presence of mind sufficient even to draw back his person from the weapon, had not Cedric, as prompt as his companion was tardy, unsheathed, with the speed of lightning, the short sword which he wore, and at a single blow severed the point of the lance from the handle. The blood rushed into the countenance of Prince John. He swore one of his deepest oaths, and was about to utter some threat corresponding in violence, when he was diverted from his purpose, partly by his own attendants, who gathered around him conjuring him to be patient, partly by a general exclamation of the crowd, uttered in loud applause of the spirited conduct of Cedric.

"Stand up, ye Saxon churls," said the fiery Prince; "for, by the light of Heaven, since I have said it, the Jew shall have his seat amongst ye!"

"By no means, an it please your Grace! It is not fit for such as we to sit with the rulers of the land," said the Jew, whose ambition for precedence, though it had led him to dispute place with the extenuated and impoverished descendant of the line of Montdidier, by no means stimulated him to an intrusion upon the privileges of the wealthy Saxons.

"Up, infidel dog, when I command you," said Prince John, "or I will have thy swarthy hide stripped off and tanned for horse furniture."

Thus urged, the Jew began to ascend the steep and narrow steps which led up to the gallery.

"Let me see," said the Prince, "who dare stop him," fixing his eye on Cedric, whose attitude intimated his intention to hurl the Jew down headlong.

The catastrophe was prevented by the clown Wamba, who, springing betwixt his master and Isaac, and exclaiming, in answer to the Prince's defiance, "Marry, that will I!" opposed to the beard of the Jew a shield of brawn, which he plucked from beneath his cloak, and with which, doubtless, he had furnished himself, lest the tournament should have proved longer than his appetite could endure abstinence. Finding the abomination of this tribe opposed to his very nose, while the Jester, at the same time, flourished his wooden sword above his head, the Jew recoiled, missed his footing, and rolled down the steps—an excellent jest to the spectators, who set up a loud laughter, in which Prince John and his attendants heartily joined.

"Deal me the prize, cousin Prince," said Wamba; "I have vanquished my foe in fair fight with sword and shield," he added, brandishing the brawn in one hand and the wooden sword in the other.

"Who and what art thou, noble champion?" said Prince John, still laughing.

"A fool by right of descent," answered the Jester; "I am Wamba, the son of Witless, who was the son of Weatherbrain, who was the son of an Alderman."

"Make room for the Jew in front of the lower ring," said Prince John, not unwilling perhaps to seize an apology to desist from his original purpose; "to place the vanquished beside the victor were false heraldry."

"Knave upon fool were worse," answered the Jester, "and Jew upon bacon worst of all."

"Gramercy! good fellow," cried Prince John, "thou pleasest me. — Here, Isaac, lend me a handful of byzants."

As the Jew, stunned by the request, afraid to refuse, and unwilling to comply, fumbled in the furred bag which hung by his girdle, and was perhaps endeavouring to ascertain how few coins might pass for a handful, the Prince stooped from his jennet and settled Isaac's doubts by snatching the pouch itself from his side; and flinging to Wamba a couple of the gold pieces which it contained, he pursued his career round the lists, leaving the Jew to the derision of those around him, and himself receiving as much applause from the spectators as if he had done some honest and honourable action.

CHAPTER 8

IN THE midst of Prince John's cavalcade he suddenly stopped, and appealing to the Prior of Jorvaulx, declared the principal business of the day had been forgotten.

"By my halidom," said he, "we have neglected, Sir Prior, to name the fair Sovereign of Love and of Beauty, by whose white hand the palm is to be distributed. For my part, I am liberal in my ideas, and I care not if I give my vote for the black-eyed Rebecca."

"Holy Virgin," answered the Prior, turning up his eyes in horror, "a Jewess! We should deserve to be stoned out of the lists; and I am not yet old enough to be a martyr. Besides, I swear by my patron saint that she is far inferior to the lovely Saxon, Rowena."

"Saxon or Jew," answered the Prince. "Saxon or Jew, dog or hog, what matters it? I say, name Rebecca, were it only to mortify the Saxon churls."

A murmur arose even among his own immediate attendants.

"This passes a jest, my lord," said De Bracy; "no knight here will lay lance in rest if such an insult is attempted."

From the tone in which this was spoken, John saw the necessity of acquiescence. "I did but jest," he said, "and you turn upon me like so many adders! Name whom you will, in the fiend's name, and please yourselves."

"Nay, nay," said De Bracy, "let the fair sovereign's throne remain unoccupied, until the conqueror shall be named, and then let him choose the lady by whom it shall be filled. It will add another grace to his triumph, and teach fair ladies to prize the love of valiant knights, who can exalt them to such distinction."

"Silence, sirs," said Waldemar, "and let the Prince assume his seat. The knights and spectators are alike impatient, the time advances, and highly fit it is that the sports should commence."

Prince John, though not yet a monarch, had in Waldemar Fitzurse all the inconveniences of a favourite minister, who, in serving his sovereign, must always do so in his own way. The Prince acquiesced, however, although his disposition was precisely of that kind which is apt to be obstinate upon trifles; and, assuming his throne, and being surrounded by his followers, gave signal to the heralds to proclaim the laws of the tournament, which were briefly as follows: —

First, the five challengers were to undertake all comers.

Secondly, any knight proposing to combat, might, if he pleased, select a special antagonist from among the challengers, by touching his shield. If he did so with the reverse of his lance, the trial of skill was made with what were called the arms of courtesy, that is, with lances at whose extremity a piece of round flat board was fixed, so that no danger was encountered, save from the shock of the horses and riders. But if the shield was touched with the sharp end of the lance, the combat was understood to be at *outrance*—that is, the knights were to fight with sharp weapons, as in actual battle.

Thirdly, when the knights present had accomplished their vow, by each of them breaking five lances, the Prince was to declare the victor in the first day's tourney, who should receive as prize a war-horse of exquisite beauty and matchless strength; and in addition he should have the honour of naming the Queen of Love and Beauty, by whom the prize should be given on the ensuing day.

Fourthly, on the second day, there should be a general tournament, in which all the knights present might take part; and being divided into two bands of equal numbers, might fight it out manfully, until the signal was given by Prince John to cease the combat. The elected Queen of Love and Beauty was then to crown the knight whom the Prince should adjudge to have borne himself best in this second day, with a coronet composed of thin gold plate, cut into the shape of a laurel crown. On this second day the knightly games ceased. But on that which was to follow, feats of archery, of bull-baiting, and other popular amusements, were to be practised, for the more immediate amusement of the populace. In this manner did Prince John endeavour to lay the foundation of a popularity, which he was perpetually throwing down by some inconsiderate act of wanton aggression upon the feelings and prejudices of the people.

The lists now presented a most splendid spectacle. The sloping galleries were crowded with all that was noble, great, wealthy, and beautiful in the northern and midland parts of England; and the contrast of the various dresses of the dignified spectators rendered the view as gay as it was rich, while the interior and lower space, filled with the substantial burgesses and yeomen of merry Englad, formed in their more plain attire, a dark fringe or border around this circle of brilliant embroidery, relieving, and, at the same time, setting off its splendour.

The heralds finished their proclamation with their usual cry of "Largesse, largesse, gallant knights!" and gold and silver pieces were showered on them from the galleries, it being a high point of chivalry to exhibit liberality towards those whom the age accounted at once the secretaries and the historians of honour. The bounty of the spectators was acknowledged by the customary shouts of "Love of Ladies—Death of Champions—Honour to the Generous—Glory to the Brave!" To which the more humble spectators added their acclamations, and a numerous band of trumpeters the flourish of their martial instruments. When these sounds had ceased, the heralds withdrew from the lists in gay and glittering procession, and none remained within them save the marshals of the field, who, armed cap-a-pie, sat on horseback, motionless as statues, at the opposite ends of the lists. Meantime, the enclosed space at the northern extremity of the lists, large as it was, was now completely crowded with knights desirous to prove their skill against the challengers, and, when viewed from the galleries, presented the appearance of a sea of waving plumage, intermixed with glistening helmets and tall lances, to the extremities of which were, in many cases, attached small pennons of about a span's breadth, which, fluttering in the air as the breeze caught them, joined with the restless motion of the feathers to add liveliness to the scene.

At length the barriers were opened, the five knights, chosen by lot, advanced slowly into the area, a single champion riding in front, and the other four following in pairs.

The champions advanced through the lists, restraining their fiery steeds, and compelling them to move slowly, while, at the same time, they exhibited their paces, together with the grace and dexterity of the riders. As the procession entered the lists, the sound of a wild barbaric music was heard from behind the tents of the challengers, where the performers were concealed. It was of Eastern origin, having been brought from the Holy Land; and the mixture of the cymbals and bells seemed to bid welcome at once, and defiance, to the knights as they advanced. With the eyes of an immense concourse of spectators fixed upon them, the five knights advanced up the platform upon which the tents of the challengers stood, and there separating themselves, each touched slightly, and with the reverse of his lance, the shield of the antagonist to whom he wished to oppose himself.

Having intimated their more pacific purpose, the champions retreated to the extremity of the lists, where they remained drawn up in a line; while the challengers, sallying each from his pavilion, mounted their horses, and, headed by Brian de Bois-Guilbert, descended from the platform, and opposed themselves individually to the knights who had touched their respective shields.

At the flourish of clarions and trumpets, they started out against each other at full gallop; and such was the superior dexterity or good fortune of the challengers, that those opposed to Bois-Guilbert, Malvoisin, and Front-de-Bœuf, rolled on the ground. The antagonist of Grantmesnil, instead of bearing his lance-point fair against the crest or the shield of his enemy, swerved so much from the direct line as to break the weapon athwart the person of his opponent —a circumstance which was accounted more disgraceful than that of being actually unhorsed, because the latter might happen from accident, whereas the former evinced awkwardness and want of management of the weapon and of the horse. The fifth knight alone maintained the honour of his party, and parted fairly with the Knight of St. John, both splintering their lances without advantage on either side.

A second and third party of knights took the field; and although they had various success, yet, upon the whole, the advantage decidedly remained with the challengers, not one of whom lost his seat or swerved from his charge —misfortunes which befell one or two of their antagonists in each encounter. Three knights only appeared on the fourth entry, who, avoiding the shields of Bois-Guilbert and Front-de-Bœuf, contented themselves with touching those of the three other knights. However, this selection did not alter the fortune of the field.

As the Saracenic music of the challengers concluded one of those long and high flourishes with which they had broken the silence of the lists, it was answered by solitary trumpet, which breathed a note of defiance from the northern extremity. All eyes were turned to see the new champion which these sounds announced, and no sooner were the barriers opened than he paced in to the lists. As far as could be judged of a man sheathed in armour, the new adventurer did not greatly exceed the middle size, and seemed to be rather slender than strongly made. His suit of armour was formed of steel richly inlaid with gold, and the device on his shield was a young oak-tree pulled up by the roots, with the Spanish word *Desdichado*, signifying Disinherited. He was mounted on a gallant black horse, and as he passed through the lists he gracefully saluted the Prince and the ladies by lowering his lance.

The champion ascended the platform by the sloping alley which led to it from the lists, and, to the astonishment of all present, riding straight up to the central pavilion, struck with the sharp end of his spear the shield of Brian de Bois-Guilbert until it rung again. All stood astonished at his presumption, but none more than the redoubted Knight whom he had thus defied to mortal combat, and who, little expecting so rude a challenge, was standing carelessly at the door of the pavilion.

"Have you confessed yourself, brother," said the Templar, "and have you heard mass this morning, that you peril your life so frankly?"

"I am fitter to meet death than thou art," answered the Disinherited Knight; for by this name the stranger had recorded himself in the books of the tourney.

"Then take your place in the lists," said Bois-Guibert, "and look your last upon the sun, for this night thou shalt sleep in paradise."

"Gramercy for thy courtesy," replied the Disinherited Knight; "and to requite it, I advise thee to take a fresh horse and a new lance, for by my honour you will need both."

Having expressed himself thus confidently, he reined his horse backward down the slope which he had ascended, and compelled him in the same manner to move backward through the lists, till he reached the northern extremity, where he remained stationary, in expectation of his antagonist. This feat of horsemanship again attracted the applause of the multitude.

When the two champions stood opposed to each other at the two extremities of the lists, the public expectation was strained to the highest pitch. Few augured the possibility that the encounter could terminate well for the Disinherited Knight, yet his courage and gallantry secured the general good wishes of the spectators.

The trumpets had no sooner given the signal, than the champions vanished from their posts with the speed of lightning, and closed in the centre of the lists with the shock of a thunderbolt. The lances burst into shivers up to the very grasp, and it seemed at the moment that both knights had fallen, for the shock had made each horse recoil backwards upon its haunches. The address of the riders recovered their steeds by use of the bridle and spur; and having glared on each other for an instant with eyes which seemed to flash fire through the bars of their visors, each made a demivolte, and, retiring to the extremity of the lists, received a fresh lance from the attendants.

A loud shout from the spectators, waving of scarfs and handkerchiefs, and general acclamations, attested the interest taken by the spectators in this encounter, the most equal, as well as the best performed, which had graced the day. But no sooner had the knights resumed their station, than the clamour of applause was hushed into a silence so deep and so dead, that it seemed the multitude were afraid even to breathe.

A few minutes' pause having been allowed, that the combatants and their horses might recover breath, Prince John with his truncheon signed to the trumpets to sound the onset. The champions a second time sprang from their stations, and closed in the centre of the lists, with the same speed, the same dexterity, the same violence, but not the same equal fortune as before.

In this second encounter, the Templar aimed at the centre of his antagonist's shield, and struck it so fair and forcibly that his spear went to shivers, and the Disinherited Knight reeled in his saddle. On the other hand, that champion had, in the beginning of his career, directed the point of his lance towards Bois-Guilbert's shield; but, changing his aim almost in the moment of encounter, he addressed it to the helmet, a mark more difficult to hit, but which, if attained, rendered the shock more irresistibile. Fair and true he hit the Norman on the visor, where his lance's point kept hold of the bars. Yet, even at this disadvantage, the Templar sustained his high reputation, and had not the girths of his saddle burst, he might not have been unhorsed. As it chanced, however, saddle, horse, and man rolled on the ground under a cloud of dust.

To extricate himself from the stirrups and a fallen steed was to the Templar scarce the work of a moment; and, stung with madness, both at his disgrace and at the acclamations with which it was hailed by the spectators, he drew his sword and waved it in defiance of his conqueror. The Disinherited Knight sprung from his steed, and also unsheathed his sword. The marshals of the field, however, spurred their horses between them, and reminded them that the laws of the tournament did not, on the present occasion, permit this species of encounter.

"We shall meet again, I trust," said the Templar, casting a resentful glance at his antagonist; "and where there are none to separate us."

"If we do not," said the Disinherited Knight, "the fault shall not be mine. On foot or horseback, with spear, with axe, or with sword, I am alike ready to encounter thee."

More and angrier words would have been exchanged, but the marshals, crossing their lances betwixt them, compelled them to separate. The Disinherited Knight returned to his first station, and Bois-Guilbert to his tent, where he remained for the rest of the day in an agony of despair.

Without alighting from his horse, the conqueror called for a bowl of wine, and opening the beaver, or lower part of his helmet, announced that he quaffed it, "To all true English hearts, and to the confusion of foreign tyrants." He then commanded his trumpet to sound a defiance to the challengers, and desired a herald to announce to them that he should make no election, but was willing to encounter them in the order in which they pleased to advance against him.

The gigantic Front-de-Bœuf, armed in sable armour, was the first who took the field. He bore on a white shield a black bull's head, half defaced by the encounters which he had undergone, and bearing the arrogant motto, *Cave, Adsum.* Over this champion the Disinherited Knight obtained a slight but decisive advantage. Both Knights broke their lances fairly, but Front-de-Bœuf, who lost a stirrup in the encounter, was adjudged to have the disadvantage.

In the stranger's third encounter, with Sir Philip Malvoisin, he was equally successful; striking that baron so forcibly on the casque, that the laces of the helmet broke, and Malvoisin, only saved from falling by being unhelmeted, was declared vanquished, like his companions.

In his fourth combat, with De Grantmesnil, the Disinherited Knight showed as much courtesy as he had hitherto evinced courage and dexterity. De Grantmesnil's horse, which was young and violent, reared and plunged in the course of the career so as to disturb the rider's aim; and the stranger, declining to take the advantage which this accident afforded him, raised his lance, and passing his antagonist without touching him, wheeled his horse and rode back again to his own end of the lists, offering his antagonist, by a herald, the chance of a second encounter. This De Grantmesnil declined, avowing himself vanquished as much by the courtesy as by the address of his opponent.

Ralph de Vipont summed up the list of the stanger's triumphs, being hurled to the ground with such force that the blood gushed from his nose and his mouth, and he was borne senseless from the lists.

The acclamations of thousands applauded the unanimous award of the Prince and marshals, announcing that day's honours to the Disinherited Knight.

CHAPTER 9

WILLIAM DE WYVIL and Stephen de Martival, the marshals of the field, were the first to offer their congratulations to the victor, praying him, at the same time, to suffer his helmet to be unlaced, or, at least, that he would raise his visor ere they conducted him to receive the prize of the day's tourney from the hands of Prince John. The Disinherited Knight, with all knightly courtesy, declined their request, alleging that he could not at this time suffer his face to be seen, for reasons which he had assigned to the heralds when he entered the lists. The marshals were perfectly satisfied by this reply; for amidst the frequent and capricious vows by which knights were accustomed to bind themselves in the days of chivalry, there were none more common than those by which they engaged to remain incognito for a certain space, or until some particular adventure was achieved.

John's curiosity was excited by the mystery observed by the stranger; and, being already displeased with the issue of the tournament, in which the challengers whom he favoured had been successively defeated by one knight, he answered haughtily to the marshals, "By the light of Our Lady's brow, this same knight hath been disinherited as well of his courtesy as of his lands, since he desires to appear before us without uncovering his face.—Wot yet, my lords," he said, turning round to his train, "who this gallant can be, that bears himself thus proudly?"

While he was yet speaking the marshals brought forward the Disinherited Knight to the foot of a wooden flight of steps which formed the ascent from the lists to Prince John's throne. But the Disinherited Knight spoke not a word in reply to the compliment of the Prince, which he only acknowledged with a profound obeisance.

The horse was led into the lists by two grooms richly dressed, the animal itself being fully accoutred with the richest war-furniture, which, however, scarcely added to the value of the noble creature in the eyes of those who were judges. Laying one hand upon the pommel of the saddle, the Disinherited Knight vaulted at once upon the back of the steed without making use of the stirrup, and, brandishing aloft his lance, rode twice around the lists, exhibiting the points and paces of the horse with the skill of a perfect horseman.

The bustling Prior of Jorvaulx had reminded Prince John, in a whisper, that the victor must now display his good judgment, instead of his valour, by selecting from among the beauties who graced the galleries, a lady who should fill the throne of the Queen of Beauty and of Love, and deliver the prize of the tourney upon the ensuing day. The Prince accordingly made a sign with his truncheon, as the Knight passed him in his second career around the lists. The Knight turned towards the throne, and sinking his lance, until the point was within a foot of the ground, remained motionless, as if expecting John's commands.

"Sir Disinherited Knight," said Prince John, "since that is the only title by which we can address you, it is now your duty, as well as privilege, to name the fair lady, who, as Queen of Honour and of Love, is to preside over next day's festival. If, as a stranger in our land, you should require the aid of other judgment to guide your own, we can only say that Alicia, the daughter of our gallant knight Waldemar Fitzurse, has at our court been long held the first in beauty as in place. Nevertheless, it is your undoubted prerogative to confer on whom you please this crown, by the delivery of which to the lady of your choice, the election of to-morrow's Queen will be formal and complete. Raise your lance."

The Knight obeyed; and Prince John placed upon its point a coronet of green satin, having around its edge a circlet of gold, the upper edge of which was relieved by arrow-points and hearts placed interchangeably, like the strawberry leaves and balls upon a ducal crown.

The Disinherited Knight passed the gallery, close to that of the Prince, in which the Lady Alicia was seated in the full pride of triumphant beauty, and, pacing forwards as slowly as he had hitherto rode swiftly around the lists, he seemed to exercise his right of examining the numerous fair faces which adorned that splendid circle.

At length the champion paused beneath the balcony in which the Lady Rowena was placed, and the expectation of the spectators was excited to the utmost.

He remained stationary for more than a minute, while the eyes of the silent audience were riveted upon his motions; and then, gradually and gracefully sinking the point of his lance, he deposited the coronet which it supported at the feet of the fair Rowena. The trumpets instantly sounded, while the heralds proclaimed the Lady Rowena the Queen of Beauty and of Love for the ensuing day, menacing with suitable penalties those who should be disobedient to her authority.

However unacceptable to Prince John, and to those around him, he saw himself nevertheless obliged to confirm the nomination of the victor, and accordingly calling to horse, he left his throne, and mounting his jennet, accompanied by his train, he again entered the lists. The Prince paused a moment beneath the gallery of the Lady Alicia, to whom he paid his compliments, then, spurring his horse, as if to give vent to his vexation, he made the animal bound forward to the gallery where Rowena was seated, with the crown still at her feet.

"Assume," he said, "fair lady, the mark of your sovereignty, to which none vows homage more sincerely than ourself, John of Anjou; and if it please you to-day, with your noble sire and friends, to grace our banquet in the Castle of Ashby, we shall learn to know the empress to whose service we devote to-morrow."

Rowena remained silent, and Cedric answered for her in his native Saxon.

"The Lady Rowena," he said, "possesses not the language in which to reply to your courtesy, or to sustain her part in your festival. I also, and the noble Athelstane of Coningsburgh, speak only the language, and practise only the manners of our fathers. We therefore decline with thanks your Highness's courteous invitation to the banquet. To-morrow, the Lady Rowena will take upon her the state to which she has been called by the free election of the victor Knight, confirmed by the acclamations of the people."

So saying, he lifted the coronet, and placed it upon Rowena's head, in token of her acceptance of the temporary authority assigned to her.

"What says he?" said Prince John, affecting not to understand the Saxon language, in which, however, he was well skilled. The purport of Cedric's speech was repeated to him in French. "It is well," he said; "to-morrow we will ourself conduct this mute sovereign to her seat of dignity.—You, at least, Sir Knight," he added, turning to the victor, who had remained near the gallery, "will this day share our banquet?"

The Knight, speaking for the first time, in a low and hurried voice, excused himself by pleading fatigue, and the necessity of preparing for tomorrow's encounter.

"It is well," said Prince John haughtily. "Although unused to such refusals, we will endeavour to digest our banquet as we may, though ungraced by the most successful in arms, and his elected Queen of Beauty."

So saying, he prepared to leave the lists with his glittering train, and turning his steed for that purpose was the signal for the breaking up and dispersion of the spectators.

CHAPTER 10

THE Disinherited Knight had no sooner reached his pavilion than squires and pages in abundance tendered their service to disarm him, to bring fresh attire, and to offer him the refreshment of the bath. Their zeal on this occasion was perhaps sharpened by curiosity, since every one desired to know who the knight was that had gained so many laurels, yet had refused, even at the command of Prince John, to lift his visor or to name his name. But their officious inquisitiveness was not gratified. The Disinherited Knight refused all other assistance save that of his own squire, or rather yeoman—a clownish-looking man, who, wrapped in a cloak of dark-coloured felt, and having his head and face half-buried in a Norman bonnet made of black fur, seemed to affect the incognito as much as his master.

The Knight had scarcely finished a hasty meal, ere his menial announced to him that five men, each leading a barbed steed, desired to speak with him. The Disinherited Knight had exchanged his armour for the long robe usually worn by those of his condition, which, being furnished with a hood, concealed the features, when such was the pleasure of the wearer, almost as completely as the visor of the helmet itself; but the twilight, which was now fast darkening, would of itself have rendered a disguise unnecessary, unless to persons to whom the face of an individual chanced to be particularly well known.

The Disinherited Knight, therefore, stepped boldly forth to the front of his tent, and found in attendance the squires of the challengers, whom he easily knew by their russet and black dresses, each of whom led his master's charger, loaded with the armour in which he had that day fought.

"According to the laws of chivalry," said the foremost of these men, "I, Baldwin de Oyley, squire to the redoubted Knight Brian de Bois-Guilbert, make offer to you, styling yourself, for the present, the Disinherited Knight, of the horse and armour used by the said Brian de Bois-Guilbert in this day's Passage of Arms, leaving it with your nobleness, to retain or to ransom the same, according to your pleasure; for such is the law of arms."

The other squires repeated nearly the same formula, and then stood to await the decision of the Disinherited Knight.

"To you four, sirs," replied the Knight, addressing those who had last spoken, "and to your honourable and valiant masters, I have one common reply. Commend me to the noble knights, your masters, and say, I should do ill to deprive them of steeds and arms which can never be used by braver cavaliers. I would I could here end my message to these gallant knights; but being, as I term myself, in truth and earnest, the Disinherited, I must be thus far bound to your masters, that they will, of their courtesy, be pleased to ransom their steeds and armour, since that which I wear I can hardly term mine own."

"We stand commissioned each of us," answered the squire of Reginald Front-de-Bœuf, "to offer a hundred zecchins in ransom of these horses and suits of armour."

"It is sufficient," said the Disinherited Knight. "Half the sum my present necessities compel me to accept; of the remaining half, distribute one moiety among yourselves, sir squires, and divide the other half betwixt the heralds and the pursuivants, and minstrels and attendants."

The squires, with cap in hand, and low reverences, expressed their deep sense of a courtesy and generosity not often practised, at least upon a scale so extensive. The Disinherited Knight then addressed his discourse to Baldwin, the squire of Brian de Bois-Guilbert. "From your master," said he, "I will accept neither arms nor ransom. Say to him in my name, that our strife is not ended –no, not until we have fought as well with swords as with lances –as well on foot as on horseback. To this mortal quarrel he has himself defied me, and I shall not forget the challenge. Meantime, let him be assured, that I hold him not as one of his companions, with whom I can with pleasure exchange courtesies, but rather as one with whom I stand upon terms of mortal defiance."

"My master," answered Baldwin, "knows how to requite scorn with scorn, and blows with blows, as well as courtesy with courtesy. Since you disdain to accept from him any share of the ransom at which you have rated the arms of the other knights, I must leave his armour and his horse here, being well assured that he will never deign to mount the one nor wear the other."

"You have spoken well, good squire," said the Disinherited Knight, "well and boldly, as it beseemeth him to speak who answers for an absent master. Leave not, however, the horse and armour here. Restore them to thy master; or, if he scorns to accept them, retain them, good friend, for thine own use. So far as they are mine, I bestow them upon you freely."

Baldwin made a deep obeisance, and retired with his companions; and the Disinherited Knight entered the pavilion.

We must now change the scene to the village of Ashby, or rather to a country house in its vicinity belonging to a wealthy Israelite, with whom Isaac, his daughter, and retinue had taken up their quarters.

In an apartment, small indeed, but richly furnished with decorations of an Oriental taste, Rebecca was seated on a heap of embroidered cushions, which, piled along a low platform that surrounded the chamber, served, like the estrada of the Spaniards, instead of chairs and stools. She was watching the motions of her father with a look of anxious and filial affection, while he paced the apartment with a dejected mien and disordered step –sometimes clasping his hands together, sometimes casting his eyes to the roof of the apartment, as one who laboured under great mental tribulation. "Oh, Jacob!" he exclaimed –"oh, all ye twelve Holy Fathers of our tribe! what a losing venture is this for one who hath duly kept every jot and tittle of the law of Moses. Fifty zecchins wrenched from me at one clutch, and by the talons of a tyrant!"

"But, father," said Rebecca, "you seemed to give the gold to Prince John willingly."

"Willingly? the blotch of Egypt upon him! –Willingly, saidst thou? Ay, as willingly as when, in the Gulf of Lyons, I flung over my merchandise to lighten the ship while she laboured in the tempest –robed the seething billows in my choice silks – perfumed their briny foam with myrrh and aloes — enriched their caverns with gold and silver work! And was not that an hour of unutterable misery, though my own hands made the sacrifice?"

"But it was a sacrifice which Heaven exacted to save our lives," answered Rebecca; "and the God of our fathers has since blessed your store and your gettings."

"Ay," answered Isaac; "but if the tyrant lays hold on them as he did to-day, and compels me to smile while he is robbing me? Oh, daughter, disinherited and wandering as we are, the worst evil which befalls our race is, that when we are wronged and plundered all the world laughs around, and we are compelled to suppress our sense of injury, and to smile tamely, when we would revenge bravely."

The evening was now becoming dark, when a Jewish servant entered the apartment, and placed upon the table two silver lamps fed with perfumed oil; the richest wines, and the most delicate refreshments, were at the same time displayed by another Israelitish domestic on a small ebony table, inlaid with silver; for, in the interior of their houses, the Jews refused themselves no expensive indulgences. At the same time the servant informed Isaac that a Nazarene (so they termed Christians, while conversing among themselves) desired to speak with him. He that would live by traffic, must hold himself at the disposal of every one claiming business with him. Isaac at once replaced on the table the untasted glass of Greek wine which he had just raised to his lips, and saying hastily to his daughter, "Rebecca, veil thyself," commanded the stranger to be admitted.

Just as Rebecca had dropped over her fine features a screen of silver gauze which reached to her feet, the door opened, and Gurth entered, wrapped in the ample folds of his Norman mantle.

"Art thou Isaac the Jew of York?" said Gurth, in Saxon.

"I am," replied Isaac, in the same language (for his traffic had rendered every tongue spoken in Britain familiar to him) – "and who art thou?"

"That is not to the purpose," answered Gurth.

"As much as my name is to thee," replied Isaac; "for without knowing thine, how can I hold intercourse with thee?"

"Easily," answered Gurth. "I, being to pay money, must know that I deliver it to the right person; thou, who are to receive it, will not, I think, care very greatly by whose hands it is delivered."

"Oh," said the Jew, "you are come to pay moneys? – Holy Father Abraham! that altereth our relation to each other. And from whom dost thou bring it?"

"From the Disinherited Knight," said Gurth, "victor in this day's tournament. It is the price of the armour supplied to him by Kirjath Jairam of Leicester, on the recommendation.

The steed is restored to thy stable. I desire to know the amount of the sum which I am to pay for the armour."

"I said he was a good youth!" exclaimed Isaac with joyful exultation. "A cup of wine will do thee no harm," he added, filling and handing to the swineherd a richer draught than Gurth has ever before tasted. "And how much money," continued Isaac, "hast thou brought with thee?"

"Holy Virgin!" said Gurth, setting down the cup, "what nectar these unbelieving dogs drink, while true Christians are fain to quaff ale as muddy and thick as the draff we give to hogs!-What money have I brought with me?" continued the Saxon, when he had finished this uncivil ejaculation, "even but a small sum -something in hand the whilst. What, Isaac! thou must bear a conscience, though it be a Jewish one."

"Nay, but," said Isaac, "thy master has won goodly steeds and rich armours with the strength of his lance and of his right hand -but 'tis a good youth -the Jew will take these in present payment, and render him back the surplus."

"My master has disposed of them already," said Gurth.

"Ah! that was wrong," said the Jew -"that was the part of a fool. No Christian here could buy so many horses and armour; no Jew except myself would give him half the values. But thou hast a hundred zecchins, with thee in that bag," said Isaac, prying under Gurth's cloak; "it is a heavy one."

"I have heads for cross-bow bolts in it," said Gurth readily.

"Well, then," said Isaac, panting and hesitating between habitual love of gain and a new-born desire to be liberal in the present instance, "if I should say that I would take eighty zecchins for the good steed and the rich armour, which leaves me not a guilder's profit, have you money to pay me?"

"Barely," said Gurth, though the sum demanded was more reasonable than he expected, "and it will leave my master nigh penniless. Nevertheless, if such be your least offer, I must be content."

"Fill thyself another goblet of wine," said the Jew. "Ah, eighty zecchins is too little. It leaveth no profit for the usages of the moneys; and, besides, the good horse may have suffered wrong in this day's encounter. Oh, it was a hard and dangerous meeting!-man and steed rushing on each other like wild bulls of Bashan! The horse cannot but have had wrong."

"And I say," replied Gurth, "he is sound, wind and limb, and you may see him now, in your stable. And I say, over and above, that seventy zecchins is enough for the armour; and I hope a Christian's word is as good as a Jew's. If you will not take seventy, I will carry this bag" (and he shook it till the contents jingled)"back to my master."

"Nay, nay!" said Isaac; "lay down the talents -the shekels - the eighty zecchins, and thou shalt see I will consider thee liberally."

Gurth at length complied, and telling out eighty zecchins upon the table, the Jew delivered out to him an acquittance for the horse and suit of armour.

Gurth folded the quittance, and put it under his cap, adding, "Peril of thy beard, Jew, see that this be full and ample!" He filled himself, unbidden, a third goblet of wine, and left the apartment without ceremony.

Gurth had descended the stair, when a figure in white, shown by a small silver lamp which she held in her hand, beckoned him into a side apartment. After a moment's pause, he obeyed the beckoning summons, and followed her into the apartment where he found to his joyful surprise that his fair guide was the beautiful Jewess whom he had seen at the tournament.

She asked him the particulars of his transaction with Isaac which he detailed accurately.

"My father did but jest with thee, good fellow," said Rebecca; "he owes thy master deeper kindness than these arms and steed could pay, were their value tenfold. What sum didst thou pay my father even now?"

"Eighty zecchins," said Gurth, surprised at the question. "In this purse," said Rebecca, "thou wilt find a hundred. Restore to thy master that which is his due, and enrich thyself with the remainder. Haste —begone —stay not to render thanks! and beware how you pass through this crowded town, where thou mayest easily lose both thy burden and thy life. —Reuben," she added, clapping her hands together, "light forth this stranger, and fail not to draw lock and bar behind him."

Reuben, a dark-browed and black-bearded Israelite, obeyed her summons, with a torch in his hand —undid the outward door of the house, and conducting Gurth across a paved court, let him out through a wicket in the entrance-gate, which he closed behind him with such bolts and chains as would well have become that of a prison.

"By St. Dunstan," said Gurth, as he stumbled up the dark avenue, "this is no Jewess, but an angel from heaven! Ten zecchins from my brave young master, twenty from this pearl of Zion —oh, happy day! Such another, Gurth, will redeem thy bondage, and make thee a brother as free of thy guild as the best. And then do I lay down my swineherd's horn and staff, and take the freeman's sword and buckler, and follow my young master to the death, without hiding either my face or my name."

CHAPTER 11

MORNING arose in unclouded splendour, and ere the sun was much above the horizon, the idlest or the most eager of the spectators appeared on the common, moving to the lists as to a general centre, in order to secure a favourable situation for viewing the continuation of the expected games.

According to due formality, the Disinherited Knight was to be considered as leader of the one body, while Brian de

Bois-Guilbert, who had been rated as having done second-best in the preceding day, was named first champion of the other band. Those who had concurred in the challenge adhered to his party of course, excepting only Ralph de Vipont, whom his fall had rendered unfit so soon to put on his armour.

About the hour of ten o'clock, the whole plain was crowded with horsemen, horsewomen, and foot-passengers, hastening to the tournament; and shortly after, a grand flourish of trumpets announced Prince John and his retinue, attended by many of those knights who meant to take share in the game, as well as others who had no such intention.

About the same time arrived Cedric the Saxon, with the Lady Rowena, unattended, however, by Athelstane. This Saxon lord had arrayed his tall and strong person in armour, in order to take his place among the combatants; and, considerably to the surprise of Cedric, had chosen to enlist himself on the part of the Knight Templar. The Saxon, indeed, had remonstrated strongly with his friend upon the injudicious choice he had made of his party; but he had only received that sort of answer usually given by those who are more obstinate in following their own course, than strong in justifying it.

No sooner was Rowena seated than a burst of music, half-drowned by the shouts of the multitude, greeted her new dignity.

The heralds then proclaimed silence until the laws of the tourney should be rehearsed. These were calculated in some degree to abate the dangers of the day—a precaution the more necessary, as the conflict was to be maintained with sharp swords and pointed lances.

This proclamation having been made, the heralds withdrew to their stations. The knights, entering at either end of the lists in long procession, arranged themselves in a double file, precisely opposite to each other, the leader of each party being in the centre of the foremost rank, a post which he did not occupy until each had carefully marshalled the ranks of his party, and stationed every one in his place. The marshals then withdrew from the lists, and William de Wyvil, with a voice of thunder, pronounced the signal words –*Laissez aller!* The trumpets sounded as he spoke; the spears of the champions were at once lowered and placed in the rests; the spurs were dashed into the flanks of the horses, and the two foremost ranks of either party rushed upon each other in full gallop, and met in the middle of the lists with a shock, the sound of which was heard at a mile's distance. The rear rank of each party advanced at a slower pace to sustain the defeated, and follow up the success of the victors of their party.

The consequences of the encounter were not instantly seen, for the dust raised by the trampling of so many steeds darkened the air, and it was a minute ere the anxious spectators could see the fate of the encounter. When the fight became visible, half the knights on each side were dismounted, some by the dexterity of their adversary's lance; some by the superior weight and strength of opponents, which had borne down both horse and man; some lay stretched on earth as if never more to rise; some had already gained their feet, and were closing hand to hand with those of their antagonists who were in the same predicament; and several on both sides, who had received wounds by which they were disabled, were stopping their blood by their scarfs, and endeavouring to extricate themselves from the tumult. The mounted knights, whose lances had been almost all broken by the fury of the encounter, were now closely engaged with their swords, shouting their war-cries, and exchanging buffets, as if honour and life depended on the issue of the combat.

The champions thus encountering each other with the utmost fury, and with alternate success, the tide of battle seemed to flow now toward the southern, now toward the northern extremity of the lists, as the one or the other party prevailed. Meantime the clang of the blows, and the shouts of the combatants, mixed fearfully with the sound of the trumpets, and drowned the groans of those who fell and lay rolling defenceless beneath the feet of the horses.

When the field became thin by the numbers on either side who had been rendered incapable of continuing the strife, the Templar and the Disinherited Knight at length encountered hand to hand, with all the fury that mortal animosity, joined to rivalry of honour, could inspire. Such was the address of each in parrying and striking, that the spectators broke forth into a unanimous and involuntary shout expressive of their delight and admiration.

But at this moment the party of the Disinherited Knight had the worst; the gigantic arm of Front-de-Bœuf on the one flank, and the ponderous strength of Athelstane on the other, bearing down and dispersing those immediately exposed to them. Finding themselves freed from their immediate antagonists, it seems to have occurred to both these knights at the same instant that they would render the most decisive advantage to their party by aiding the Templar in his contest with his rival. Turning their horses, therefore, at the same moment, the Norman spurred against the Disinherited Knight on the one side, and the Saxon on the other. It was utterly impossible that the object of this unequal and unexpected assault could have sustained it, had he not been warned by a general cry from the spectators, who could not but take interest in one exposed to such disadvantage.

"Beware! beware! Sir Disinherited!" was shouted so universally, that the knight became aware of his danger, and, striking a full blow at the Templar, he reined back his steed in the same moment, so as to escape the charge of Athelstane and Front-de-Bœuf. These knights, therefore, their aim being thus eluded, rushed from opposite sides betwixt the object of their attack and the Templar, almost running their horses against each other ere they could stop their career. Recovering their horses, however, and wheeling them round, the whole three pursued their united purpose of bearing to the earth the Disinherited Knight.

Nothing could have saved him, except the remarkable strength and activity of the noble horse which he had won on the preceding day.

This stood him in the more stead, as the horse of Bois-Guilbert was wounded, and those of Front-de-Bœuf and Athelstane were both tired with the weight of their gigantic masters, clad in complete armour, and with the preceding exertions of the day. The masterly horsemanship of the Disinherited Knight and the activity of the noble animal which he mounted, enabled him for a few minutes to keep at sword's point his three antagonists, turning and wheeling with the agility of a hawk upon the wing, keeping his enemies as far separate as he could, and rushing now against the one, now against the other, dealing sweeping blows with his sword, without waiting to receive those which were aimed at him in return.

There was among the ranks of the Disinherited Knight a champion in black armour, mounted on a black horse, large of size, tall, and to all appearance powerful and strong, like the rider by whom he was mounted. This knight, who bore on his shield no device of any kind, had hitherto evinced very little interest in the event of the fight, beating off with seeming ease those combatants who attacked him, but neither pursuing his advantages nor himself assailing any one. In short, he had hitherto acted the part rather of a spectator than of a party in the tournament, a circumstance which procured him among the spectators the name of *Le Noir Fainéant*, or the Black Sluggard.

At once this knight seemed to throw aside his apathy, when he discovered the leader of his party so hard bestead; for, setting spurs to his horse which was quite fresh, he came to his assistance like a thunderbolt, exclaiming, in a voice like a trumpet-call, "*Desdichado*, to the rescue!" It was high time; for, while the Disinherited Knight was pressing upon the Templar, Front-de-Bœuf had got nigh to him with his uplifted sword; but ere the blow could descend, the Sable Knight dealt a stroke on his head, which, glancing from the polished helmet, lighted with violence scarcely abated on the chamfron of the steed, and Front-de-Bœuf rolled on the ground, both horse and man equally stunned by the fury of the blow. *Le Noir Fainéant* then turned his horse upon Athelstane of Conings-burgh; and his own sword having been broken in his encounter with Front-de-Bœuf, he wrenched from the hand of the bulky Saxon the battle-axe which he wielded, and, like one familiar with the use of the weapon, bestowed him such a blow upon the crest that Athelstane also lay senseless on the field. Having achieved this double feat, for which he was the more highly applauded that it was totally unexpected from him, the knight seemed to resume the sluggishness of his character, returning calmly to the northern extremity of the lists, leaving his leader to cope as he best could with Brian de Bois-Guilbert. This was no longer matter of so much difficulty as formerly. The Templar's horse had bled much, and gave way under the shock of the Disinherited Knight's charge. Brian de Bois-Guilbert rolled on the field, encumbered with the stirrup, from which he was unable to draw his foot. His antagonist sprung from horseback, waved his fatal sword over the head of his adversary, and commanded him to yield himself; when Prince John, more moved by the Templar's dangerous situation than he had been by that of his rival, saved him the morti-fication of confessing himself vanquished by casting down his warder, and putting an end to the conflict.

Thus ended the memorable field of Ashby-de-la-Zouche, one of the most gallantly contested tournaments of that age;

for although only four knights, including one who was smothered by the heat of his armour, had died upon the field, yet upwards of thirty were desperately wounded, four or five of whom never recovered. Several more were disabled for life; and those who escaped best carried the marks of the conflict to the grave with them. Hence it is always mentioned in the old records as the Gentle and Joyous Passage of Arms of Ashby.

It being now the duty of Prince John to name the knight who had done best, he had no excuse for resisting the claim of the Disinherited Knight, whom, therefore, he named the champion of the day.

"Disinherited Knight," said Prince John, "since by that title only you will consent to be known to us, we a second time award to you the honours of this tournament, and announce to you your right to claim and receive from the hands of the Queen of Love and Beauty, the Chaplet of Honour which your valour has justly deserved." The Knight bowed low and gracefully, but returned no answer

While the trumpets sounded, while the heralds strained their voices in proclaiming honour to the brave and glory to the victor, while ladies waved their silken kerchiefs and embroidered veils, and while all ranks joined in a clamorous shout of exultation, the marshals conducted the Disinherited Knight across the lists to the foot of that throne of honour which was occupied by the Lady Rowena.

On the lower step of this throne the champion was made to kneel down. Rowena, descending from her station with a graceful and dignified step, was about to place the chaplet which she held in her hand upon the helmet of the champion, when the marshals exclaimed with one voice, "It must not be thus; his head must be bare." The knight muttered faintly a few words, which were lost in the hollow of his helmet, but their purport seemed to be a desire that his casque might not be removed.

Whether from love of form, or from curiosity, the marshals paid no attention to his expression of reluctance, but unhelmed him by cutting the laces of his casque and undoing the fastening of his gorget. When the helmet was removed, the well-formed yet sun-burnt features of a young man of twenty-five were seen, amidst a profusion of short fair hair. His countenance was as pale as death, and marked in one or two places with streaks of blood.

Rowena had no sooner beheld him than she uttered a faint shriek; but at once summoning up the energy of her disposition, she placed upon the drooping head of the victor the splendid chaplet which was the destined reward of the day, and pronounced in a clear and distinct tone, these words, "I bestow on thee this chaplet, Sir Knight, as the meed of valour assigned to this day's victor." Here she paused a moment, and then firmly added, "And upon brows more worthy could a wreath of chivalry never be placed!"

The knight stooped his head and kissed the hand of the lovely Sovereign by whom his valour had been rewarded; and then, sinking yet farther forward, lay prostrate at her feet.

There was a general consternation. Cedric, who had been struck mute by the sudden appearance of his banished son, now rushed forward, as if to separate him from Rowena. But this had been already accomplished by the marshals of the field, who, guessing the cause of Ivanhoe's swoon, had hastened to undo his armour, and found that the head of a lance had penetrated his breastplate, and inflicted a wound in his side.

CHAPTER 12

THE sound of the trumpets soon recalled those spectators who had already begun to leave the field; and proclamation was made that Prince John, unwilling that so many good yeomen should depart without a trial of skill, was pleased to appoint them, before leaving the ground, to execute the competition of archery intended for the morrow. To the best archer a prize was to be awarded, being a bugle-horn, mounted with silver, and a silken baldric richly ornamented with a medallion of St. Hubert, the patron of silvan sport.

More than thirty yeomen at first presented themselves as competitors, several of whom were rangers and underkeepers in the royal forests of Needwood and Charnwood. When, however, the archers understood with whom they were to be matched, upwards of twenty withdrew from the contest, unwilling to encounter the dishonour of almost certain defeat.

The diminished list of competitors for silvan fame still amounted to eight. Prince John stepped from his royal seat to view more nearly the persons of these chosen yeomen, several of whom wore the royal livery. Having satisfied his curiosity by this investigation, he looked for the object of his resentment, whom he observed standing on the same spot, and with the same composed countenancew wich he had exhibited upon the preceding day.

"Fellow," said Prince John, "I guessed by thy insolent babble thou wert no true lover of the long-bow, and I see thou darest not adventure thy skill among such merry men as stand yonder."

"Under favour, sir," replied the yeoman, "I have another reason for refraining to shoot, besides the fearing discomfiture and disgrace."

"And what is thy other reason?" said Prince John, who, for some cause which perhaps he could not himself have explained, felt a painful curiosity respecting this individual.

"Because," replied the woodsman, "I know not if these yeomen and I are used to shoot at the same marks; and because, moreover, I know not how your Grace might relish the winning of a third prize by one who has unwittingly fallen under your displeasure."

Prince John coloured as he put the question, "What is thy name, yeoman?"

"Locksley," answered the yeoman.

"Then, Locksley," said Prince John, "thou shalt shoot in thy turn, when these yeomen have displayed their skill. If thou carriest the prize, I will add to it twenty nobles; but if thou losest it, thou shalt be stripped of thy Lincoln green, and scourged out of the lists with bowstrings, for a wordy and insolent braggart."

"And how if I refuse to shoot on such a wager?" said the yeoman. – "Your Grace's power, supported, as it is, by so many men-at-arms, may indeed easily strip and scourge me, but cannot compel me to bend or to draw my bow."

"If thou refusest my fair proffer," said the Prince, "the Provost of the lists shall cut thy bowstring, break thy bow and arrows, and expel thee from the presence as a faint-hearted craven."

"This is no fair chance you put on me, proud Prince," said the yeoman, "to compel me to peril myself against the best archers of Leicester and Staffordshire, under the penalty of infamy if they should overshoot me. Nevertheless, I will obey your pleasure."

"Look to him close, men-at-arms," said Prince John, "his heart is sinking; I am jealous lest he attempt to escape the trial. – And do you, good fellows, shoot boldly round; a buck and a butt of wine are ready for your refreshment in yonder tent, when the prize is won."

A target was placed at the upper end of the southern avenue which led to the lists. The contending archers took their station in turn, at the bottom of the southern access, the distance between that station and the mark allowing full distance for what was called a shot at rovers. The archers, having previously determined by lot their order of precedence, were to shoot each three shafts in succession.

One by one the archers, stepping forward, delivered their shafts yeomanlike and bravely. Of twenty-four arrows, shot in succession, ten were fixed in the target, and the others ranged so near it that, considering the distance of the mark, it was accounted good archery. Of the ten shafts which hit the target two within the inner ring were shot by Hubert, a forester in the service of Malvoisin, who was accordingly pronounced victorious.

"Now, Locksley," said Prince John to the bold yeoman, with a bitter smile, "wilt thou try conclusions with Hubert, or wilt thou yield up bow, baldric, and quiver to the Provost of the sports?"

"Sith it be no better," said Locksley, "I am content to try my fortune; on condition that when I have shot two shafts at yonder mark of Hubert's, he shall be bound to shoot one at that which I shall propose."

"That is but fair," answered Prince John, "and it shall not be refused thee. –If thou dost beat this braggart, Hubert, I will fill the bugle with silver pennies for thee."

"A man can do but his best," answered Hubert; "but my grandsire drew a good long bow at Hastings, and I trust not to dishonour his memory."

The former target was now removed, and a fresh one of the same size placed in its room. Hubert, who, as victor in the first trial of skill, had the right to shoot first, took his aim with great deliberation, long measuring the distance with his eye, while he held in his hand his bended bow, with the arrow placed on the string. At length he made a step forward, and raising the bow at the full stretch of his left arm, till the centre or grasping-place was nigh level with his face, he drew his bowstring to his ear. The arrow whistled through the air and lighted within the inner ring of the target, but not exactly in the centre.

"You have not allowed for the wind, Hubert," said his antagonist, bending his bow, "or that had been a better shot."

So saying, and without showing the least anxiety to pause upon his aim, Locksley stepped to the appointed station, and shot his arrow as carelessly in appearance as if he had not even looked at the mark. He was speaking almost at the instant that the shaft left the bowstring, yet it alighted in the target two inches nearer to the white spot which marked the centre than that of Hubert.

"By the light of heaven!" said Prince John to Hubert, "an thou suffer that runagate knave to overcome thee, thou art worthy of the gallows!"

Hubert had but one set speech for all occasions. "An your highness were to hang me," he said, "a man can but do his best. Nevertheless, my grandsire drew a good bow–"

"The foul fiend on thy grandsire and all his generation!" interrupted John; "shoot, knave, and shoot thy best, or it shall be the worse for thee!"

Thus exhorted, Hubert resumed his place, and not neglecting the caution which he had received from his adversary, he made the necessary allowance for a very light air of wind, which had just arisen, and shot so successfully that his arrow alighted in the very centre of the target.

"A Hubert! a Hubert!" shouted the populace, more interested in a known person than in a stranger. "In the clout!– in the clout!–a Hubert for ever!"

"Thou canst not mend that shot, Locksley," said the Prince, with an insulting smile.

"I will notch his shaft for him, however," replied Locksley.

And letting fly his arrow with a little more precaution than before, it lighted right upon that of his competitor, which

it split to shivers. The people who stood around were so astonished at his wonderful dexterity, that they could not even
give vent to their surprise in their usual clamour. "This must
be the devil, and no man of flesh and blood," whispered the
yeomen to each other; "such archery was never seen since a
bow was first bent in Britain."

"And now," said Locksley, "I will crave your Grace's permission to plant such a mark as is used in the North Country;
and welcome every brave yeoman who shall try a shot at
it to win a smile from the bonny lass he loves best."

He then turned to leave the lists. "Let your guards attend
me," he said, "if you please; I go but to cut a rod from the
next willowbush."

Prince John made a signal that some attendants should
follow him in case of his escape; but the cry of "Shame!
shame!" which burst from the multitude, induced him to
alter his ungenerous purpose.

Locksley returned almost instantly with a willow wand
about six feet in length, perfectly straight, and rather thicker
than a man's thumb. He began to peel this with great composure, observing at the same time that to ask a good woodsman to shoot at a target so broad as had hitherto been used,
was to put shame upon his skill. "For his own part," he
said, "and in the land where he was bred, men would as soon
take for their mark King Arthur's round table, which held
sixty knights around it. A child of seven years old," he said,
"might hit yonder target with a headless shaft; but," added
he, walking deliberately to the other end of the lists, and
sticking the willow wand upright in the ground, "he that hits
that rod at five-score yards, I call him an archer fit to bear
both bow and quiver before a king, an it were the stout King
Richard himself."

"My grandsire," said Hubert, "drew a good bow at the
battle of Hastings, and never shot at such a mark in his

life, and neither will I. If this yeoman can cleave that rod, I give him the bucklers—or rather, I yield to the devil that is in his jerkin, and not to any human skill; a man can but do his best, and I will not shoot where I am sure to miss. I might as well shoot at the edge of our parson's whittle, or at a wheat straw, or at a sunbeam, as at a twinkling white streak which I can hardly see."

"Cowardly dog!" said Prince John.—"Sirrah Locksley, do thou shoot; but if thou hittest such a mark, I will say thou art the first man ever did so. Howe'er it be, thou shalt not crow over us with a mere show of superior skill."

"I will do my best, as Hubert says," answered Locksley; "no man can do more."

So saying, he again bent his bow, but on the present occasion looked with attention to his weapon, and changed the string, which he thought was no longer truly round, having been a little frayed by the two former shots. He then took his aim with some deliberation, and the multitude awaited the event in breathless silence. The archer vindicated their opinion of his skill—his arrow split the willow rod against which it was aimed. A jubilee of acclamations followed; and even Prince John, in admiration of Locksley's skill, lost for an instant his dislike to his person. "These twenty nobles," he said, "which, with the bugle, thou hast fairly won, are thine own; we will make them fifty, if thou wilt take livery and service with us as a yeoman of our bodyguard, and be near to our person. For never did so strong a hand bend a bow, or so true an eye direct a shaft."

"Pardon me, noble Prince," said Locksley; "but I have vowed, that if ever I take service, it should be with your royal brother King Richard. These twenty nobles I leave to Hubert, who has this day drawn as brave a bow as his grandsire did at Hastings. Had his modesty not refused the trial, he would have hit the wand as well as I."

Hubert shook his head as he received with reluctance the bounty of the stranger, and Locksley, anxious to escape further observation, mixed with the crowd, and was seen no more.

The victorious archer would not perhaps have escaped John's attention so easily, had not that Prince had other subjects of anxious and more important meditation pressing upon his mind at that instant. He called upon his chamberlain as he gave the signal for retiring from the lists, and commanded him instantly to gallop to Ashby, and seek out Isaac the Jew. "Tell the dog," he said, "to send me, before sundown, two thousand crowns. He knows the security; but thou mayest show him this ring for a token. The rest of the money must be paid at York within six days. If he neglects, I will have the unbelieving villain's head. Look that thou pass him not on the way, for the circumcised slave was displaying his stolen finery amongst us."

So saying, the Prince resumed his horse, and returned to Ashby, the whole crowd breaking up and dispersing upon his retreat.

CHAPTER 13

WHEN Cedric the Saxon saw his son drop down senseless in the lists at Ashby, his first impulse was to order him into the custody and care of his own attendants; but the words choked in his throat. He could not bring himself to acknowledge, in presence of such an assembly, the son whom he had renounced and disinherited. He ordered, however, Oswald to keep an eye upon him, and directed that officer, with two of his serfs, to convey Ivanhoe to Ashby as soon as the crowd had dispersed. Oswald, however, was anticipated in this good office. The crowd dispersed, indeed, but the knight was nowhere to be seen.

It was in vain that Cedric's cupbearer looked around for his young master. He saw the bloody spot on which he had lately sunk down, but himself he saw no longer; it seemed as if the fairies had conveyed him from the spot. Perhaps Oswald (for the Saxons were very superstitious) might have adopted some such hypothesis, to account for Ivanhoe's disappearance, had he not suddenly cast his eye upon a person attired like a squire, in whom he recognized the features of his fellow-servant Gurth. Anxious concerning his master's fate, and in despair at his sudden disappearance, the swineherd was searching for him everywhere, and had neglected, in doing so, the concealment on which his own safety depended.

The only information which the cupbearer could collect from the bystanders was, that the knight had been raised with care by certain well-attired grooms, and placed in a litter belonging to a lady among the spectators, which had immediately transported him out of the press. Oswald, on receiving this intelligence, resolved to return to his master for further instructions, carrying along with him Gurth, whom he considered in some sort as a deserter from the service of Cedric.

The Saxon had been under very intense and agonizing apprehensions concerning his son; for Nature had asserted her rights, in spite of the patriotic stoicism which laboured to disown her. But no sooner was he informed that Ivanhoe was in careful, and probably in friendly hands, than the paternal anxiety which had been excited by the dubiety of his fate, gave way anew to the feeling of injured pride and resentment, at what he termed Wilfred's filial disobedience.

Immediately upon retiring from the castle, the Saxon thanes, with their attendants, took horse; and it was during the bustle which attended their doing so, that Cedric, for the first time, cast his eyes upon the deserter Gurth.

"The gyves!" he said, "the gyves!—Oswald—Hundebert!—dogs and villains!—why leave ye the knave unfettered?"

"Without daring to remonstrate, the companions of Gurth bound him with a halter, as the readiest cord which occurred. He submitted to the operation without remonstrance, except that, darting a reproachful look at his master, he said, "This comes of loving your flesh and blood better than mine own."

"To horse, and forward!" said Cedric.

At the convent of St. Withold's, the Abbot received the noble Saxons with the profuse and exuberant hospitality of their nation, wherein they indulged to a late or rather an early hour; nor did they take leave of their reverend host the next morning until they had shared with him a sumptuous refection.

CHAPTER 14

THE travellers had now reached the verge of the wooded country, and were about to plunge into its recesses, held dangerous at that time from the number of outlaws whom oppression and poverty had driven to despair, and who occupied the forests in such large bands as could easily bid defiance the the feeble police of the period.

As the travellers journeyed on their way, they were alarmed by repeated cries for assistance; and when they rode up to the place from whence they came, they were surprised to find a horse-litter placed upon the ground, beside which sat a young woman, richly dressed in the Jewish fashion, while an old man, whose yellow cap proclaimed him to belong to the same nation, walked up and down with gestures expressive of the deepest despair, and wrung his hands, as if affected by some strange disaster.

To the inquiries of Athelstane and Cedric, the old Jew could for some time only answer by invoking the protection of all the patriarchs of the Old Testament successively against the sons of Ishmael, who were coming to smite them, hip and thigh, with the edge of the sword. When he began to come to himself out of this agony of terror, Isaac of York (for it was our old friend) was at length able to explain, that he had hired a bodyguard of six men at Ashby, together with mules for carrying the litter of a sick friend. This party had undertaken to escort him as far as Doncaster. They had come thus far in safety; but having received information from a woodcutter that there was a strong band of outlaws lying in wait in the woods before them, Isaac's mercenaries had not only taken flight, but had carried off with them the horses which bore the litter, and left the Jew and his daughter without the means either of defence or of retreat, to be plundered, and probably murdered, by the banditti, whom they expected every moment would bring down upon them. "Would it but please your valours," added Isaac, in a tone of deep humiliation, "to permit the poor Jews to travel under your safeguard, I swear by the tables of our law, that never has favour been conferred upon a child of Israel since the days of our captivity which shall be more gratefully acknowledged."

"The man is old and feeble," said Rowena to her guardian, "the maiden young and beautiful, their friend sick and in peril of his life; Jews though they be, we cannot as Christians leave them in this extremity. Let them unload two of the sumpter-mules, and put the baggage behind two of the serfs. The mules may transport the litter, and we have led horses for the old man and his daughter."

Cedric readily assented to what she proposed, and Athelstane only added the condition, "that they should travel in the rear of the whole party, where Wamba," he said, "might attend them with his shield of boar's brawn."

"I have left my shield in the tilt-yard," answered the Jester, "as has been the fate of many a better knight than myself."

Athelstane coloured deeply, for such had been his own fate on the last day of the tournament; while Rowena, who was pleased in the same proportion, as if to make amends for the brutal jest of her unfeeling suitor, requested Rebecca to ride by her side.

"It were not fit I should do so," answered Rebecca, with proud humility, "where my society might be held a disgrace to my protectress."

By this time the change of baggage was hastily achieved; for the single word "outlaws" rendered every one sufficiently alert, and the approach of twilight made the sound yet more impressive. Amid the bustle, Gurth was taken from horseback, in the course of which removal he prevailed upon the Jester to slack the cord with which his arms were bound. It was so negligently refastened, perhaps intentionally, on the part of Wamba, that Gurth found no difficulty in freeing his arms altogether from bondage, and then, gliding into the thicket, he made his escape from the party.

The path upon which the party travelled was now so narrow as not to admit, with any sort of convenience, above two riders abreast, and began to descend into a dingle, traversed by a brook whose banks were broken, swampy, and overgrown with dwarf willows. Cedric and Athelstane, who were at the head of their retinue, saw the risk of being attacked at this pass; but neither of them having had much practice in war, no better mode of preventing the danger occurred to them than that they should hasten through the defile as fast as possible. Advancing, therefore, without much order, they had just crossed the brook with a part of their followers, when they were assailed in front, flank, and rear at once, with an impetuosity to which, in their confused and ill-prepared condition, it was impossible to offer effectual resistance. The shout of "A white dragon!–a white dragon! Saint George for merry England!" war-cries adopted by the assailants, as belonging to their assumed character of Saxon outlaws, was heard on every side, and on every side enemies appeared with a rapidity of advance and attack which seemed to multiply their numbers.

Both the Saxon chiefs were made prisoners at the same moment.

The attendants, embarrassed with baggage, surprised and terrified at the fate of their masters, fell an easy prey to the assailants; while the Lady Rowena, in the centre of the cavalcade, and the Jew and his daughter in the rear, experienced the same misfortune.

Of all the train none escaped except Wamba, who showed upon the occasion much more courage than those who pretended to greater sense. He possessed himself of a sword belonging to one of the domestics, who was just drawing it with a tardy and irresolute hand, laid it about him like a lion, drove back several who approached him, and made a brave though ineffectual attempt to succour his master. Finding himself overpowered, the Jester at length threw himself from his horse, plunged into the thicket, and favoured by the general confusion, escaped from the scene of action.

Yet the valiant Jester, as soon as he found himself safe, hesitated more than once whether he should not turn back and share the captivity of a master to whom he was sincerely attached.

"I have heard men talk of the blessings of freedom," he said to himself, "but I wish any wise man would teach me what use to make of it now that I have it."

As he pronounced these words aloud, a voice very near him called out in a low and cautious tone, "Wamba!" and, at the same time, a dog, which he recognized to be Fangs, jumped up and fawned upon him. "Gurth!" answered Wamba, with the same caution, and the swineherd immediately stood before him.

"What is the matter?" said he eagerly; "what means these cries, and that clashing of swords?"

"Only a trick on the times," said Wamba; "they are all prisoners."

"Who are prisoners?" exclaimed Gurth impatiently.

"My lord, and my lady, and Athelstane, and Hundibert, and Oswald."

"In the name of God!" said Gurth, "how came they prisoners? and to whom?"

"Our master was too ready to fight," said the Jester, "and Athelstane was not ready enough, and no other person was ready at all. And they are prisoners to green cassocks and black visors. And they lie all tumbled about on the green, like the crab-apples that you shake down to your swine. And I would laugh at it," said the honest Jester, "if I could for weeping." And he shed tears of unfeigned sorrow.

Gurth's countenance kindled. "Wamba," he said, "thou hast a weapon, and thy heart was ever stronger than thy brain, – we are only two, but a sudden attack from men of resolution will do much. Follow me!"

"Whither? and for what purpose?" said the Jester.

"To rescue Cedric – follow me!"

As the Jester was about to obey, a third person suddenly made his appearance, and commanded them both to halt. From his dress and arms, Wamba would have conjectured him to be one of those outlaws who had just assailed his master; but, besides that he wore no mask, the glittering baldric across his shoulder, with the rich bugle-horn which it supported, as well as the calm and commanding expression of his voice and manner, made him, notwithstanding the twilight, recognize Locksley the yeoman, who had been victorious, under such disadvantageous circumstances, in the contest for the prize of archery.

"What is the meaning of all this?" said he; "or who is it that rifle, and ransom, and make prisoners, in these forests?"

"You may look at their cassocks close by," said Wamba, "and see whether they be thy children's coats or no –for they are as like thine own as one green pea-cod is to another."

"I will learn that presently," answered Locksley; "and I charge ye, on peril of your lives, not to stir from the place where ye stand, until I have returned. Obey me, and it shall be the better for you and your masters. –Yet stay, I must render myself as like these men as possible."

So saying he unbuckled his baldric with the bugle, took a feather from his cap, and gave them to Wamba; then drew a vizard from his pouch, and, repeating his charges to them to stand fast, went to execute his purposes of reconnoitring.

"Shall we stand fast, Gurth?" said Wamba; "or shall we e'en give him leg-bail? In my foolish mind, he had all the equipage of a thief too much in readiness, to be himself a true man."

"Let him be the devil," said Gurth, "an he will. We can be no worse off waiting his return. If he belong to that party, he must already have given them the alarm, and it will avail nothing either to fight or fly. Besides, I have late experience, that arrant thieves are not the worst men in the world to have to deal with."

The yeoman returned in the course of a few minutes.

"Friend Gurth," he said, "I have mingled among yon men, and have learnt to whom they belong, and whither they are bound. There is, I think, no chance that they will proceed to any actual violence against their prisoners. For three men to attempt them at this moment were little else than madness; for they are good men of war, and have, as such, placed sentinels to give the alarm when any one approaches. But I trust soon to gather such a force as may act in defiance of all their precautions. You are both servants, and, as I think, faithful servants, of Cedric the Saxon, the friend of the rights of Englishmen. He shall not want English hands to help him in this extremity. Come then with me, until I gather more aid."

So saying, he walked through the wood at a great pace, followed by the jester and the swineherd. It was not consistent with Wamba's humour to travel long in silence.

"I think," said he, looking at the baldric and bugle which he still carried, "that I saw the arrow shot which won this gay prize, and that not so long since Christmas."

"And I," said Gurth, "could take it on my halidom that I have heard the voice of the good yeoman who won it by night as well as by day, and that the moon is not three days older since I did so."

"Mine honest friends," replied the yeoman, "who or what I am is little to the present purpose; should I free your master, you will have reason to think me the best friend you have ever had in your lives. And whether I am known by one name or another, or whether I can draw a bow as well or better than a cow-keeper, or whether it is my pleasure to walk in sunshine or by moonlight, are matters which, as they do not concern you, so neither need ye busy yourselves respecting them."

"Our heads are in the lion's mouth," said Wamba, in a whisper to Gurth, "get them out how we can."

"Hush–be silent," said Gurth. "Offend him not by thy folly, and I trust sincerely that all will go well."

CHAPTER 15

IT was after three hours' good walking that the servants of Cedric, with their mysterious guide, arrived at a small opening in the forest, in the centre of which grew an oak-tree of enormous magnitude, throwing its twisted branches in every direction. Beneath this tree four or five yeomen lay stretched on the ground, while another, as sentinel, walked to and fro in the moonlight shade.

Upon hearing the sound of feet approaching, the watch instantly gave the alarm, and the sleepers as suddenly started up and bent their bows. Six arrows placed on the string were pointed towards the quarter from which the travellers approached, when their guide, being recognized, was welcomed with every token of respect and attachment, and all signs and fears of a rough reception at once subsided.

"Where is the Miller?" was his first question.

"On the road towards Rotherham."

"With how many?" demanded the leader, for such he seemed to be.

"With six men, and good hope of booty, if it please St. Nicholas."

"Devoutly spoken," said Locksley, "and where is Allan-a-dale?"

"Walked up towards the Watling-street, to watch for the Prior of Jorvaulx."

"That is well thought on also," replied the Captain;—"and where is the Friar?"

"In his cell."

"Thither will I go," said Locksley. "Disperse and your companions. Collect what force you can, for there's game afoot that must be hunted hard, and will turn to bay. Meet me here by daybreak. And stay," he added, "I have forgotten what is most necessary of the whole—two of you take the road quickly towards Torquilstone, the Castle of Front-de-Bœuf. A set of gallants, who have been masquerading in such guise as our own, are carrying a band of prisoners thither. Watch them closely, for even if they reach the castle before we collect our force, our honour is concerned to punish them, and we will find means to do so. Keep a close watch on them therefore; and dispatch one of your comrades, the lightest of foot, to bring the news of the yeomen thereabout."

They promised implicit obedience, and departed with alacrity on their different errands. In the meanwhile, their leader and his two companions, who now looked upon him with great respect, as well as some fear, pursued their way to the Chapel of Copmanhurst.

When they had reached the little moonlight glade, having in front the reverend though ruinous chapel, and the rude hermitage, so well suited to ascetic devotion, Wamba whispered to Gurth, "If this be the habitation of a thief, it makes good the old proverb, The nearer the church the farther from God. –And by my cockscomb," he added, "I think it be even so—hearken but to the black sanctus which they are singing in the hermitage!"

In fact the anchorite and his guest were performing, at the full extent of their very powerful lungs, an old drinking song.

Locksley's loud and repeated knocks at length disturbed the anchorite and his guest. "By my beads," said the hermit, stopping short in a grand flourish, "here come more benighted guests. I would not for my cowl that they found us in this goodly exercise. All men have their enemies, good Sir Sluggard; and there be those malignant enough to construe the hospitable refreshment which I have been offering to you, a weary traveller, for the matter of three short hours, into sheer drunkenness and debauchery, vices alike alien to my profession and my disposition".

"Mad priest," answered the voice from without, "open to Locksley!"

"All's safe –all's right," said the hermit to his companion.

"But who is he?" said the Black Knight; "it imports me much to know."

"Who is he?" answered the hermit; "I tell thee he is a friend."

"But what friend?" answered the knight; "for he may be friend to thee and none of mine."

"What friend?" replied the hermit; "that, now, is one of the questions that is more easily asked than answered. What friend? –why, he is, now that I bethink me a little, the very same honest keeper I told thee of a while since."

"Ay, as honest a keeper as thou art a pious hermit," replied the knight, "I doubt it not. But undo the door to him before he beat it from its hinges."

The dogs, in the meantime, which had made a dreadful baying at the commencement of the disturbance, seemed now to recognize the voice of him who stood without; for, totally changing their manner, they scratched and whined at the door, as if interceding for his admission. The hermit speedily unbolted his portal, and admitted Locksley, with his two companions.

"Why, hermit," was the yeoman's first question as soon as he beheld the knight, "what boon companion hast thou here?"

"A brother of our order," replied the friar, shaking his head; "we have been at our orisons all night."

"He is a monk of the church militant, I think," answered Locksley; "and there be more of them abroad. I tell thee, friar, thou must lay down the rosary and take up the quarter-staff; we shall need every one of our merry men, whether clerk or layman. But," he added, taking him a step aside, "art thou mad, to give admittance to a knight thou dost not know? Hast thou forgot our articles?"

"Not know him!" replied the friar boldly; "I know him as well as the beggar knows his dish."

"And what is his name, then?" demanded Locksley.

"His name," said the hermit –"his name is Sir Anthony of Scrabelstone. As if I would drink with a man, and did not know his name!"

"Thou hast been drinking more than enough, friar," said the woodsman, "and, I fear, prating more than enough too."

"Good yeoman," said the knight, coming forward, "be not wroth with my merry host. He did but afford me the hospitality which I would have compelled from him if he had refused it."

"Thou compel!" said the friar. "Wait but till I have changed this grey gown for a green cassock, and if I make not a quarter-staff ring twelve upon thy pate, I am neither true clerk nor good woodsman."

While he spoke thus, he stripped off his gown, and appeared in a close black buckram doublet and drawers, over which he speedily did on a cassock of green, and hose of the same colour. "I pray thee truss my points," said he to Wamba, "and thou shalt have a cup of sack for thy labour."

"Gramercy for thy sack," said .Wamba; "but think'st thou it is lawful for me to aid you to transmew thyself from a holy hermit into a sinful forester?"

"Never fear," said the hermit; "I will but confess the sins of my green cloak to my grey friar's frock, and all shall be well again."

"Amen!" answered the Jester; "a broadcloth penitent should have a sackcloth confessor, and your frock may absolve my motley doublet into the bargain."

So saying, he accommodated the friar with his assistance in tying the endless number of points, as the laces which attached the hose to the doublet were then termed.

While they were thus employed, Locksley led the knight a little apart, and addressed him thus:—"Deny it not, Sir Knight —you are he who decided the victory to the advantage of the English against the strangers on the second day of the tournament at Ashby."

"And what follows if you guess truly, good yeoman?" replied the knight.

"I should in that case hold you," replied the yeoman, "a friend to the weaker party."

"Such is the duty of a true knight at least," replied the Black Champion; "and I would not willingly that there were reason to think otherwise of me."

"But for my purpose," said the yeoman, "thou shouldst be as well a good Englishman as a good knight; for that which I have to speak concerns, indeed, the duty of every honest man, but is more especially that of a true-born native of England."

"You can speak to no one," replied the knight, "to whom England, and the life of every Englishman, can be dearer than to me."

"I would willingly believe so," said the woodsman, "for never had this country such need to be supported by those who love her. Hear me, and I will tell thee of an enterprise in which, if thou be'st really that which thou seemest, thou mayest take an honourable part. A band of villains, in the disguise of better men than themselves, have made themselves master of the person of a noble Englishman, called Cedric the Saxon, together with his ward, and his friend Athelstane of Coningsburgh, and have transported them to a castle in this forest, called Torquilstone. I ask of thee, as a good knight and a good Englishman, wilt thou aid in their rescue?"

"I am bound by my vow to do so," replied the knight; "but I would willingly know who you are who request my assistance in their behalf?"

"I am," said the forester, "a nameless man; but I am the friend of my country, and of my country's friends. With this account of me you must for the present remain satisfied, the more especially since you yourself desire to continue unknown. Believe, however, that my word, when pledged, is as inviolate as if I wore golden spurs."

"I willingly believe it," said the knight. "I have been accustomed to study men's countenances, and I can read in thine honesty and resolution. I will therefore ask thee no further questions, but aid thee in setting at freedom these oppressed captives; which done, I trust we shall part better acquainted, and well satisfied with each other."

CHAPTER 16

WHILE these measures were being taken in behalf of Cedric and his companions, the armed men by whom the latter had been seized hurried their captives along towards the place of security, where they intended to imprison them. But darkness came on fast, and the paths of the wood seemed but imperfectly known to the marauders. They were compelled to make several long halts, and once or twice to return on their road to resume the direction, which they wished to pursue. The summer morn had dawned upon them ere they could travel in full assurance that they held the right path. But confidence returned with light, and the cavalcade now moved rapidly forward.

Meanwhile, the following dialogue took place between the two leaders of the banditti.

"It is time thou shouldst leave us, Sir Maurice," said the Templar to De Bracy, "in order to prepare the second part of thy mystery. Thou art next, thou knowest, to act the Knight Deliverer."

"I have thought better of it," said De Bracy. "I will not leave thee till the prize is fairly deposited in Front-de-Bœuf's castle. There will I appear before the Lady Rowena in mine own shape, and trust that she will set down to the vehemence of my passion the violence of which I have been guilty."

"And what has made thee change thy plan, De Bracy?" replied the Knight Templar.

"That concerns thee nothing," answered his companion.

"I would hope, however, Sir Knight," said the Templar, "that this alteration of measures arises from no suspicion of my honourable meaning, such as Fitzurse endeavoured to instil into thee?"

"My thoughts are my own," answered De Bracy. "The fiend laughs, they say, when one thief robs another; and we know, that were he to spit fire and brimstone instead, it would never prevent a Templar from following his bent."

"Or the leader of a Free Company," answered the Templar, "from dreading, at the hands of a comrade and friend, the injustice he does to all mankind."

"This is unprofitable and perilous recrimination," answered De Bracy. "Suffice it to say, I know the morals of the Temple Order, and I will not give thee the power of cheating me out of the fair prey for which I have run such risks."

"Psha," replied the Templar, "what hast thou to fear? Thou knowest the vows of our order."

"Right well," said De Bracy, "and also how they are kept. Come, Sir Templar, the laws of gallantry have a liberal interpretation in Palestine, and this is a case in which I will trust nothing to your conscience."

"Hear the truth, then," said the Templar: "I care not for your blue-eyed beauty. There is in that train one who will make me a better mate."

"What! wouldst thou stoop to the waiting damsel?" said De Bracy.

"No, Sir Knight," said the Templar haughtily. "To the waiting-woman will I not stoop. I have a prize among the captives as lovely as thine own."

"By the Mass, thou meanest the fair Jewess!" said De Bracy.

"And if I do," said Bois-Guilbert, "who shall gainsay me?"

"No one that I know," said De Bracy, "unless it be your vow of celibacy, or a check of conscience for an intrigue with a Jewess."

"For my vow," said the Templar, "our Grand Master hath granted me a dispensation. And for my conscience, a man that has slain three hundred Saracens need not reckon up every little failing, like a village girl at her first confession upon Good Friday eve."

"Thou knowest best thine own privileges," said De Bracy. "Yet, I would have sworn thy thought had been more on the old usurer's money bags, than on the black eyes of the daughter."

"I can admire both," answered the Templar; "besides, the old Jew is but half-prize. I must share his spoils with Front-de-Bœuf, who will not lend us the use of his castle for nothing. I must have something that I can term exclusively my own by this foray of ours, and I have fixed on the lovely Jewess as my peculiar prize. But, now thou knowest my drift, thou wilt resume thine own original plan, wilt thou not? Thou hast nothing, thou seest, to fear from my interference."

"No," replied De Bracy, "I will remain beside my prize. What thou sayest is passing true, but I like not the privileges acquired by the dispensation of the Grand Master, and the merit acquired by the slaughter of three hundred Saracens. You have too good a right to a free pardon, to render you very scrupulous about peccadilloes."

It was in vain that Cedric expostulated with his guards, who had too many good reasons for their silence to be induced to break it either by his wrath or his expostulations. They continued to hurry along, travelling at a very rapid rate, until, at the end of an avenue of huge trees, arose Torquilstone, now the hoary and ancient castle of Reginald Front-de-Bœuf. It was a fortress of no great size, consisting of a donjon, or large and high square tower, surrounded by buildings of inferior height, which were encircled by an inner courtyard. Around the exterior wall was a deep moat, supplied with water from a neighbouring rivulet. Front-de-Bœuf, whose character placed him often at feud with his enemies, had made considerable additions to the strength of his castle, by building towers upon the outward wall, so as to flank it at every angle. The access, as usual in castles of the period, lay through an arched barbican, or outwork, which was terminated and defended by a small turret at each corner.

De Bracy winded his horn three times, and the archers and cross-bow men, who had manned the wall upon seeing their approach, hastened to lower the drawbridge, and admit them. The prisoners were compelled by their guards to alight, and were conducted to an apartment where a hasty repast was offered them, of which none but Athelstane felt any inclination to partake. Neither had the descendant of the Confessor much time to do justice to the good cheer placed before them, for their guards gave him and Cedric to understand that they were to be imprisoned in a chamber apart from Rowena. Resistance was vain; and they were compelled to follow to a large room, which, rising on clumsy Saxon pillars, resembled those refectories and chapter-houses which may be still seen in the most ancient parts of our most ancient monasteries.

The Lady Rowena was next separated from her train, and conducted, with courtesy, indeed, but still without consulting her inclination, to a distant apartment. The same alarming distinction was conferred on Rebecca, in spite of her father's entreaties, who offered even money, in this extremity of distress, that she might be permitted to abide with him. "Base unbeliever," answered one of his guards, "when thou hast seen thy lair, thou wilt not wish thy daughter to partake it." And, without further discussion, the old Jew was forcibly dragged off in a different direction from the other prisoners. The domestics, after being carefully searched and disarmed, were confined in another part of the castle; and Rowena was refused even the comfort she might have derived from the attendance of her handmaiden Elgitha.

Cedric paced the apartment, filled with indignant reflections on the past and on the present, while the apathy of his companion served, instead of patience and philosophy, to defend him against everything save the inconvenience of the present moment; and so little did he feel even this last, that he was only from time to time roused to a reply by Cedric's animated and impassioned appeal to him.

"Yes," said Cedric, half speaking to himself, and half addressing himself to Athelstane, "it was in this very hall that my father feasted with Torquil Wolfganger, when he entertained the valiant and unfortunate Harold, then advancing against the Norwegians, who had united themselves to the rebel Tosti. It was in this hall that Harold returned the magnanimous answer to the ambassador of his rebel brother. Oft have I heard my father kindle as he told the tale. The envoy of Tosti was admitted, when this ample room could scarce contain the crowd of noble Saxon leaders, who were quaffing the blood-red wine around their monarch."

While the Saxon was plunged in these painful reflections, the door of their prison opened, and gave entrance to a sewer, holding his white rod of office. This important person advanced into the chamber with a grave pace, followed by four attendants, bearing in a table covered with dishes, the sight and smell of which seemed to be an instant compensation to Athelstane for all the inconvenience he had undergone. The persons who attended on the feast were masked and cloaked.

"What mummery is this?" said Cedric; "think you that we are ignorant whose prisoners we are, when we are in the castle of your master? Tell him," he continued, willing to use this opportunity to open a negotiation for his freedom—"tell your master, Reginald Front-de-Bœuf, that we know no reason he can have for withholding our liberty, excepting his unlawful desire to enrich himself at our expense. Tell him that we yield to his rapacity, as in similar circumstances we should do to that if a literal robber. Let him name the ransom at which he rates our liberty, and it shall be paid, provided the exaction is suited to our means."

The sewer made no answer, but bowed his head.

"And tell Sir Reginald Front-de-Bœuf," said Athelstane, "that I send him my mortal defiance, and challenge him to combat with me, on foot or horseback, at any secure place, within eight days after our liberation; which, if he be a true knight, he will not, under these circumstances, venture to refuse or to delay."

"I shall deliver to the knight your defiance," answered the sewer; "meanwhile I leave you to your food."

The captives had not long enjoyed their refreshment, however, ere their attention was disturbed even from this most serious occupation by the blast of a horn winded before the gate. It was repeated three times, with as much violence as if it had been blown before an enchanted castle by the destined knight, at whose summons halls and towers, barbican and battlement, were to roll off like a morning vapour. The Saxons started from the table, and hastened to the window. But their curiosity was disappointed, for these outlets only looked upon the court of the castle, and the sound came from beyond its precincts. The summons, however, seemed of importance, for a considerable degree of bustle took place in the castle.

CHAPTER 17

The poor Jew had been hastily thrust into a dungeon-vault of the castle, the floor of which was deep beneath the level of the ground, and very damp, being lower than even the moat itself. The only light was received through one or two loop-holes far above the reach of the captive's hand. These apertures admitted, even at mid-day, only a dim and uncertain light, which was changed for utter darkness long before the rest of the castle had lost the blessing of day. Chains and shackles, which had been the portion of former captives, from whom active exertions to escape had been apprehended, hung rusted and empty on the walls of the prison; and in the rings of one of those sets of fetters there remained two mouldering bones, which seemed to have been once those of the human leg, as if some prisoner had been left not only to perish there, but to be consumed to a skeleton.

At one end of this ghastly apartment was a large fire-grate, over the top of which were stretched some transverse iron bars half devoured with rust.

The Jew remained without altering his position for nearly three hours, at the expiry of which steps were heard on the dungeon stair. The bolts screamed as they were withdrawn, the hinges creaked as the wicket opened, and Reginald Front-de-Bœuf, followed by the two Saracen slaves of the Templar, entered the prison.

"Let my daughter Rebecca go forth to York," pleaded Isaac, "with your safe-conduct, noble knight, and so soon as man and horse can return, my treasure –" here he groaned deeply, but added, after the pause of a few seconds, "my treasure shall be told down on this very floor."

"I would," said the Norman, somewhat relenting, "that I had known of this before. I thought your race had loved nothing save their money-bags."

"Think not so vilely of us, Jews though we be," said Isaac, eager to improve the moment of apparent sympathy, "the hunted fox, the tortured wild-cat, loves its young—the despised and persecuted race of Abraham love their children!"

"Be it so," said Front-de-Bœuf; "I will believe it in future, Isaac, for thy very sake. But it aids us not now; I cannot help what has happened, or what is to follow. My word is passed to my comrade in arms, nor would I break it for ten Jews and Jewesses to boot. Besides, why shouldst thou think evil is to come to the girl, even if she came Bois-Guilbert's booty?"

"There will, there must!" exclaimed Isaac, wringing his hands in agony; "when did Templars breathe aught but cruelty to men and dishonour to women?"

"Dog of an infidel," said Front-de-Bœuf, with sparkling eyes, and not sorry, perhaps, to seize a pretext for working himself into a passion, "blaspheme not the Holy Order of the Temple of Zion, but take thought instead to pay me the ransom thou hast promised, or woe betide thy Jewish throat!"

"Robber and villain!" said the Jew, retorting the insults of his oppressor with passion, which, however impotent, he now found it impossible to bridle, "I will pay thee nothing — not one silver penny will I pay thee, unless my daughter is delivered to me in safety and honour!"

"Art thou in thy senses, Israelite?" said the Norman sternly; "has thy flesh and blood a charm against heated iron and scalding oil?"

"I care not!" said the Jew, rendered desperate by paternal affection; "do thy worst. My daughter is my flesh and blood, dearer to me a thousand times than those limbs which thy cruelty threatens. No silver will I give thee, unless I were to pour it molten down thy avaricious throat — no, not a silver penny will I give thee, Nazarene, were it to save thee from the deep damnation thy whole life has merited! Take my life if thou wilt, and say the Jew, amidst his tortures, knew how to disappoint the Christian."

"We shall see that," said Front-de-Bœuf; "for by the blessed rood, which is the abomination of thy accursed tribe, thou shalt feel the extremities of fire and steel! — Strip him, slaves, and chain him down upon the bars."

In spite of the feeble struggles of the old man, the Saracens had already torn from him his upper garment, and were proceeding totally to disrobe him, when the sound of a bugle, twice winded without the castle, penetrated even to the recesses of the dungeon, and immediately after loud voices were heard calling for Sir Reginald Front-de-Bœuf. Unwilling to be found engaged in his hellish occupation, the savage Baron gave the slaves a signal to restore Isaac's garment, and, quitting the dungeon with his attendants, he left the Jew to thank God for his own deliverance, or to lament over his daughter's captivity, and probable fate, as his personal or parental feelings might prove strongest.

CHAPTER 18

THE apartment to which the Lady Rowena had been introduced was fitted up with some rude attempts at ornament and magnificence, and her being placed there might be considered as a peculiar mark of respect not offered to the other prisoners. But the wife of Front-de-Bœuf, for whom it had been originally furnished, was long dead, and decay and neglect had impaired the few ornaments with which her taste had adorned it. The tapestry hung down from the walls in many places, and in others was tarnished and faded under the effects of the sun, or tattered and decayed by age. Desolate, however, as it was, this was the apartment of the castle which had been judged most fitting for the accommodation of the Saxon heiress; and here she was left to meditate upon her fate, until the actors in this nefarious drama had arranged the several parts which each of them was to perform. This had been settled in a council held by Front-de-Bœuf, De Bracy, and the Templar, in which, after a long and warm debate concerning the several advantages which each insisted upon deriving from his peculiar share in this audacious enterprise, they had at length determined the fate of their unhappy prisoners.

It was about the hour of noon, therefore, when De Bracy, for whose advantage the expedition had been first planned' appeared to prosecute his views upon the hand and possessions of the Lady Rowena.

The interval had not entirely been bestowed in holding council with his confederates, for De Bracy had found leisure to decorate his person with all the foppery of the times. His green cassock and vizard were now flung aside. His long luxuriant hair was trained to flow in quaint tresses down his richly-furred cloak. His beard was closely shaved, his doublet reached to the middle of his leg, and the girdle which secured it, and at the same time supported his ponderous sword, was embroidered and embossed with gold work. We have already noticed the extravagant fashion of the shoes at this period, and the points of Maurice de Bracy's might have challenged the prize of extravagance with the gayest, being turned up and twisted like the horns of a ram. Such was the dress of a gallant of the period; and, in the present instance, that effecf was aided by the handsome person and good demeanour ot the wearer, whose manners partook alike of the grace of a courtier and the frankness of a soldier.

He saluted Rowena by doffing his velvet bonnet, garnished with a golden brooch, representing St. Michael trampling down the Prince of Evil. With this, he gently motioned the lady to a seat; and, as she still retained her standing posture, the knight ungloved his right hand and motioned toconduct her thither. But Rowena declined, by her gesture, the proffered compliment, and replied, "If I be in the presence of my jailer, Sir Knight—nor will circumstances allow me to think otherwise—it best becomes his prisoner to remain standing till she learns her doom."

"Alas! fair Rowena," returned De Bracy, "you are in presence of your captive, not your jailer; and it is from your fair eyes that De Bracy must receive that doom which you fondly expect from him."

"I know you not, sir," said the lady, drawing herself up with all the pride of offended rank and beauty—"I know you not;

and the insolent familiarity with which you apply to me the jargon of a troubadour, forms no apology for the violence of a robber."

"To thyself," answered De Bracy, "to thine own charms be ascribed whate'er I have done."

"I repeat to you, Sir Knight, that I know you not, and that no man wearing chain and spurs ought thus to intrude himself upon the presence of an unprotected lady."

"That I am unknown to you," said De Bracy, "is indeed my misfortune; yet let me hope that De Bracy's name has not been always unspoken, when minstrels or heralds have praised deeds of chivalry, whether in the lists or in the battlefield."

"To heralds and to minstrels, then, leave thy praise, Sir Knight," replied Rowena—"more suiting for their mouths than for thine own—and tell me which of them shall record in song, or in book of tourney, the memorable conquest of this night, a conquest obtained over an old man followed by a few timid hinds; and its booty, an unfortunate maiden, transported against her will to the castle of a robber?"

"You speak well, lady," said the Norman; "and in the bold language which best justifies bold action, I tell thee, thou shalt never leave this castle, or thou shalt leave it as Maurice de Bracy's wife. I am not wont to be baffled in my enterprises; nor need a Norman noble scrupulously to vindicate his conduct to the Saxon maiden whom he distinguishes by the offer of his hand. Thou art proud, Rowena, and thou art the fitter to be my wife. By what other means couldst thou be raised to high honour and to princely place, saving by my alliance? How else wouldst thou escape from the mean precincts of a country grange, where Saxons herd with the swine which form their wealth, to take thy seat, honoured as thou shouldst be, and shalt be, amid all in England that is distinguished by beauty or dignified by power?"

"Sir Knight," replied Rowena, "the grange which you contemn hath been my shelter from infancy; and, trust me, when I leave it — should that day ever arrive — it shall be with one who has not learnt to despise the dwelling and manners in which I have been brought up."

"I guess your meaning, lady," said De Bracy, "though you may think it lies too obscure for my apprehension. But dream not that Richard Cœur-de-Lion will ever resume his throne, far less that Wilfred of Ivanhoe, his minion, will ever lead thee to his footstool, to be there welcomed as the bride of a favourite. Another suitor might feel jealousy while he touched this string; but my firm purpose cannot be changed by a passion so childish and so hopeless. Know, lady, that this rival is in my power, and that it rests but with me to betray the secret of his being within the castle to Front-de-Bœuf, whose jealousy will be more fatal than mine."

"Wilfred here?" said Rowena, in disdain; "that is as true as that Front-de-Bœuf is his rival."

De Bracy looked at her steadily for an instant.

"Wert thou really ignorant of this?" said he; "didst thou not know that Wilfred of Ivanhoe travelled in the litter of the Jew? — a meet conveyance for the crusader whose doughty arm was to reconquer the Holy Sepulchre!" And he laughed scornfully.

"And if he is here," said Rowena, compelling herself to a tone of indifference, though trembling with an agony of apprehension which she could not suppress, "in what is he the rival of Front-de-Bœuf? or what has he to fear beyond a short imprisonment, and an honourable ransom, according to the use of chivalry?"

"Rowena," said De Bracy, "art thou too deceived by the common error of thy sex, who think there can be no rivalry but that respecting their own charms? Knowest thou not there is a jealousy of ambition and of wealth, as well as of love;

and that this our host, Front-de-Bœuf, will push from his road him who opposes his claim to the fair barony of Ivanhoe, as readily, eagerly, and unscrupulously as if he were preferred to him by some blue-eyed damsel? But smile on my suit, lady, and the wounded champion shall have nothing to fear from Front-de-Bœuf, whom else thou mayest mourn for, as in the hands of one who has never shown compassion."

"Save him, for the love of Heaven!" said Rowena, her firmness giving way under terror for her lover's impending fate.

"I can–I will–it is my purpose," said De Bracy; "for when Rowena consents to be the bride of De Bracy, who is it shall dare to put forth a violent hand upon her kinsman — the son of her guardian–the companion of her youth? But it is thy love must buy his protection. I am not romantic fool enough to further the fortune, or avert the fate, of one who is likely to be a successful obstacle between me and my wishes. Use thine influence with me in his behalf, and he is safe; refuse to employ it, Wilfred dies, and thou thyself art not the nearer to freedom."

De Bracy was interrupted by the horn, "hoarse-winded blowing far and keen," which had at the same time alarmed the other inmates of the castle, and interrupted their several plans of avarice and of license. Of them all, perhaps, De Bracy least regretted the interruption, for his conference with the Lady Rowena had arrived at a point where he found it equally difficult to prosecute or to resign his enterprise.

CHAPTER 19

WHILE the scenes we have described were passing in other parts of the castle, the Jewess Rebecca awaited her fate in a distant and sequestered turret. Hither she had been led by two of her disguised ravishers, and on being thrust into the little cell she found herself in the presence of an old sibyl, who kept murmuring to herself a Saxon rhyme, as if to beat time to the revolving dance which her spindle was performing upon the floor. The hag raised her head as Rebecca entered, and scowled at the fair Jewess with the malignant envy with which old age and ugliness, when united with evil conditions, are apt to look upon youth and beauty.

The men quickly retired, leaving Rebecca in company with the old woman, upon whose presence she had been thus unwillingly forced.

"What devil's deed have they now in the wind?" said the old hag, murmuring to herself, yet from time to time casting a sidelong and malignant glance at Rebecca. "But it is easy to guess—bright eyes, black locks, and a skin like paper, ere the priest stains it with his black unguent—ay, it is easy to guess why they send her to this lone turret, whence a shriek could no more be heard than at the depth of five hundred fathoms beneath the earth. Thou wilt have owls for thy neighbours, fair one; and their screams will be heard as far, and as much regarded, as thine own. Outlandish, too," she said, marking the dress and turban of Rebecca. —"What country art thou of? —a Saracen? or an Egyptian? Why dost not answer? —thou canst weep, canst thou not speak?"

"Be not angry, good mother," said Rebecca.

"Thou need'st say no more," replied Urfried; "men know a fox by the train, and a Jewess by her tongue."

"For the sake of mercy," said Rebecca, "tell me what I am to expect as the conclusion of the violence which hath dragged me hither! Is it my life they seek, to atone for my religion? I will lay it down cheerfully."

"Thy life, minion?" answered the sibyl; "what would taking thy life pleasure them? Trust me, thy life is in no peril. Such usage shalt thou have as was once thought good enough for a noble Saxon maiden. And shall a Jewess, like thee, repine because she hath no better? Look at me. I was as young and twice as fair as thou when Front-de-Bœuf, father of this Reginald, and his Normans, stormed this castle. My father and his seven sons defended their inheritance from story to story, from chamber to chamber—there was not a room, not a step of the stair, that was not slippery with their blood. They died–they died every man; and ere their bodies were cold, and ere their blood was dried, I had become the prey and the scorn of the conqueror!"

"Is there no help?–are there no means of escape?" said Rebecca. "Richly, richly would I requite thine aid."

"Think not of it," said the hag. "From hence there is no escape but through the gates of death; and it is late," she added, shaking her grey head, "ere these open to us. Yet it is comfort to think that we leave behind us on earth those who shall be wretched as ourselves. Fare thee well, Jewess! Jew or Gentile, thy fate would be the same; for thou hast to do with them that have neither scruple nor pity. Fare thee well, I say. My thread is spun out–thy task is yet to begin."

"Stay! stay! for Heaven's sake!" said Rebecca; "stay, though it be to curse and to revile me—thy presence is yet some protection."

"The presence of the mother of God were no protection," answered the old woman. "There she stands," pointing to a rude image of the Virgin Mary; "see if she can avert the fate that awaits thee."

She left the room as she spoke, her features writhed into a sort of sneering laugh, which made them seem even more hideous than their habitual frown. She locked the door behind her; and Rebecca might hear her curse every step for its steepness, as slowly and with difficulty she descended the turret stair.

The prisoner trembled and changed colour, when a step was heard, and the door of the turret-chamber slowly opened, and a tall man, dressed as one of those banditti to whom they owed their misfortune, slowly entered, and shut the door behind him. His cap, pulled down upon his brows, concealed the upper part of his face, and he held his mantle in such a manner as to muffle the rest. In this guise, as if prepared for the execution of some deed, at the thought of which he was himself ashamed, he stood before the affrighted prisoner; yet, ruffian as his dress bespoke him, he seemed at a loss to express what purpose had brought him thither, so that Rebecca, making an effort upon herself, had time to anticipate his explanation. She had already unclasped two costly bracelets and a collar, which she hastened to proffer to the supposed outlaw, concluding naturally that to gratify his avarice was to bespeak his favour.

"Take these," she said, "good friend, and for God's sake be merciful to me and my aged father! These ornaments are of value, yet are they trifling of what he would bestow to obtain our dismissal from this castle, free and uninjured."

"Fair flower of Palestine," replied the outlaw, "these pearls are orient, but they yield in whiteness to your teeth; the diamonds are brilliant, but they cannot match your eyes; and ever since I have taken up this wild trade, I have made a vow to prefer beauty to wealth."

"Do not do yourself such wrong," said Rebecca; "take ransom, and have mercy! Gold will purchase your pleasure, –to misuse us, could only bring thee remorse. My father will willingly satiate thy utmost wishes; and if thou wilt act wisely, thou mayest purchase with our spoils thy restoration to civil society –mayest obtain pardon for past errors, and be placed beyond the necessity of committing more."

"It is well spoken," replied the outlaw in French, finding it difficult probably to sustain, in Saxon, a conversation which Rebecca had opened in that language; "but know, bright lily of the vale of Baca! that thy father is already in the hands of a powerful alchemist, who knows how to convert into gold and silver even the rusty bars of a dungeon grate. Thy ransom must be paid by love and beauty, and in no other coin will I accept it."

"Thou art no outlaw," said Rebecca, in the same language in which he addressed her. "No outlaw had refused such offers; no outlaw in this land uses the dialect in which thou hast spoken. Thou art no outlaw, but a Norman –a Norman, noble perhaps in birth –oh, be so in thy actions, and cast off this fearful mask of outrage and violence!"

"And thou, who canst guess so truly," said Brian de Bois-Guilbert, dropping the mantle from his face, "art no true daughter of Israel, but in all, save youth and beauty, a very witch of Endor. I am not an outlaw, then, fair rose of Sharon. And I am one who will be more prompt to hang thy neck and arms with pearls and diamonds, which so well become them, than to deprive thee of these ornaments."

"What wouldst thou have of me," said Rebecca, "if not my wealth? We have nought in common between us. You are a Christian; I am a Jewess. Our union were contrary to the laws alike of the church and the synagogue."

As she spoke, she threw open the latticed window which led to the bartizan, and in an instant after stood on the very verge of the parapet, with not the slightest screen between her and the tremendous depth below. Unprepared for such a desperate effort, for she had hitherto stood perfectly motionless, Bois-Guilbert had neither time to intercept nor to stop her.

As he offered to advance, she exclaimed, "Remain where thou art, proud Templar, or at thy choice advance!–one foot nearer, and I plunge myself from the precipice. My body shall be crushed out of the very form of humanity upon the stones of that courtyard, ere it become the victim of thy brutality!"

She clasped her hands and extended them towards Heaven, as if imploring mercy on her soul before she made the final plunge. The Templar hesitated, and a resolution which had never yielded to pity or distress gave way to his admiration of her fortitude. "Come down," he said, "rash girl! I swear by earth, and sea, and sky, I will offer thee no offence. If not for thyself, yet for thy father's sake forbear. I will be his friend, and in this castle he will need a powerful one."

"Alas!" said Rebecca, "I know it but too well –dare I trust thee?"

"May my arms be reversed, and my name dishonoured," said Brian de Bois-Guilbert, "if thou shalt have reason to complain of me! Many a law, many a commandment have I broken, but my word never."

"I will then trust thee," said Rebecca, "thus far"; and she descended from the verge of the battlement, but remained standing close by one of the embrasures, or *machicolles*, as they were then called. "Here," she said, 'I take my stand. Remain where thou art; and if thou shalt attempt to diminish by one step the distance now between us, thou shalt see that the Jewish maiden will rather trust her soul wiih God than her honour to the Templar!"

Bois-Guilbert, proud himself and high-spirited, thought he had never beheld beauty so animated and so commanding.

"Let there be peace between us, Rebecca," he said. "That bugle-sound announces something which may require my presence. Think on what I have said. Farewell! I will soon return, and hold further conference with thee."

He re-entered the turret-chamber, and descended the stair, leaving Rebecca scarcely more terrified at the prospect of the death to which she had been so lately exposed, than at the furious ambition of the bold bad man in whose power she found herself so unhappily placed. When she entered the turret-chamber, her first duty was to return thanks to the God of Jacob for the protection which He had afforded her, and to implore its continuance for her and for her father. Another

name glided into her petition –it was that of the wounded
Christian, whom fate had placed in the hands of bloodthirsty
men, his avowed enemies. Her heart indeed checked her, as
if, even in communing with the Deity in prayer, she mingled
in her devotions the recollection of one with whose fate hers
could have no alliance –a Nazarene, and an enemy to her
faith. But the petition was already breathed; nor could all
the narrow prejudices of her sect induce Rebecca to wish it
recalled.

CHAPTER 20

When the Templar reached the hall of the castle, he found
De Bracy already there.

They were soon after joined by Front-de-Bœuf.

"Let us see the cause of this cursed clamour," said he;
"here is a letter, and, if I mistake not, it is in Saxon."

He looked at it, turning it round and round as if he had
really some hopes of coming at the meaning by inverting the
position of the paper, and then handed it to De Bracy.

"It may be magic spells for aught I know," said De Bracy,
who possessed his full proportion of the ignorance which charac-
terized the chivalry of the period. "Our chaplain attempted
to teach me to write," he said; "but all my letters were
formed like spear-heads and sword-blades, and so the old
shaveling gave up the task."

"Give it me," said the Templar. "We have that of the
priestly character, that we have some knowledge to enlighten
our valour."

"Let us profit by your most reverend knowledge, then,"
said De Bracy; "what says the scroll?"

"It is a formal letter of defiance," answered the Templar;
"but, by our Lady of Bethlehem, if it be not a foolish jest,

it is the most extraordinary cartel that ever was sent across the drawbridge of a baronial castle."

"Jest!" said Front-de-Boeuf; "I would gladly know who dares jest with me in such a matter!—Read it, Sir Brian."

The Templar accordingly read it as follows:—

"I, Wamba, the son of Witless, Jester to a noble and free-born man, Cedric of Rotherwood, called the Saxon,—And I, Gurth, the son of Beowulph, the swineherd—"

"Thou art mad," said Front-de-Bœuf, interrupting the reader.

"By St. Luke, it is so set down," answered the Templar. Then resuming his task, he went on:—"I, Gurth, the son of Beowulph, swineherd unto the said Cedric, with the assistance of our allies and confederates, who make common cause with us in this our feud, namely, the good knight, called for the present *Le Noir Fainéant*, and the stout yeoman, Robert Locksley, called Cleave-the-wand, Do you, Reginald Front-de-Boeuf, and your allies and accomplices whomsoever, to wit, that whereas you have, without cause given or feud declared, wrongfully and by mastery seized upon the person of our lord and master the said Cedric; also upon the person of a noble and freeborn damsel, the Lady Rowena of Hargott-standstede; also upon the person of a noble and freeborn man, Athelstane of Coningsburgh; also upon the persons of certain freeborn men, their *cnichts;* also upon certain serfs, their born bondsmen; also upon a certain Jew, named Isaac of York, together with his daughter, a Jewess, and certain horses and mules: Which noble persons, with their *cnichts* and slaves, and also with the horses and mules, Jew and Jewess beforesaid, were all in peace with his majesty, and travelling as liege subjects upon the king's highway; therefore we require and demand that the said noble persons, namely, Cedric of Rotherwood, Rowena of Hargottstandstede, Athel-stane of Coningsburgh, with their servants, *cnichts*, and followers, also the horses and mules, Jew and Jewess aforesaid, together with all goods and chattels to them pertaining, be, within an hour after the delivery hereof, delivered to us, or to those whom we shall appoint to receive the same, and that untouched and unharmed in body and goods. Failing of which, we do pronounce to you, that we hold ye as robbers and traitors, and will wager our bodies against ye in battle, siege, or otherwise, and do our utmost to your annoyance and destruction. Wherefore may God have you in His keeping. – Signed by us upon the eve of St. Withold's day, under the great trysting oak in the Hart-hill Walk, the above being written by a holy man, Clerk to God, our Lady, and St. Dunstan, in the Chapel of Copmanhurst."

The knights heard this uncommon document read from end to end, and then gazed upon each other in silent amazement, as being utterly at a loss to know what it could portend. De Bracy was the first to break silence by an uncontrollable fit of laughter, wherein he was joined, though with more moderation, by the Templar. Front-de-Bœuf, on the contrary, seemed impatient of their ill-timed jocularity.

"I give you plain warning," he said, "fair sirs, that you had better consult how to bear yourselves under these circumstances, than give way to such misplaced merriment."

"Front-de-Bœuf has not recovered his temper since his late overthrow," said De Bracy to the Templar. "He is cowed at the very idea of a cartel, though it come but from a fool and a swineherd."

"By St. Michael," answered Front-de-Bœuf, "I would thou couldst stand the whole brunt of this adventure thyself, De Bracy. These fellows dared not have acted with such inconceivable impudence, had they not been supported by some strong bands. – Here, fellow," he added, to one of his attendants, "hast thou sent out to see by what force this precious challenge is to be supported?"

"There are at least two hundred men assembled in the woods," answered a squire who was in attendance.

"Send to thy neighbours," said the Templar, "let them assemble their people, and come to the rescue of three knights besieged by a jester and a swineherd in the baronial castle of Reginald Front-de-Bœuf!"

"You jest, Sir Knight," answered the baron; "but to whom should I send? Malvoisin is by this time at York with his retainers, and so are my other allies; and so should I have been, but for this infernal enterprise."

"Then send to York and recall our people," said De Bracy. "If they abide the shaking of my standard, or the sight of my Free Companions, I will give them credit for the boldest outlaws ever bent bow in greenwood."

"And who shall bear such a message?" said Front-de-Bœuf; "they will beset every path, and rip the errand out of his bosom. —"I have it," he added, after pausing for a moment. "Sir Templar, thou canst write as well as read, and if we can but find the writing materials of my chaplain, who died a twelvemonth since in the midst of his Christmas carousals—"

"So please ye," said the squire, who was still in attendance, "I think old Urfried has them somewhere in keeping, for love of the confessor. He was the last man, I have heard her tell, who ever said aught to her which man ought in courtesy to address to maid or matron."

"Go, search them out, Engelred," said Front-de-Bœuf; "and then, Sir Templar, thou shalt return an answer to this bold challenge."

"I would rather do it at the sword's point than at that of the pen," said Bois-Guilbert; "but be it as you will."

He sat down accordingly, and indited, in the French language, an epistle in the following tenor:—

"Sir Reginald Front-de-Bœuf, with his noble and knightly allies and confederates, receive no defiances at the hands of slaves, bondsmen, or fugitives. If the person calling himself the Black Knight have indeed a claim to the honours of chivalry, he ought to know that he stands degraded by his present association, and has no right to ask reckoning at the hands of good men of noble blood. Touching the prisoners we have made, we do in Christian charity require you to send a man of religion, to receive their confession and reconcile them with God, since it is our fixed intention to execute them this morning before noon, so that their heads being placed on the battlements, shall show to all men how lightly we esteem those who have bestirred themselves in their rescue. Wherefore, as above, we require you to send a priest to reconcile them to God, in doing which you shall render them the last earthly service."

This letter being folded, was delivered to the squire, and by him to the messenger who waited without, as the answer to that which he had brought.

The yeoman having thus accomplished his mission, returned to the headquarters of the allies, which were for the present established under a venerable oak-tree, about three arrow-flights distant from the castle. Here Wamba and Gurth, with their allies the Black Knight and Locksley, and the jovial hermit, awaited with impatience an answer to their summons. Around, and at a distance from them, were seen many a bold yeoman, whose silvan dress and weather-beaten countenances showed the ordinary nature of their occupation. More than two hundred had already assembled, and others were fast coming in. Those whom they obeyed as leaders were only distinguished from the others by a feather in the cap, their dress, arms, and equipments being in all other respects the same.

Besides these bands, a less orderly and a worse armed force, consisting of the Saxon inhabitants of the neighbouring township, as well as many bondsmen and servants from Cedric's extensive estate, had already arrived, for the purpose of assisting in his rescue. Few of these were armed otherwise than with such rustic weapons as necessity sometimes converts to military purposes. Boer-spears, scythes, flails, and the like, were their chief arms; for the Normans, with the usual policy of conquerors, were jealous of permitting to the vanquished Saxons the possession or the use of swords and spears. These circumstances rendered the assistance of the Saxons far from being so formidable to the besieged as the strength of the men themselves, their superior numbers, and the animation inspired by a just cause, might otherwise well have made them. It was to the leaders of this motley army that the letter of the Templar was now delivered.

Reference was at first made to the chaplain for an expostulation of its contents.

"By the crook of St. Dunstan," said that worthy ecclesiastic, "which hath brought more sheep within the sheepfold than the crook of e'er another saint in Paradise, I swear that I cannot expound unto you this jargon, which, whether it be French or Arabic, is beyond my guess."

He then gave the letter to Gurth, who shook his head gruffly, and passed it to Wamba. The Jester looked at each of the four corners of the paper with such a grin of affected intelligence as a monkey is apt to assume upon similar occasions, then cut a caper, and gave the letter to Locksley.

"If the long letters were bows, and the short letters broad arrows, I might know something of the matter," said the brave yeoman; "but as the matter stands, the meaning is as safe, for me, as the stag that's at twelve miles' distance."

"I must be clerk, then," said the Black Knight; and taking the letter from Locksley, he first read it over to himself, and then explained the meaning in Saxon to his confederates.

"Execute the noble Cedric!" exclaimed Wamba; "by the rood, thou must be mistaken, Sir Knight."

"Not I, my worthy friend," replied the knight; "I have explained the words as they are here set down."

"Then, by St. Thomas of Canterbury," replied Gurth, "we will have the castle, should we tear it down with our hands!"

"We have nothing else to tear it with," replied Wamba; "but mine are scarce fit to make mammocks of freestone and mortar."

"'Tis but a contrivance to gain time," said Locksley; "they dare not do a deed for which I could exact a fearful penalty."

"I would," said the Black Knight, "there were some one among us who could obtain admission into the castle, and discover how the case stands with the besieged. Methinks, as they require a confessor to be sent this holy hermit might at once exercise his pious vocation, and procure us the information we desire."

"A plague on thee, and thy advice!" said the pious hermit. "I tell thee, Sir Slothful Knight, that when I doff my friar's frock, my priesthood, my sanctity, my very Latin, are put off along with it; and when in my green jerkin, I can better kill twenty deer than confess one Christian."

"I fear," said the Black Knight, "I fear greatly, there is no one here that is qualified to take upon him, for the nonce, this same character of father confessor?"

All looked on each other, and were silent.

"I see," said Wamba, after a short pause, "that the fool must be still the fool, and put his neck in the venture which wise men shrink from. You must know, my dear cousins and countrymen, that I wore russet before I wore motley, and was bred to be a friar, until a brainfever came upon me and left me just wit enough to be a fool. I trust, with the assistance of the good hermit's frock, together with the priesthood, sanctity, and learning which are stitched into the cowl of it,

I shall be found qualified to administer both worldly and ghostly comfort to our worthy master Cedric, and his companions in adversity."

"Hath he sense enough, think'st thou?" said the Black Knight, addressing Gurth.

"I know not," said Gurth; "but if he hath not, it will be the first time he hath wanted wit to turn his folly to account."

"On with the frock, then, good fellow," quoth the Knight, "and let thy master send us an account of their situation within the castle. Their numbers must be few, and it is five to one they may be accessible by a sudden and bold attack. Time wears –away with thee."

"And, in the meantime," said Locksley, "we will beset the place so closely that not so much as a fly shall carry news from thence. So that, my good friend," he continued, addressing Wamba, "thou mayest assure these tyrants, that whatever violence they exercise on the persons of their prisoners, shall be most severely repaid upon their own."

"*Pax vobiscum*," said Wamba, who was now muffled in his religious disguise.

And so saying, he imitated the solemn and stately deportment of a friar, and departed to execute his mission.

CHAPTER 21

WHEN the Jester, arrayed in the cowl and frock of the hermit, and having his knotted cord twisted round his middle, stood before the portal of the castle of Front-de-Bœuf, the warder demanded of him his name and errand.

"*Pax vobiscum*," answered the Jester, "I am a poor brother of the Order of St. Francis, who comes hither to do my office to certain unhappy prisoners now secured within this castle."

"Thou art a bold friar," said the warder, "to come hither, where, saving our own drunken confessor, a cock of thy feather hath not crowed these twenty years."

"Yet I pray thee, do mine errand to the lord of the castle," answered the pretended friar; "trust me it will find good acceptance with him, and the cock shall crow that the whole castle shall hear him."

"Gramercy," said the warder, "but if I come to shame for leaving my post upon thine errand, I will try whether a friar's grey gown be proof against a grey-goose shaft."

With this threat he left his turret, and carried to the hall of the castle his unwonted intelligence, that a holy friar stood before the gate and demanded instant admission. With no small wonder he received his master's commands to admit the holy man immediately; and, having previously manned the entrance to guard against surprise, he obeyed, without further scruple, the commands which he had received. The harebrained self-conceit which had emboldened Wamba to undertake this dangerous office, was scarce sufficient to support him when he found himself in the presence of a man so dreadful, and so much dreaded, as Reginald Front-de-Bœuf, and he brought out his *Pax vobiscum*, to which he, in a good measure, trusted for supporting his character, with more anxiety and hesitation than had hitherto accompanied it. But Front-de-Bœuf was accustomed to see men of all ranks tremble in his presence, so that the timidity of the supposed father did not give him any cause of suspicion. "Who and whence art thou, priest?" said he.

"*Pax vobiscum*," reiterated the Jester; "I am a poor servant of St. Francis, who, travelling through this wilderness, have fallen among thieves (as Scripture hath it), *quidam viator incidit in lat ones*, which thieves have sent me unto this castle in order to do my ghostly office on two persons condemned by your honourable justice."

"Ay, right," answered Front-de-Bœuf; "and canst thou tell me, holy father, the number of those banditti?"

"Gallant sir," answered the Jester, "*nomen illis legio* –their name is legion."

"Tell me in plain terms what numbers there are, or, priest, thy cloak and cord will ill protect thee."

"Alas!" said the supposed friar, "*cor meum eructavit* –that is to say, I was like to burst with fear! but I conceive they may be, what of yeomen, what of commons, at least five hundred men."

"What!" said the Templar, who came into the hall that moment, "muster the wasps so thick here? It is time to stifle such a mischievous brood." Then taking Front-de-Bœuf aside, "Knowest thou the priest?"

"He is a stranger from a distant convent," said Front-de-Bœuf; "I know him not."

"Then trust him not with thy purpose in words," answered the Templar. "Let him carry a written order to De Bracy's company of Free Companions, to repair instantly to their master's aid. In the meantime, and that the shaveling may suspect nothing, permit him to go freely about his task of preparing these Saxon bogs for the slaughter-house."

"It shall be so," said Front-de-Bœuf. And he forthwith appointed a domestic to conduct Wamba to the apartment where Cedric and Athelstane were confined.

The impatience of Cedric had been rather enhanced than diminished by his confinement. He walked from one end of the hall to the other, with the attitude of one who advances to charge an enemy, or to storm the breach of a beleaguered place, sometimes ejaculating to himself, sometimes addressing Athelstane, who stoutly and stoically awaited the issue of the adventure, digesting, in the meantime, the liberal meal he had made at noon.

"*Pax vobiscum,*" said the Jester, entering the apartment; "the blessing of St. Dunstan, St. Denis, St. Duthoc, and all other saints whatsoever, be upon ye and about ye."

"Enter freely," answered Cedric to the supposed friar; "with what intent art thou come hither?"

"To bid you prepare yourselves for death," answered the Jester.

"It is impossible!" replied Cedric, starting. "Fearless, and wicked as they are, they dare not attempt such open and gratuitous cruelty!"

"Alas!" said the Jester, "to restrain them by their sense of humanity, is the same as to stop a runaway horse with a bridle of silk thread. Bethink thee, therefore, noble Cedric, and you also gallant Athelstane, what crimes you have committed in the flesh; for this very day will ye be called to answer at a higher tribunal."

"Hearest thou this, Athelstane?" said Cedric. "We must rouse up our hearts to this last action, since better it is we should die like men than live like slaves."

"I am ready," answered Athelstane, "to stand the worst of their malice, and shall walk to my death with as much composure as ever I did to my dinner."

"Let us then unto our holy gear, father," said Cedric.

"Wait yet a moment, good uncle," said the Jester, in his natural tone; "better look long, before you leap in the dark."

"By my faith," said Cedric, "I should know that voice!"

"It is that of your trusty slave and jester," answered Wamba, throwing back his cowl. "Had you taken a fool's advice formerly, you would not have been here at all. Take a fool's advice now, and you will not be here long."

"How mean'st thou, knave?" answered the Saxon.

"Even thus," replied Wamba; "take thou this frock and cord, which are all the orders I ever had, and march quietly out of the castle, leaving me your cloak and girdle to take the long leap in thy stead."

"Leave thee in my stead!" said Cedric, astonished at the proposal; "why, they would hang thee, my poor knave."

"E'en let them do as they are permitted," said Wamba. "I trust—no disparagement to your birth—that the son of Witless may hang in a chain with as much gravity as the chain hung upon his ancestor the alderman."

"Go, then, noble Cedric," said Athelstane; "neglect not this opportunity. Your presence without may encourage friends to our rescue; your remaining here would ruin us all."

"And is there any prospect, then, of rescue from without?" said Cedric, looking to the Jester.

"Prospect, indeed!" echoed Wamba. "Let me tell you, when you fill my cloak, you are wrapped in a general's cassock. Five hundred men are there without, and I was this morning one of their chief leaders. My fool's cap was a casque, and my bauble a truncheon. Well, we shall see what good they will make by exchanging a fool for a wise man. Truly, I fear they will lose in valour what they may gain in discretion. And so farewell, master, and be kind to poor Gurth and his dog Fangs; and let my cock's comb hang in the hall at Rotherwood, in memory that I flung away my life for my master, like a faithful fool."

The exchange of dress was now accomplished, when a sudden doubt struck Cedric.

"I know no language," he said, "but my own, and a few words of their mincing Norman. How shall I bear myself like a reverend brother?"

"The spell lies in two words," replied Wamba—"*Pax vobiscum* will answer all queries. If you go or come, eat or drink, bless or ban, *Pax vobiscum* carries you through it all. It is as useful to a friar as a broomstick to a witch, or a wand to a conjurer. Speak it but thus, in a deep grave tone—*Pax vobiscum!*—

it is irresistible. Watch and ward, knight and squire, foot and horse, it acts as a charm upon them all."

"If such prove the case," said his master, "my religious orders are soon taken—*Pax vobiscum*. I trust I shall remember the password.—Noble Athelstane, farewell; and farewell, my poor boy, whose heart might make amends for a weaker head. I will save you, or return and die with you. Farewell."

"Farewell, noble Cedric," said Athelstane; "remember it is the true part of a friar to accept refreshment, if you are offered any."

"Farewell, uncle," added Wamba; "and remember *Pax vobiscum*."

Thus exhorted, Cedric sallied forth upon his expedition; and it was not long ere he had occasion to try the force of that spell which his Jester had recommended as omnipotent. In a low-arched and dusky passage, by which he endeavoured to work his way to the hall of the castle, he was interrupted by a female form.

"*Pax vobiscum!*" said the pseudo-friar, and was endeavouring to hurry past, when a soft voice replied, "*Et vobis-quœso, domine reverendissime, pro misericordia vestra.*"

"I am somewhat deaf," replied Cedric, in good Saxon, and at the same time muttered to himself, "A curse on the fool and his *Pax vobiscum!* I have lost my javelin at the first cast."

"I pray you of dear love, reverend father," she replied in his own language, "that you will deign to visit with your ghostly comfort a wounded prisoner of this castle, and have such compassion upon him and us as thy holy office teaches. Never shall good deed so highly advantage thy convent."

"Daughter," anwered Cedric, much embarrassed, "my time in this castle will not permit me to exercise the duties of mine office. I must presently forth; there is life and death upon my speed."

"Yet, father, let me entreat you by the vow you have taken on you," replied the suppliant, "not to leave the oppressed and endangered without counsel or succour."

"May the fiend fly away with me, and leave me in Ifrin with the souls of Odin and of Thor!" answered Cedric impatiently, and would probably have proceeded in the same tone of total departure from his spiritual character, when the colloquy was interrupted by the harsh voice of Urfried, the old crone of the turret.

"How, minion," said she to the female speaker. "is this the manner in which you requite the kindness which permitted thee to leave thy prison cell yonder? Puttest thou the reverend man to use ungracious language to free himself from the importunities of a Jewess?"

"A Jewess!" said Cedric, availing himself of the information to get clear of their interruption. "Let me pass, woman! stop me not at your peril. I am fresh from my holy office, and would avoid pollution."

"Come this way, father," said the old hag; "thou art a stranger in this castle, and canst not leave it without a guide. Come hither, for I would speak with thee. -And you, daughter of and accursed race, go to the sick man's chamber, and tend him until my return; and woe betide you if you again quit it without my permission!"

Rebecca retreated. Her importunities had prevailed upon Urfried to suffer her to quit the turret; and Urfried had employed her services, where she herself would most gladly have paid them, by the bedside of the wounded Ivanhoe. With an understanding awake to their dangerous situation, and prompt to avail herself of each means of safety which occurred, Rebecca had hoped something from the presence of a man of religion, who, she learned from Urfried, had penetrated into this godless castle. She watched the return of the supposed ecclesiastic, with the purpose of addressing him, and interesting him in favour of the prisoners –with what imperfect success the reader has been just acquainted.

CHAPTER 22

WHEN Urfried had, with clamours and menaces, driven Rebecca back to the apartment from which she had sallied, she proceeded to conduct the unwilling Cedric into a small apartment, the door of which she heedfully secured. Then fetching from a cupboard a stoup of wine and two flagons, she placed them on the table, and said in a tone rather asserting a fact than asking a question. "Thou art Saxon, father. –Deny it not," she continued, observing that Cedric hastened not to reply; "the sounds of my native language are sweet to mine ears, though seldom heard save from the tongues of the wretched and degraded serfs on whom the proud Normans impose the meanest drudgery of this dwelling. Thou art a Saxon, father – a Saxon, and, save as thou art a servant of God, a freeman. Thine accents are sweet in mine ear."

"Do not Saxon priests visit this castle, then?" replied Cedric; "it were, methinks, their duty to comfort the outcast and oppressed children of the soil."

"They come not; or if they come, they better love to revel at the boards of their conquerors," answered Urfried, "than to hear the groans of their countrymen. So, at least, report speaks of them; of myself I can say little. This castle, for ten years, has opened to no priest save the debauched Norman chaplain who partook the nightly revels of Front-de-Bœuf; and he has been long gone to render an account of his stewardship. But thou art a Saxon –a Saxon priest, and I have one question to ask of thee,"

"I am a Saxon," answered Cedric, "but unworthy, surely, of the name of priest. Let me begone on my way; I swear I will return, or send one of our fathers more worthy to hear your confession."

"Stay yet a while," said Urfried; "the accents of the voice which thou hearest now will soon be choked with the cold earth, and I would not descend to it like the beast I have lived. But wine must give me strength to tell the horrors of my tale." She poured out a cup, and drank it with a frightful avidity, which seemed desirous of draining the last drop in the goblet. "It stupefies," she said, looking upwards as she finished her draught, "but it cannot cheer. Partake it, father, if you would hear my tale without sinking down upon the pavement." Cedric would have avoided pledging her in this ominous conviviality, but the sign which she made to him expressed impatience and despair. He complied with her request, and answered her challenge in a large wine-cup. She then proceeded with her story, as if appeased by his complaisance.

"I was not born," she said, "father, the wretch that thou now seest me. I was free, was happy, was honoured, loved, and was beloved. I am now a slave, miserable and degraded; the sport of my masters' passions while I had yet beauty — the object of their contempt, scorn, and hatred since it has passed away. Dost thou wonder, father, that I should hate mankind, and, above all, the race that has wrought this change in me? Can the wrinkled, decrepit hag before thee, whose wrath must vent itself in impotent curses, forget she was once the daughter of the noble Thane of Torquilstone, before whose frown a thousand vassals trembled?"

"Thou the daughter of Torquil Wolfganger!" said Cedric, receding as he spoke; "thou the daughter of my father's friend and companion in arms!"

"Thy father's friend!" echoed Urfried; "then Cedric called the Saxon stands before me, for the noble Hereward of Rotherwood had but one son, whose name is well known among his countrymen. But if thou art Cedric of Rotherwood, why this religious dress? –hast thou too despaired of saving thy country, and sought refuge from oppression in the shade of the convent?"

"It matters not who I am," said Cedric; "proceed, unhappy woman, thy tale of horror and guilt! Guilt there must be –there is guilt even in thy living to tell it."

"There is," answered the woman. "In these halls stained with the blood of my father and my brethren I have lived, the paramour of their murderer."

"Wretched woman!" exclaimed the Saxon.

"Cedric!" answered Urfried, "thou hast shown me the means of revenge, and be assured I will embrace them. There is a force without beleaguering this accursed castle. Hasten to lead them to the attack; and when thou shalt see a red flag wave from the turret on the eastern angle of the donjon, press the Normans hard –they will then have enough to do within, and you may win the wall in spite both of bow and mangonel. Begone, I pray thee; follow thine own fate, and leave me to mine."

Cedric would have inquired further into the purpose which she thus darkly announced, but the stern voice of Front-de-Bœuf was heard, exclaiming. "Where tarries this loitering priest? By the scallop-shell of Compostella, I will make a martyr of him if he loiters here to hatch treason among my domestics!"

The old woman vanished through a private door, and Cedric, with some difficulty, compelled himself to make obeisance to the haughty Baron, who returned his courtesy with a slight inclination of the head.

"Thy penitents, father, have made a long shrift; it is the better for them, since it is the last they shall ever make. Hast thou prepared them for death?"

"I found them," said Cedric, in such French as he could command, "expecting the worst, from the moment they knew into whose power they had fallen."

"How now, Sir Friar," replied Front-de-Bœuf, "thy speech, methinks, smacks of a Saxon tongue?"

"I was bred in the convent of St. Withold of Burton," answered Cedric.

"Ay?" said the Baron. "It had been better for thee to have been a Norman, and better for my purpose too; but need has no choice of messengers. That St. Withold's of Burton is a howlet's nest worth the harrying. The day will soon come that the frock shall protect the Saxon as little as the mail-coat."

"God's will be done," said Cedric, in a voice tremulous with passion, which Front-de-Bœuf imputed to fear.

"Follow me through this passage, then, that I may dismiss thee by the postern."

And as he strode on his way before the supposed friar, Front-de-Bœuf thus schooled him in the part which he desired he should act.

"Thou seest, Sir Friar, yon herd of Saxon swine, who have dared to environ this castle of Torquilstone. Tell them whatever thou hast a mind of the weakness of this fortalice, or aught else that can detain them before it for twenty-four hours. Meantime bear thou this scroll—But soft—canst read, Sir Priest?"

"Not a jot I," answered Cedric, "save on my breviary; and then I know the characters, because I have the holy service by heart, praised be Our Lady and St. Withold!"

"The fitter messenger for my purpose. Carry thou this scroll to the castle of Philip de Malvoisin; say it cometh from me, and is written by the Templar Brian de Bois-Guilbert, and that I pray him to send it to York with all the speed man and horse can make. Meanwhile, tell him to doubt nothing;

he shall find us whole and sound behind our battlement. Shame on it, that we should be compelled to hide thus by a pack of runagates, who are wont to fly even at the flash of our pennons and the tramp of our horses!"

Front-de-Bœuf led the way to a postern, where, passing the moat on a single plank, they reached a small barbican, or exterior defence, which communicated with the open field by a well-fortified sally-port.

"Begone, then; and if thou wilt do mine errand, and return hither when it is done, thou shalt see Saxon flesh cheap as ever was hog's in the shambles of Sheffield. And, hark thee, thou seemest to be a jolly confessor—come hither after the onslaught, and thou shalt have as much Malvoisie as would drench thy whole convent."

"Assuredly we shall meet again," answered Cedric.

"Something in hand the whilst," continued the Norman, and, as they parted at the postern door, he thrust into Cedric's reluctant hand a gold byzant, adding, "Remember, I will flay off both cowl and skin, if thou failest in thy purpose."

"And full leave will I give thee to do both," answered Cedric, leaving the postern, and striding forth over the free field with a joyful step, "if, when we meet next, I deserve not better at thine hand." Turning then back towards the castle, he threw the piece of gold towards the donor, exclaiming at the same time, "False Norman, thy money perish with thee!"

Front-de-Bœuf heard the words imperfectly, but the action was suspicious. "Archers," he called to the warders on the outward battlements, "send me an arrow through yon monk's frock! Yet stay," he said, as his retainers were bending their bows, "it avails not; we must thus far trust him since we have no better shift. I think he dares not betray me. At the worst I can but treat with these Saxon dogs whom I have safe in kennel. —Ho! Giles jailer, let them bring Cedric of Rother-wood before me, and the other churl, his companion—him I mean of Coningsburgh—Athelstane there, or what call they him?"

Front-de-Bœuf took a long draught of wine, and then addressed his prisoners—for the manner in which Wamba drew the cap over his face, the change of dress, the gloomy and broken light, and the Baron's imperfect acquaintance with the features of Cedric (who avoided his Norman neighbours, and seldom stirred beyond his own domains), prevented him from discovering that the most important of his captives had made his escape.

"Gallants of England," said Front-de-Bœuf, "how relish ye your entertainment at Torquilstone? Have ye forgotten how ye requited the unmerited hospitality of the royal John? By God and St. Denis, an ye pay not the richer ransom, I will hang ye up by the feet from the iron bars of these windows, till the kites and hooded crows have made skeletons of you! Speak out, ye Saxon dogs—what bid ye for your worthless lives?—How say you, you of Rotherwood?"

"Not a doit I," answered poor Wamba; "and for hanging up by the feet, my brain has been topsy-turvy, they say, ever since the biggin was bound first round my head; so turning me upside down may peradventure restore it again."

"Saint Genevieve!" said Front-de-Bœuf, "what have we got here?"

And with the back of his hand he struck Cedric's cap from the head of the Jester, and throwing open his collar, discovered the fatal badge of servitude, the silver collar round his neck.

"Giles—Clement—dogs and varlets!" exclaimed the furious Norman, "what have you brought here?"

"I think I can tell you," said De Bracy, who just entered the apartment. "This is Cedric's clown, who fought so manful a skirmish with Isaac of York about a question of precedence."

"Go," said Front-de-Bœuf to two of his attendants, "fetch me the right Cedric hither, and I pardon your error for once;

the rather that you but mistook a fool for a Saxon franklin."

"Ay, but," said Wamba, "your chivalrous excellency will
find there are more fools than franklins among us."

"Saint of Heaven!" exclaimed De Bracy, "he must have
escaped in the monk's garments!"

"Fiends of hell!" echoed Front-de-Bœuf; "it was then the
boar of Rotherwood whom I ushered to the postern, and dismissed with my own hands!—And thou," he said to Wamba,
"whose folly could overreach the wisdom of idiots yet more
gross than thyself, I will give thee holy orders—I will shave
thy crown for thee!—Here, let them tear the scalp from his
head, and then pitch him headlong from the battlements—
Thy trade is to jest, canst thou jest now?"

The conversation was interrupted by the arrival of a menial,
who announced that a monk demanded admittance at the
postern gate.

"In the name of Saint Bennet, the prince of these bull-
beggars," said Front-de-Bœuf, "have we a real monk this
time, or another imposter? Search him, slaves; for an ye suffer
a second imposter to be palmed upon you, I will have your
eyes torn out, and hot coals put into the sockets."

"Let me endure the extremity of your anger, my lord,"
said Giles, "if this be not a real shaveling. Your squire Jocelyn
knows him well, and will vouch him to be brother Ambrose,
a monk in attendance upon the Prior of Jorvaulx."

"Admit him," said Front-de-Bœuf; "most likely he brings
us news from his jovial master. Surely the devil keeps holiday,
and the priests are relieved from duty, that they are strolling
thus wildly through the country. Remove these prisoners—
and, Saxon, think on what thou hast heard."

The Saxon prisoners were accordingly removed, just as they
introduced the monk Ambrose, who appeared to be in great
perturbation.

"This is the real *Deus vobiscum*," said Wamba as he passed the reverend brother; "the others were but counterfeits."

"Holy Mother," said the monk, as he addressed the assembled knights, "I am at last safe, and in Christian keeping!"

"Safe thou art," replied De Bracy; "and for Christianity, here is the stout Baron Reginald Front-de-Bœuf, whose utter abomination is a Jew and the good Knight Templar, Brian de Bois-Guilbert, whose trade is to slay Saracens. If these are not good marks of Christianity, I know no other which they bear about them."

"Ye are friends and allies of our reverend father in God, Aymer, Prior of Jorvaulx," said the monk, without noticing the tone of De Bracy's reply; "ye owe him aid both by knightly faith and holy charity; for what saith the blessed Saint Augustin, in his treatise *De Civitate Dei*—"

"Brother priest," said the Templar, "tell us plainly, is thy master, the Prior, made prisoner, and to whom?"

"Surely," said Ambrose, "he is in the hands of the men of Belial, infesters of these woods, and contemners of the holy text, 'Touch not mine anointed, and do my prophets nought of evil.'"

"Here is a new argument for our swords, sirs," said Front-de-Bœuf, turning to his companions; "and so, instead of reaching us any assistance, the Prior of Jorvaulx requests aid at our hands? —a man is well helped of these lazy churchmen when he hath most to do! But speak out, priest, and say at once, what doth thy master expect from us?"

"So please you," said Ambrose, "violent hands having been imposed on my reverend superior, contrary to the holy ordinance which I did already quote, and the men of Belial having rifled his mails and budgets, and stripped him of two hundred marks of pure refined gold, they do yet demand of him a large sum besides, ere they will suffer him to depart from their uncircumcised hands. Wherefore the reverend father in

God prays you, as his dear friends, to rescue him, either by paying down the ransom at which they hold him, or by force of arms, at your best discretion."

"The foul fiend quell the Prior!" said Front-de-Bœuf; "how can we do aught by valour to free him, that are cooped up here by ten times our number, and expect assault every moment?

"And that was what I was about to tell you," said the monk, "had your hastings allowed me time. But, God help me, I am old, and these foul onslaughts distract an aged man's brain. Nevertheless, it is of verity that they assemble a camp, and raise a bank against the walls of this castle."

"To the battlements!" cried De Bracy, "and let us mark what these knaves do without;" and so saying, he opened a latticed window which led to a sort of bartizan or projecting balcony, and immediately called from thence to those in the apartment—"Saint Denis, but the old monk hath brought true tidings! They bring forward mantelets and pavisses, and the archers muster on the skirts of the wood like a dark cloud before a hailstorm."

Reginald Front-de-Bœuf also looked out upon the field, and immediately snatched his bugle, and, after winding a long and loud blast, commanded his men to their posts on the walls.

"De Bracy, look to the eastern side, where the walls are lowest. —Noble Bois-Gilbert, thy trade hath well taught thee how to attack and defend, look thou to the western side. —I myself will take post at the barbican. Yet, do not confine your exertions to any one spot, noble friends! —we must this day be everywhere, and multiply ourselves, were it possible, so as to carry by our presence succour and relief wherever the attack is hottest. Our numbers are few, but activity and courage may supply that defect, since we have only to do with rascal clowns."

"But, noble knights," exclaimed Father Ambrose, amidst the bustle and confusion occasioned by the preparations for defence, "will none of ye hear the message of the reverend father in God, Aymer, Prior of Jorvaulx? –I beseech thee to hear me, noble Sir Reginald!"

"Go patter thy petition to heaven," said the fierce Norman, "for we on earth have no time to listen to them. –Ho! there, Anselm! see that seething pitch and oil are ready to pour on the heads of these audacious traitors. Look that the cross-bowmen lack not bolts. Fling abroad my banner with the old bull's head –the knaves shall soon find with whom they have to do this day!"

"But, noble sir," continued the monk, persevering in his endeavours to draw attention, "consider my vow of obedience, and let me discharge myself of my Superior's errand."

"Away with this prating dotard," said Front-de-Bœuf; lock him up in the chapel, to tell his beads till the broil be over. It will be a new thing to the saints in Torquilstone to hear aves and paters; they have not been so honoured, I trow, since they were cut out of stone."

The Templar had in the meantime been looking out on the proceedings of the besiegers, with rather more attention than the brutal Front-de-Bœuf or his giddy companion.

"By the faith of mine order," he said, "these men approach with more touch of discipline than could have been judged, however they come by it. See ye how dexterously they avail themselves of every cover which a tree or bush affords, and shun exposing themselves to the shot of our crossbows? I spy neither banner nor pennon among them, and yet will I gage my golden chain that they are led on by some noble knight or gentleman, skilful in the practice of wars."

"I espy him," said De Bracy; "I see the waving of a knight's crest and the gleam of his armour. See yon tall man in the black mail, who is busied marshalling the farther troop of the rascaille yeomen –by Saint Denis, I hold him to be the same whom we called *Le Noir Fainéant*, who overthrew, thee, Front-de-Bœuf, in the lists at Ashby."

"So much the better," said Front-de-Bœuf, "that he comes here to give me my revenge. Some hilding fellow he must be, who dared not stay to assert his claim to the tourney prize which chance had assigned him. I should in vain have sought for him where knights and nobles seek their foes, and right glad am I he hath here shown himself among yon villain yeomanry."

The demonstrations of the enemy's immediate approach cut off all further discourse. Each knight repaired to his post, and they awaited with calm determination the threatened assault.

CHAPTER 23

WHEN Ivanhoe sank down, and seemed abandoned by all the world, it was the importunity of Rebecca which prevailed on her father to have the gallant young warrior transported from the lists to the house which for the time the Jews inhabited in the suburbs of Ashby.

Rebecca lost no time in causing the patient to be transported to their temporary dwelling, and proceeded with her own hands to examine and to bind up his wounds.

When Ivanhoe reached the habitation of Isaac, he was still in a state of unconsciousness, owing to the profuse loss of blood which had taken place during his exertions in the lists. Rebecca examined the wound, and informed her father that if fever could be averted, there was nothing to fear for the guest's life, and that he might with safety travel to York with them on the ensuing day. Isaac looked a little blank at this annunciation. His charity would willingly have stopped short at Ashby, or at most would have left the wounded Christian to be tended in the house where he was residing at present, with an assurance to the Hebrew to whom it belonged that all expenses should be duly charged. To this, however, Rebecca opposed many reasons, of which we shall only mention two that had peculiar weight against Isaac. The one was, that she would on no account put the phial of precious balsam into the hands of another physician; the other, that this wounded knight, Wilfred of Ivanhoe, was an intimate favourite of Richard Cœur-de-Lion, and that, in case the monarch should return, Isaac, who had supplied his brother John with treasure to prosecute his rebellious purposes, would stand in no small need of a powerful protector who enjoyed Richard's favour.

The fair Jewess, though sensible her patient now regarded her as one of a race of reprobation, ceased not to pay the same patient and devoted attention to his safety and convalescence. She informed him of the necessity they were under of removing to York, and of her father's resolution to transport him thither, and tend him in his own house until his health should be restored.

He was deposited in the horse-litter which had brought him from the lists, and every precaution taken for his travelling with ease. In one circumstance only even the entreaties of Rebecca were unable to secure sufficient attention to the accommodation of the wounded knight. Isaac, like the enriched traveller of Juvenal's tenth satire, had ever the fear of robbery before his eyes, conscious that he would be alike accounted fair game by the marauding Norman noble and by the Saxon outlaw. He therefore journeyed at a great rate, and made short halts and shorter repasts, so that he passed by Cedric and Athelstane, who had several hours the start of him, but who had been delayed by their protracted feasting at the convent of Saint Withold's.

The Jew's haste proved somewhat more than good speed. The rapidity with which he insisted on travelling bred several disputes between him and the party whom he had hired to attend him as a guard. These men were Saxons, and not free by any means from the national love of ease and good living which the Normans stigmatized as laziness and gluttony. Reversing Shylock's position, they had accepted the employment in hopes of feeding upon the wealthy Jew, and were very much displeased when they found themselves disappointed, by the rapidity with which he insisted on their proceeding. They remonstrated also upon the risk of damage to their horses by these forced marches. Finally, there arose betwixt Isaac and his satellites a deadly feud, concerning the quantity of wine and ale to be allowed for consumption at each meal. And thus it happened, that when the alarm of danger approached, and that which Isaac feared was likely to come upon him, he was deserted by the discontented mercenaries on whose protection he had relied, without using the means necessary to secure their attachment.

In this deplorable condition the Jew, with his daughter and her wounded patient, were found by Cedric, as has already been noticed, and soon afterwards fell into the power of De Bracy and his confederates. Little notice was at first taken of the horse-litter, and it might have remained behind but for the curiosity of De Bracy, who looked into it under the impression that it might contain the object of his enterprise, for Rowena had not unveiled herself. But De Bracy's astonishment was considerable, when he discovered that the litter contained a wounded man, who, conceiving himself to have fallen into the power of Saxon outlaws, with whom his name might be a protection for himself and his friends, frankly avowed himself to be Wilfred of Ivanhoe.

The ideas of chivalrous honour, which, amidst his wildness and levity, never utterly abandoned De Bracy, prohibiting him from doing the knight any injury in his defenceless condition, and equally interdicted his betraying him to Front-de-Bœuf, who would have had no scruples to put to death, under any circumstances, the rival claimant of the fief of Ivanhoe. On the other hand, to liberate a suitor preferred by the Lady Rowena, as the events of the tournament, and indeed Wilfred's previous banishment from his father's house, had made matter of notoriety, was a pitch far above the flight of De Bracy's generosity. A middle course betwixt good and evil was all which he found himself capable of adopting, and he commanded two of his own squires to keep close by the litter, and to suffer no one to approach it. If questioned, they were directed by their master to say that the empty litter of the Lady Rowena was employed to transport one of their comrades who had been wounded in the scuffle. On arriving at Torquilstone, while the Knight Templar and the lord of that castle were each intent upon their own schemes, the one on the Jew's treasure, and the other on his daughter, De Bracy's squires conveyed Ivanhoe, still under the name of a wounded comrade, to a distant apartment.

CHAPTER 24

THE Black Knight and Locksley readily agreed with Cedric that a storm, under whatever disadvantages, ought to be attempted, as the only means of liberating the prisoners now in the hands of the cruel Front-de-Bœuf.

"The royal blood of Alfred is endangered," said Cedric.

"The honour of a noble lady is in peril," said the Black Knight.

"And, by the Saint Christopher at my baldric," said the good yeoman, "were there no other cause than the safety of that poor faithful knave Wamba, I would jeopard a joint ere a hair of his head were hurt."

"And now, good Locksley," said the Black Knight, "were it not well that noble Cedric should assume the direction of this assault?"

"Not a jot I," returned Cedric. "I will fight among the foremost; but my honest neighbours well know I am not a trained soldier in the discipline of wars, or the attack of strongholds."

"Since it stands thus with noble Cedric," said Locksley, "I am most willing to take on me the direction of the archery; and ye shall hang me up on my own trysting-tree, and the defenders be permitted to show themselves over the wall without being stuck with as many shafts as there are cloves in a gammon of bacon at Christmas."

"Well said, stout yeoman," answered the Black Knight; "and if I be thought worthy to have a charge in these matters, and can find among these brave men as many as are willing to follow a true English knight –for so I may surely call myself –I am ready, with such skill as my experience has taught me, to lead them to the attack of these walls."

The parts being thus distributed to the leaders, they commenced the first assault.

When the barbican was carried, the Sable Knight sent notice of the happy event to Locksley, requesting him at the same time to keep such a strict observation on the castle as might prevent the defenders from combining their force for a sudden sally, and recovering the outwork which they had lost.

The knight employed the interval in causing to be constructed a sort of floating bridge, or long raft, by means of which he hoped to cross the moat in despite of the resistance of the enemy. This was a work of some time, which the leaders the less regretted, as it gave Ulrica leisure to execute her plan of diversion in their favour, whatever that might be.

When the raft was completed, the Black Knight addressed the besiegers: –"It avails not waiting here longer, my friends; the sun is descending to the west, and I have that upon my hands which will not permit me to tarry with you another day. Besides, it will be a marvel if the horsemen come not upon us from York, unless we speedily accomplish our purpose.

Wherefore, one of ye go to Locksley, and bid him commence a discharge of arrows on the opposite side of the castle, and move forward as if about to assault it; and you, true English hearts, stand by me, and be ready to thrust the raft endlong over the moat whenever the postern on our side is thrown open. Follow me boldly across, and aid me to burst yon sally-port in the main wall of the castle. As many of you as like not this service, or are but ill armed to meet it, do you man the top of the outwork, draw your bowstrings to your ears, and mind you quell with your shot whatever shall appear to man the rampart. –Noble Cedric, wilt thou take the direction of those which remain?"

"Not so, by the soul of Hereward!" said the Saxon. "Lead I cannot; but may posterity curse me in my grave, if I follow not with the foremost wherever thou shalt point the way. The quarrel is mine, and well it becomes me to be in the van of the battle."

"Yet, bethink thee, noble Saxon," said the knight, "thou hast neither hauberk, nor corselet, nor aught but that light helmet, target, and sword."

"The better!" answered Cedric; "I shall be the lighter to climb these walls. And –forgive the boast, Sir Knight –thou shalt this day see the naked breast of a Saxon as boldly presented to the battle as ever ye beheld the steel corselet of a Norman."

"In the name of God, then," said the knight, "fling open the door, and launch the floating bridge."

The portal, which led from the inner wall of the barbican to the moat, and which corresponded with a sally-port in the main wall of the castle, was now suddenly opened. The temporary bridge was then thrust forward, and soon flashed in the waters, extending its length between the castle and outwork, and forming a slippery and precarious passage for two men abreast to cross the moat. Well aware of his importance of taking the foe by surprise, the Black Knight, closely followed by Cedric, threw himself upon the bridge, and reached the opposite side. Here he began to thunder with his axe upon the gate of the castle, protected in part from the shot and stone cast by the defenders by the ruins of the former drawbridge, which the Templar had demolished in his retreat from the barbican, leaving the counterpoise still attached to the upper part of the portal. The followers of the knight had no such shelter. Two were instantly shot with cross-bow bolts, and two more fell into the moat; the others retreated back into the barbican.

The situation of Cedric and of the Black Knight was now truly dangerous, and would have been still more so, but for the constancy of the archers in the barbican, who ceased not to shower their arrows upon the battlements, distracting the attention of those by whom they were manned, and thus affording a respite to their two chiefs from the storm of missiles which must otherwise have overwhelmed them. But their situation was eminently perilous, and was becoming more so with ever moment.

"Shame on ye all!" cried De Bracy to the soldiers around him; do ye call yourselves cross-bowmen, and let these two dogs keep their station under the walls of the castle? Heave over the coping stones from the battlement, an better may not be –get pick-axe and levers, and down with that huge pinnacle!" pointing to a heavy piece of stone carved-work that projected from the parapet.

At this moment the besiegers caught sight of the red flag upon the angle of the tower which Ulrica had described to Cedric. The stout yeoman Locksley was the first who was aware of it, as he was hasting to the outwork, impatient to see the progress of the assault.

"Saint George!" he cried, "Merry Saint George for England! –To the charge, bold yeomen! –why leave ye the good knight and noble Cedric to storm the pass alone? –Make in, mad priest, show thou canst fight for thy rosary –make in, brave yeomen! –the castle is ours, we have friends within. See yonder flag, it is the appointed signal –Torquilstone is ours! Think of honour, think of spoil. One effort, and the place is ours!"

With that he bent his good bow, and sent a shaft right through the breast of one of the men-at-arms who, under De Bracy's direction, was loosening a fragment from one of the battlements to precipitate on the heads of Cedric and the Black Knight. A second soldier caught from the hands of the dying man the iron crow, with which he heaved at and had loosened the stone pinnacle, when, receiving an arrow through his head-piece, he dropped from the battlements into the moat a dead man. The men-at-arms were daunted, for no armour seemed proof against the shot of this tremendous archer.

"Do you give ground, base knaves?" said De Bracy; "*Mount joye Saint Denis!* –Give me the lever!"

And, snatching it up, he again assailed the loosened pinnacle, which was of weight enough, if thrown down, not only to have destroyed the remnant of the drawbridge, which sheltered the two foremost assailants, but also to have sunk the rude float of planks over which they had crossed. All saw the danger, and the boldest, even the stout Friar himself, avoided setting foot on the raft. Thrice did Locksley bend his shaft against De Bracy, and thrice did his arrow bound back from the knight's armour of proof.

"Curse on thy Spanish steel-coat!" said Locksley; "had English smith forged it, these arrows had gone through, an as if it had been silk or sendal." He then began to call out, "Comrades! friends! noble Cedric! bear back, and let the ruin fall."

His warning voice was unheard, for the din which the knight himself occasioned by his strokes upon the postern would have drowned twenty war-trumpets. The faithful Gurth indeed sprang forward on the planked bridge, to warn Cedric of his impending fate, or to share it with him. But his warning would have come too late; the massive pinnacle already tottered, and De Bracy, who still heaved at his task, would have accomplished it, had not the voice of the Templar sounded close in his ears, –

"All is lost, De Bracy; the castle burns."

"Thou art mad to say so!" replied the knight.

"It is all in a light flame on the western side. I have striven in vain to extinguish it."

With the stern coolness which formed the basis of his character, Brian de Bois-Guilbert communicated this hideous intelligence, which was not so calmly received by his astonished comrade.

"Saints of Paradise!" said De Bracy; "what is to be done? I vow to Saint Nicholas of Limoges a candlestick of pure gold –"

"Spare thy vow," said the Templar, "and mark me. Lead thy men down, as if to a sally; throw the postern gate open— there are but two men who occupy the float, fling them into the moat, and push across for the barbican. I will charge from the main gate, and attack the barbican on the outside; and if we can regain that post, be assured we shall defend ourselves until we are relieved, or at least till they grant us fair quarter."

"It is well thought upon," said De Bracy. "I will play my part –Templar, thou wilt not fail me?"

"Hand and glove, I will not!" said Bois-Guilbert. "But haste thee, in the name of God!"

De Bracy hastily drew his men together, and rushed down to the postern gate, which he caused instantly to be thrown open. But scarce was this done ere the portentous strength of the Black Knight forced his way inward in despite of De Bracy and his followers. Two of the foremost instantly fell, and the rest gave way notwithstanding all their leader's efforts to stop them.

"Dogs!" said De Bracy, "will ye let *two* men win our only pass for safety?"

"He is the devil!" said a veteran man-at-arms, bearing back from the blows of their sable antagonist.

"And if he be the devil," replied De Bracy, "would you fly from him into the mouth of hell? The castle burns behind us, villains!—let despair give you courage; or let me forward! I will cope with this champion myself."

And well and chivalrous did De Bracy that day maintain the fame he had acquired in the civil wars of that dreadful period. The vaulted passage to which the postern gave entrance, and in which these two redoubted champions were now fighting hand to hand, rung with the furious blows which they dealt each other, De Bracy with his sword, the Black Knight with his ponderous axe. At length the Norman received a blow, which, though its force was partly parried by his shield, for otherwise never more would De Bracy have again moved limb, descended yet with such violence on his crest, that he measured his length on the paved floor.

"Yield thee, De Bracy," said the Black Champion, stooping over him, and holding against the bars of his helmet the fatal poniard with which the knights dispatched their enemies (and which was called the dagger of mercy)—"yield thee, Maurice de Bracy, rescue or no rescue, or thou art but a dead man."

"I will not yield," replied De Bracy faintly, "to an unknown conqueror. Tell me thy name, or work thy pleasure on me; it shall never be said that Maurice de Bracy was prisoner to a nameless churl."

The Black Knight whispered something in the ear of the vanquished.

"I yield me to be true prisoner, rescue or no rescue," answered the Norman, exchanging his tone of stern and determined obstinacy for one of deep though sullen submission.

"Go to the barbican," said the victor, in a tone of authority, "and there wait my further orders."

"Yet first, let me say," said De Bracy, "what it imports thee to know. Wilfred of Ivanhoe is wounded, and a prisoner, and will perish in the burning castle without present help."

"Wilfred of Ivanhoe!" exclaimed the Black Knight—"prisoner, and perish! The life of every man in the castle shall answer it if a hair of his head be singed. Show me his chamber!"

"Ascend yonder winding stair," said De Bracy; "it leads to his apartment. Wilt thou not accept my guidance?" he added, in a submissive voice.

"No. To the barbican, and there wait my orders. I trust thee not, De Bracy."

During this combat and the brief conversation which ensued, Cedric, at the head of a body of men, among whom the Friar was conspicuous, had pushed across the bridge as soon as they saw the postern open, and drove back the dispirited and despairing followers of De Bracy, of whom some asked quarter, some offered vain resistance, and the greater part fled towards the courtyard. De Bracy himself arose from the ground, and cast a sorrowful glance after his conqueror. "He trusts me not!" he repeated; "but have I deserved his trust?" He then lifted his sword from the floor, took off his helmet in token of submission, and, going to the barbican, gave up his sword to Locksley, whom he met by the way.

As the fire augmented, symptoms of it became soon apparent in the chamber where Ivanhoe was watched and tended by the Jewess Rebecca. He had been awakened from his brief slumber by the noise of the battle; and his attendant, who had, at his anxious desire, placed herself at the window to watch and report to him the fate of the attack, was for some time prevented from observing either by the increase of the smouldering and stifling vapour. At length the volumes of smoke which rolled into the apartment, the cries for water which were heard even above the din of the battle, made them sensible of the progress of this new danger.

"The castle burns," said Rebecca; "it burns! What can we do to save ourselves?"

"Fly, Rebecca, and save thine own life," said Ivanhoe, "for no human aid can avail me."

"I will not fly," answered Rebecca; "we will be saved or perish together. And yet, great God!—my father, my father —what will be his fate?"

At this moment the door of the apartment flew open, and the Templar presented himself—a ghastly figure, for his gilded armour was broken and bloody, and the plume was partly shorn away, partly burnt from his casque. "I have found thee," said he to Rebecca; "thou shalt prove I will keep my word to share weal and woe with thee. There is but one path to safety; I have cut my way through fifty dangers to point it to thee—up, and instantly follow me!"

"Alone," answered Rebecca, "I will not follow thee. If thou were born of woman—if thou hast but a touch of human charity in thee—if thy heart be not hard as thy breastplate—save my aged father—save this wounded knight!"

"A knight," answered the Templar, with his characteristic calmness—"a knight, Rebecca, must encounter his fate, whether it meet him in the shape of sword or flame; and who recks how or where a Jew meets with his?"

"Savage warrior," said Rebecca, "rather will I perish in the flames than accept safety from thee!"

"Thou shalt not choose, Rebecca. Once didst thou foil me, but never mortal did so twice."

So saying, he seized on the terrified maiden, who filled the air with her shrieks, and bore her out of the room in his arms in spite of her cries, and without regarding the menaces and defiance which Ivanhoe thundered against him. "Hound of the Temple—stain to thine Order—set free the damsel!

Traitor of Bois-Guilbert, it is Ivanhoe commands thee!—
Villain, I will have thy heart's blood!"

"I had not found thee, Wilfred," said the Black Knight,
who at that instant entered the apartment, "but for thy
shouts."

"If thou be'st true knight," said Wilfred, "think not of
me. Pursue yon ravisher—save the Lady Rowena—look to the
noble Cedric!"

"In their turn," answered he of the fetterlock, "but thine
is first."

And seizing upon Ivanhoe, he bore him off with as much
ease as the Templar had carried off Rebecca, rushed with
him to the postern, and having there delivered his burden
to the care of two yeomen, he again entered the castle to
assist in the rescue of the other prisoners.

Through this scene of confusion, Cedric rushed in quest
of Rowena; while the faithful Gurth, following him closely
through the *mêlée*, neglected his own safety while he strove
to avert the blows that were aimed at his master. The noble
Saxon was so fortunate as to reach his ward's apartment
just as she had abandoned all hope of safety, and, with a
crucifix clasped in agony to her bosom, sat in expectation
of instant death. He committed her to the charge of Gurth,
to be conducted in safety to the barbican, the road to which
was now cleared of the enemy, and not yet interrupted by
the flames. This accomplished, the loyal Cedric hastened in
quest of his friend Athelstane, determined, at every risk to
himself, to save that last scion of Saxon royalty. But ere
Cedric penetrated as far as the old hall in which he had
himself been a prisoner, the inventive genius of Wamba had
procured liberation for himself and his companion in adversity.

When the noise of the conflict announced that it was at
the hottest, the Jester began to shout, with the utmost power
of his lungs, "Saint George and the dragon!—Bonny Saint

George for merry England!—The castle is won!" And these sounds he rendered yet more fearful, by banging against each other two pieces of rusty armour. A guard ran to tell the Templar that foemen had entered the hall. Meantime the prisoners made their escape into the court.

Animated by despair, and supported by the example of their indomitable leader, the remaining soldiers of the castle fought with the utmost valour; and, being well-armed, succeeded more than once in driving back the assailants, though much inferior in numbers. Rebecca, placed on horseback before one of the Templar's Saracen slaves, was in the midst of the little party; and Bois-Guilbert, notwithstanding the confusion of the bloody fray, showed every attention to her safety. Repeatedly he was by her side, and, neglecting his own defence, held before her the fence of his triangular steel-plated shield; and anon starting from his position by her, he cried his war-cry, dashed forward, struck to earth the most forward of the assailants, and was on the same instant once more at her bridle-rein.

Athelstane, who, as the reader knows, was slothful, but not cowardly, beheld the female form whom the Templar protected thus sedulously, and doubted not that it was Rowena whom the knight was carrying off, in despite of all resistance which could be offered.

"By the soul of Saint Edward," he said, "I will rescue her from yonder over-proud knight, and he shall die by my hand!"

To snatch a mace from the pavement, on which it lay beside one whose dying grasp had just relinquished it, to rush on the Templar's band, and to strike in quick succession to the right and left, levelling a warrior at each blow, was, for Athelstane's great strength, now animated with unusual fury, but the work of a single moment; he was soon within two yards of Bois-Guilbert, whom he defied in his loudest tone.

"Turn, false-hearted Templar! let her go whom thou art unworthy to touch –turn, limb of a band of murdering and hypocritical robbers!"

"Dog!" said the Templar grinding his teeth, "I will teach thee to blaspheme the holy Order of the Temple of Zion"; and with these words, half-wheeling his steed, he made a demi-courbette towards the Saxon, and rising in the stirrups, so as to take full advantage of the descent of the horse, he discharged a fearful blow upon the head to Athelstane.

Well said Wamba that silken bonnet keeps out no steel blade. So trenchant was the Templar's weapon that it shore asunder, as it had been a willow twig, the tough and plaited handle of the mace, which the ill-fated Saxon reared to parry the blow, and, descending on his head, levelled him with the earth.

"*Ha! Beau-séant!*" exclaimed Bois-Guilbert, "thus be it to the maligners of the Temple knights!" Taking advantage of the dismay which was spread by the fall of Athelstane, and calling aloud, "Those who would save themselves, follow me!" he pushed across the drawbridge, dispersing the archers who would have intercepted them. He was followed by his Saracens, and some five or six men-at-arms, who had mounted their horses. The Templar's retreat was rendered perilous by the numbers of arrows shot off at him and his party; but this did not prevent him from galloping round to the barbican, of which, according to his previous plan, he supposed it possible De Bracy might have been in possession.

"De Bracy! De Bracy!" he shouted, "art thou there?"

"I am here," replied De Bracy, "but I am a prisoner."

"Can I rescue thee?" cried Bois-Guilbert.

"No," replied De Bracy; "I have rendered me, rescue or no rescue. I will be true prisoner. Save thyself –there are hawks abroad –put the seas betwixt you and England. I dare not say more."

"Well," answered the Templar, "an thou wilt tarry there, remember I have redeemed word and glove. Be the hawks where they will, methinks the walls of the Preceptory of Templestowe will be cover sufficient, and thither will I, like heron to her haunt."

Having thus spoken, he galloped off with his followers.

The fire was spreading rapidly through all parts of the castle, when Ulrica, who had first kindled it, appeared on a turret, in the guise of one of the ancient furies, yelling forth a war-song, such as was of yore raised on the field of battle by the scalds of the yet heathen Saxons. Her long dishevelled grey hair flew back from her uncovered head; the inebriating delight of gratified vengeance contended in the eyes with the fire of insanity; and she brandished the distaff which she held in her hand, as if she had been one of the Fatal Sisters who spin and abridge the thread of human life.

The towering flames had now surmounted every obstruction, and rose to the evening skies one huge and burning beacon, seen far and wide through the adjacent country. Tower after tower crashed down, with blazing roof and rafter, and the combatants were driven from the courtyard. The vanquished, of whom very few remained, scattered and escaped into the neighbouring wood. The victors, assembling in large bands, gazed with wonder, not unmixed with fear, upon the flames, in which their own ranks and arms glanced dusky red. The maniac figure of the Saxon Ulrica was for a long time visible on the lofty stand she had chosen, tossing her arms abroad with wild exultation, as if she reigned empress of the conflagration which she had raised. At length, with a terrific crash, the whole turret gave way, and she perished in the flames which had consumed her tyrant. An awful pause of horror silenced each murmur of the armed spectators, who, for the space of several minutes, stirred not a finger, save to sign the cross. The voice of Locksley was then heard, "Shout, yeoman! –

the den of tyrants is no more! Let each bring his spoil to
our chosen place of rendezvous at the Trysting-tree in the
Harthill-walk; for there, at break of day, will we make just
partition among our own bands, together with our worthy
allies in this great deed of vengeance."

CHAPTER 25

MOUNTED upon a mule, the gift of the Outlaw, with two
tall yeomen to act as his guard and guides, the Jew had set
out for the Preceptory of Templestowe, for the purpose of
negotiating his daughter's redemption. The Preceptory was
but a day's journey from the demolished castle of Torquilstone,
and the Jew had hoped to reach it before nightfall; accordingly, having dismissed his guides at the verge of the forest,
and rewarded them with a piece of silver, he began to press
on with such speed as his weariness permitted him to exert.
But his strength failed him totally ere he had reached within
four miles of the Temple Court; racking pains shot along
his back and through his limbs; and the excessive anguish
which he felt at heart being now augmented by bodily suffering,
he was rendered altogether incapable of proceeding farther
than a small market-town, where dwelt a Jewish Rabbi of
his tribe, eminent in the medical profession, and to whom
Isaac was well known. Nathan Ben Israel received his suffering
countryman with that kindness which the Law prescribed,
and which the Jews practised to each other. He insisted on
his betaking himself to repose, and used such remedies as were
then in most repute to check the progress of the fever.

On the morrow, when Isaac proposed to arise and pursue
his journey, Nathan remonstrated against his purpose, both
as his host and as his physician. It might cost him, he said,

his life. But Isaac replied, that more than life and death depended upon his going that morning to Templestowe.

"To Templestowe!" said his host with surprise; again felt his pulse, and then muttered to himself, "His fever is abated, yet seems his mind somewhat alienated and disturbed."

"And why not to Templestowe?" answered his patient.

"I know it well," said Nathan; "but wottest thou that Lucas de Beaumanoir, the chief of their Order, and whom they term Grand Master, is now himself at Templestowe?"

Isaac then explained to Nathan the pressing cause of his journey. The Rabbi listened with interest, and testified his sympathy after the fashion of his people, rending his clothes, and saying. "Ah, my daughter! ah, my daughter! Alas! for the beauty of Zion! Alas! for the captivity of Israel!"

Isaac accordingly bade his friend farewell, and about an hour's riding brought him before the Preceptory of Templestowe.

The Grand Master was a man advanced in age, as was testified by his long grey beard, and the shaggy eyebrows overhanging eyes, of which, however, years had been unable to quench the fire. A formidable warrior, his thin and severe features retained the soldier's fierceness of expression; an ascetic bigot, they were no less marked by the emaciation of abstinence, and the spiritual pride of the self-satisfied devotee.

"Conrade," said the Grand Master to his Preceptor, "dear companion of my toils, to thy faithful bosom alone I can confide my sorrows. To thee alone can I tell how oft, since I came to this kingdom, I have desired to be dissolved and to be with the just. Not one object in England hath met mine eye which it could rest upon with pleasure, save the tombs of our brethren beneath the massive roof of our Temple Church in yonder proud capital."

"It is but true," answered Conrade Mont-Fitchet—"it is but too true."

At this moment a squire clothed in a threadbare vestment entered the garden and bowed profoundly before the Grand Master.

"A Jew stands without the gate, noble and reverend father," he said, "who prays to speak with brother Brian de Bois-Guilbert."

"Thou wert right to give me knowledge of it," said the Grand Master;—It imports us especially to know of this Bois-Guilbert's proceedings."

"Report speaks him brave and valiant," said Conrade.

"And truly is he so spoken of," said the Grand Master. "But brother Brian came into our Order a moody and disappointed man, stirred, I doubt me, to take our vows and to renounce the world, not in sincerity of soul, but as one whom some touch of light discontent had driven into penitence.— Damian," he continued, "lead the Jew to our presence."

The squire departed with a profound reverence, and in a few minutes returned, marshalling in Isaac of York. No naked slave, ushered into the presence of some mighty prince, could approach his judgment-seat with more profound reverence and terror than that with which the Jew drew near to the presence of the Grand Master. When he had approached within the distance of three yards, Beaumanoir made a sign with his staff that he should come no farther. The Jew kneeled down on the earth, which he kissed in token of reverence; then rising, stood before the Templars, his hands folded on his bosom, his head bowed on his breast, in all the submission of Oriental slavery.

"Damian," said the Grand Master, "retire, and have a guard ready to await our sudden call; and suffer no one to enter the garden until we shall leave it."—The squire bowed and retreated.—"Jew," continued the haughty old man, "mark me. It suits not our condition to hold with thee long communication, nor do we waste words or time upon any one. Wherefore be brief in thy answers to what questions I shall ask thee, and let thy words be of truth; for if thy tongue doubles with me, I will have it torn from thy misbelieving jaws."

The Jew was about to reply, but the Grand Master went on.

"Peace, unbeliever!—not a word in our presence, save in answer to our questions. What is thy business with our brother Brian de Bois-Guilbert?"

"I am bearer of a letter," stammered out the Jew, "so please your reverend valour, to that good knight, from Prior Aymer of the Abbey of Jorvaulx."

"Said I not these were evil times, Conrade?" said the Master. "A Cistercian Prior sends a letter to a soldier of the Temple, and can find no more fitting messenger than an unbelieving Jew.—Give me the letter."

The Jew, with trembling hands, undid the folds of his Armenian cap, in which he had deposited the Prior's tablets for the greater security, and was about to approach, with hand extended and body crouched, to place it within the reach of his grim interrogator.

"Back, dog!" said the Grand Master; "I touch not misbelievers, save with the sword,—Conrade, take thou the letter from the Jew, and give it to me."

He then perused the letter in haste, with an expression of surprise and horror; read it over again slowly; then holding it out to Conrade with one hand, and slightly striking it with the other, exclaimed, "Here is goodly stuff for one Christian man to write to another, and both members, and no inconsiderable members, of religious professions!"

Mont-Fitchet took the letter from his Superior, and was about to peruse it. "Read it aloud, Conrade," said the Grand Master,—"and do thou" (to Isaac) "attend to the purport of it, for we will question thee concerning it."

Conrade read the letter, which was in these words: "Aymer, by divine grace, Prior of the Cistercian house of Saint Mary's of Jorvaulx, to Sir Brian de Bois-Guilbert, a Knight of the holy Order of the Temple, wisheth health, with the bounties of King Bacchus and of my Lady Venus. Touching our present condition, dear Brother, we are a captive in the hands of certain lawless and godless men, who have not feared to detain our person and put us to ransom; whereby we have also learned of Front-de-Bœuf's misfortune, and that thou hast escaped with that fair Jewish sorceress, whose black eyes have bewitched thee. We are heartily rejoiced of thy safety. Nevertheless, we pray thee to be on thy guard in the matter of this second Witch of Endor; for we are privately assured that your Great Master, who careth not a bean for cherry cheeks and black eyes, comes from Normandy to diminish your mirth and amend your misdoings. Wherefore we pray you heartily to beware, and to be found watching, even as the Holy Text hath it, *Invenientur vigilantes*. And the wealthy Jew her father, Isaac of York, having prayed of me letters in his behalf, I gave him these, earnestly advising, and in a sort entreating, that you do hold the damsel to ransom, seeing he will pay you from his bags as much as may find fifty damsels upon safer terms, whereof I trust to have my part when we make merry together, as true brothers, not forgetting the wine-cup.

"Till which merry meeting, we wish you farewell. Given from this den of thieves, about the hour of matins,

"AYMER PR. S. M. JORVOLCIENCIS"

"What sayest thou to this, Conrade?" said the Grand Master. "Den of thieves!—and a fit residence is a den of thieves for such a Prior. No wonder that the hand of God is upon us, and that in the Holy Land we lose place by place, foot by foot, before the infidels, when we have such churchmen as this Aymer. And what meaneth he, I trow, by this second Witch of Endor?" said he to his confidant.

Conrade was better acquainted (perhaps by practice) with the jargon of gallantry than was his Superior; and he expounded the passage which embarrassed the Grand Master, to be a sort of language used by worldly men towards those whom they loved *par amours*. But the explanation did not satisfy the bigoted Beaumanoir.

Turning to Isaac, he said, "Thy daughter, then, is prisoner with Brian de Bois-Guilbert?"

"Ay, reverend valorous sir," stammered poor Isaac; "and whatsoever ransom a poor man may pay for her deliverance—"

"Peace!" said the Grand Master. "This thy daughter hath practised the art of healing, hath she not?"

"Ay, gracious sir," answered the Jew, with more confidence; "and knight and yeoman, squire and vassal, may bless the goodly gift which Heaven hath assigned to her. Many a one can testify that she hath recovered them by her art, when every other human aid hath proved vain; but the blessing of the God of Jacob was upon her."

"Thy daughter worketh the cures, I doubt not," thus he went on to address the Jew, "by words and sigils, and periapts, and other cabalistical mysteries."

"Nay, reverend and brave Knight," answered Isaac, "but in chief measure by a balsam of marvellous virtue."

"Where had she that secret?" said Beaumanoir.

"It was delivered to her," answered Isaac reluctantly, "by Miriam, a sage matron of our tribe."

"Ah, false Jew?" said the Grand Master; "was it not from that same witch Miriam, the abomination of whose enchantments has been heard of throughout every Christian land?" exclaimed the Grand Master, crossing himself. "Her body was burnt at the stake, and her ashes were scattered to the four winds; and so be it with me and mine Order, if I do not as much to her pupil, and more also! I will teach her to throw spell and incantation over the soldiers of the blessed

Temple. –There, Damian, spurn this Jew from the gate—shoot him dead if he oppose or turn again. With his daughter we will deal as the Christian law and our own high office warrant."

Poor Isaac was hurried off accordingly, and expelled from the Preceptory –all his entreaties, and even his offers, unheard and disregarded. He could do no better than return to the house of the Rabbi, and endeavour, through his means, to learn how his daughter was to be disposed of. He had hitherto feared for her honour; he was now to tremble for her life. Meanwhile, the Grand Master ordered to his presence the Preceptor of Templestowe.

CHAPTER 26

THE Tribunal, erected for the trial of the innocent and un-happy Rebecca, occupied the dais or elevated part of the upper end of the great hall –a platform, which we have already described as the place of honour, destined to be occupied by the most distinguished inhabitants or guests of an ancient mansion.

On an elevated seat, directly before the accused, sat the Grand Master of the Temple, in full and ample robes of flowing white, holding in his hand the mystic staff which bore the symbol of the Order. At his feet was placed a table, occupied by two scribes, chaplains of the Order, whose duty it was to reduce to formal record the proceedings of the day. The black dresses, bare scalps, and demure looks of these churchmen formed a strong contrast to the warlike appearance of the knights who attended, either as residing in the Preceptory, or as come thither to attend upon their Grand Master. The Preceptors, of whom there were four present, occupied seats lower in height, and somewhat drawn back behind that of their superior; and the knights, who enjoyed no such rank in the Order, were placed on benches still lower, and preserving the same distance from the Preceptors as these from the Grand Master. Behind them, but still upon the dais or elevated portion of the hall, stood the esquires of the Order, in white dresses of an inferior quality.

The remaining and lower part of the hall was filled with guards, holding partisans, and with other attendants whom curiosity had drawn thither, to see at once a Grand Master and a Jewish sorceress. By far the greater part of those inferior persons were, in one rank or other, connected with the order, and were accordingly distinguished by their black dresses. But peasants from the neighbouring country were not refused admittance, for it was the pride of Beaumanoir to render the edifying spectacle of the justice which he administered as public as possible. His large blue eyes seemed to expand as he gazed around the assembly, and his countenance appeared elated by the conscious dignity, and imaginary merit, of the part which he was about to perform. A psalm, raised by a hundred masculine voices accustomed to combine in the choral chant, arose to the vaulted roof of the hall, and rolled on amongst its arches with the pleasing yet solemn sound of the rushing of mighty waters.

The Grand Master then addressed the assembly:

"Reverend and valiant men, Knights, Preceptors, and Companions of this Holy Order, my brethren and my children! – you also, well-born and pious Esquires, who aspire to wear this holy Cross! – and you also, Christian brethren, of every degree! – Be it known to you, that it is not defect of power in us which hath occasioned the assembling of this congregation; for, however unworthy in our person, yet to us is committed, with this batoon, full power to judge and to try all that regards the weal of this our Holy Order. We have therefore summoned to our presence a Jewish woman, by name Rebecca, daughter of Isaac of York – a woman infamous for sortileges and for witcheries; whereby she hath maddened the

blood and besotted the brain, not of a churl, but of a Knight —
not of a secular Knight, but of one devoted to the service of
the Holy Temple — not of a Knight Companion, but of a Preceptor of our Order, first in honour as in place. Our brother,
Brian de Bois-Guilbert, is well known to ourselves, and to
all degrees who now hear me, as a true and zealous champion
of the Cross, by whose arm many deeds of valour have been
wrought in the Holy Land, and the holy places purified from
pollution by the blood of those infidels who defiled them. If
we were told that such a man, so honoured, and so honourable, suddenly casting away regard for his character, his
vows, his brethren, and his prospects, had associated to himself
a Jewish damsel, wandered in this lewd company through
solitary places, defended her person in preference to his own,
and, finally, was so utterly blinded and besotted by his folly,
as to bring her even to one of our own Preceptories, what
should we say but that the noble knight was possessed by
some evil demon, or influenced by some wicked spell? — Stand
forth, therefore, and bear witness, ye who have witnessed these
unhappy doings, that we may judge of the sum and bearing
thereof; and judge whether our justice may be satisfied with
the punishment of this infidel woman, or if we must go on,
with a bleeding heart, to the further proceedings against our
brother."

Several witnesses were called upon to prove the risks to
which Bois-Guilbert exposed himself in endeavouring to save
Rebecca from the blazing castle, and his neglect of his personal
defence in attending to her safety.

The Preceptor of Templestowe was then called on to describe
the manner in which Bois-Guilbert and the Jewess arrived
at the Preceptory. The evidence of Malvoisin was skilfully
guarded. But while he apparently studied to spare the feelings
of Bois-Guilbert, he threw in, from time to time, such hints
as seemed to infer that he laboured under some temporary

alienation of mind, so deeply did he appear to be enamoured of the damsel whom he brought along with him. With sighs of penitence, the Preceptor avowed his own contrition for having admitted Rebecca and her lover within the walls of the Preceptory. "But my defence," he concluded, "has been made in my confession to our most reverend father, the Grand Master; he knows my motives were not evil, though my conduct may have been irregular. Joyfully will I submit to any penance he shall assign me."

"Thou hast spoken well, Brother Albert," said Beaumanoir; "thy motives were good, since thou didst judge it right to arrest thine erring brother in his career of precipitate folly. But thy conduct was wrong – as he that would stop a runaway steed, and seizing by the stirrup instead of the bridle, receiveth injury himself, instead of accomplishing his purpose. Thirteen pater-nosters are assigned by our pious founder for matins, and nine for vespers; be those services doubled by thee. Thrice a week are Templars permitted the use of flesh; but do thou keep fast for all the seven days. This do for six weeks to come, and thy penance is accomplished."

With a hypocritical look of the deepest submission, the Preceptor of Templestowe bowed to the ground before his Superior, and resumed his seat.

Herman of Goodalricke was the Fourth Preceptor present; the other three were Conrade, Malvoisin, and Bois-Guilbert himself. Herman was an ancient warrior, whose face was marked with scars inflicted by the sabre of Moslemah, and had great rank and consideration among his brethren. He arose and bowed to the Grand Master, who instantly granted him license of speech. "I would crave to know, most reverend father, of our valiant brother, Brian de Bois-Guilbert, what he says to these wondrous accusations, and with what eye he himself now regards his unhappy intercourse with this Jewish maiden?"

"Brian de Bois-Guilbert," said the Grand Master, "thou hearest the question which our Brother of Goodalricke desirest thou shouldst answer. I command thee to reply to him."

Bois-Guilbert made an effort to suppress his rising scorn and indignation, the expression of which, he was well aware, would have little availed him. "Brian de Bois-Guilbert," he answered, "replies not, most reverend father, to such wild and vague charges. If his honour be impeached, he will defend it with his body, and with that sword which has often fought for Christendom."

"We forgive thee, Brother Brian," said the Grand Master; "though that thou hast boasted thy warlike achievements before us, is a glorifying of thine own deeds, and cometh of the Enemy, who tempteth us to exalt our own worship. But thou hast our pardon, judging thou speakest less of thine own suggestion than from the impulse of him whom, by Heaven's leave, we will quell and drive forth from our assembly." A glance of disdain flashed from the dark fierce eyes of Bois-Guilbert, but he made no reply. "And now," pursued the Grand Master, "since our Brother of Goodalricke's question has been thus imperfectly answered, pursue we our quest, brethren, and with our patron's assistance we will search to the bottom of this mystery of iniquity. Let those who have aught to witness of the life and conversation of this Jewish woman, stand forth before us." There was a bustle in the lower part of the hall, and when the Grand Master inquired the reason, it was replied, there was in the crowd a bedridden man, whom the prisoner had restored to the perfect use of his limbs by a miraculous balsam.

The poor peasant, a Saxon by birth, was dragged forward to the bar, terrified at the penal consequences which he might have incurred by the guilt of having been cured of the palsy by a Jewish damsel. Perfectly cured he certainly was not, for he supported himself forward on crutches to give evidence. Most unwilling was his testimony, and given with many tears; but he admitted that two years since, when residing at York, he was suddenly afflicted with a sore disease, while labouring for Isaac the rich Jew, in his vocation of a joiner – that he had been unable to stir from his bed until the remedies applied by Rebecca's directions, and especially a warming and spicy-smelling balsam, had in some degree restored him to the use of his limbs. Moreover, he said, she had given him a pot of that precious ointment, and furnished him with a piece of money withal, to return to the house of his father, near to Templestowe. "And may it please your gracious reverence," said the man, "I cannot think the damsel meant harm by me, though she hath the ill hap to be a Jewess; for even when I used her remedy, I said the Pater and the Creed, and it never operated a whit less kindly."

"Peace, slave," said the Grand Master, "and begone! It well suits brutes like thee to be tampering and trinketing with hellish cures, and to be giving your labour to the sons of mischief. I tell thee, the fiend can impose diseases for the very purpose of removing them, in order to bring into credit some diabolical fashion of cure. Hast thou that unguent of which thou speakest?"

The peasant, fumbling in his bosom with a trembling hand, produced a small box, bearing some Hebrew characters on the lid, which was, with most of the audience, a sure proof that the devil had stood apothecary. Beaumanoir, after crossing himself, took the box into his hand, and, learned in most of the Eastern tongues, read with ease the motto on the lid, – *The Lion of the Tribe of Judah hath conquered*. "Strange powers of Sathanas," said he, "which can convert Scripture into blasphemy, mingling poison with our necessary food! Is there no leech here who can tell us the ingredients of this mystic unguent?"

Two mediciners, as they called themselves, the one a monk, the other a barber, appeared, and avouched they knew nothing of the materials, excepting that they savoured of myrrh and camphire, which they took to be Oriental herbs. But with the true professional hatred to a successful practitioner of their art, they insinuated that, since the medicine was beyond their own knowledge, it must necessarily have been compounded from an unlawful and magical pharmacopoeia. When this medical research was ended, the Saxon peasant desired humbly to have back the medicine which he had found so salutary; but the Grand Master frowned severely at the request. "What is thy name, fellow?" said he to the cripple.

"Higg, the son of Snell," answered the peasant.

"Then Higg, son of Snell," said the Grand Master, "I tell thee it is better to be bedridden, than to accept the benefit of unbelievers' medicine that thou mayest arise and walk; better to despoil infidels of their treasure by the strong hand, than to accept of them benevolent gifts, or do them service for wages. Go thou, and do as I have said."

"Alack," said the peasant, "an it shall not displease your reverence, the lesson comes too late for me, for I am but a maimed man; but I will tell my two brethren, who serve the rich Rabbi Nathan Ben Samuel, that your mastership says it is more lawful to rob him than to render him faithful service."

Higg, the son of Snell, withdrew into the crowd, but, interested in the fate of his benefactress, lingered until he should learn her doom, even at the risk of again encountering the frown of that severe judge, the terror of which withered his very heart within him.

At this period of the trial, the Grand Master commanded Rebecca to unveil herself. She withdrew her veil, and looked on them with a countenance in which bashfulness contended with dignity. Her exceeding beauty excited a murmur of surprise, and the younger knights told each other with their eyes, in silent correspondence, that Brian's best apology was in the power of her real charms, rather than of her imaginary witchcraft. But Higg, the son of Snell, felt most deeply the effect produced by the sight of the countenance of his benefactress.

"Let me go forth," he said to the warders at the door of the hall —"let me go forth! To look at her again will kill me, for I have had a share in murdering her."

"Peace, poor man," said Rebecca, when she heard his exclamation; "thou hast done me no harm by speaking the truth — thou canst not aid me by thy complaints or lamentations. Peace, I pray thee; go home and save thyself."

Higg was about to be thrust out by the compassion of the warders, who were apprehensive lest his clamorous grief should draw upon them reprehension, and upon himself punishment. But he promised to be silent, and was permitted to remain. The evidence of two men that followed would have been, in modern days, divided into two classes — those which were immaterial, and those which were actually and physically impossible. But both were, in those ignorant and superstitious times, easily credited as proofs of guilt. They set forth that Rebecca was heard to mutter to herself in an unknown tongue; that the songs she sung were of a strangely sweet sound, which made the ears of the hearer tingle and his heart throb; that her garments were of a strange and mystic form, unlike those of women of good repute; that she had rings impressed with cabalistical devices, and that strange characters were broidered on her veil.

All these circumstances, so natural and so trivial, were gravely listened to as proofs, or, at least, as affording strong suspicions, that Rebecca had unlawful correspondence with mystical powers.

But there was less equivocal testimony, which the credulity of the assembly, or of the greater part, greedily swallowed, however incredible. One of the soldiers had seen her work a cure upon a wounded man, brought with them to the castle of Torquilstone. She did, he said, make certain signs upon the wound, and repeated certain mysterious words, which he blessed God he understood not, when the iron head of a square cross-bow bolt disengaged itself from the wound, the bleeding was stanched, the wound was closed, and the dying man was, within a quarter of an hour, walking upon the ramparts, and assisting the witness in managing a mangonel, or machine for hurling stones. This legend was probably founded upon the fact that Rebecca had attended on the wounded Ivanhoe when in the castle of Torquilstone. But it was more difficult to dispute the accuracy of the witness, as, in order to produce real evidence in support of his verbal testimony, he drew from his pouch the very bolt-head which, according to his story, had been miraculously extracted from the wound; and as the iron weighed a full ounce, it completely confirmed the tale, however marvellous.

His comrade had been a witness from a neighbouring battlement of the scene betwixt Rebecca and Bois-Guilbert, when she was upon the point of precipitating herself from the top of the tower. Not to be behind his companion, this fellow stated that he had seen Rebecca perch herself upon the parapet of the turret, and there take the form of a milk-white swan, under which appearance she flitted three times round the castle of Torquilstone; then again settle on the turret, and once more assume the female form.

The Grand Master had collected the suffrages, and now in a solemn tone demanded of Rebecca what she had to say against the sentence of condemnation, which he was about to pronounce.

"To invoke your pity," said the lovely Jewess, with a voice somewhat tremulous with emotion, "would, I am aware, be as useless as I should hold it mean. To state that to relieve the

sick and wounded of another religion, cannot be displeasing
to the acknowledged Founder of both our faiths, were also
unavailing. To plead that many things which these men (whom
may Heaven pardon!) have spoken against me are impossible,
would avail me but little, since you believe in their possibility.
And still less would it advantage me to explain that the pecu-
liarities of my dress, language, and manners are those of my
people – I had well-nigh said of my country, but, alas! we
have no country. Nor will I even vindicate myself at the expense
of my oppressor, who stands there listening to the fictions and
surmises which seem to convert the tyrant into the victim.
God be judge between him and me! but rather would I submit
to ten such deaths as your pleasure may denounce against
me, than listen to the suit which that man of Belial has urged
upon me—friendless, defenceless, and his prisoner. But he is
of your own faith, and his lightest affirmance would weigh
down the most solemn protestations of the distressed Jewess.
I will not therefore return to himself the charge brought
against me, but to himself – yes, Brian de Bois-Guilbert, to
thyself I appeal, whether these accusations are not false? as
monstrous and calumnious as they are deadly?"

There was a pause; all eyes turned to Brian de Bois-Guilbert. He was silent.

"Speak," she said, "if thou art a man – if thou art a Christian,
speak! I conjure thee, by the habit which thou dost wear, by
the name thou dost inherit, by the knighthood thou dost
vaunt, by the honour of thy mother, by the tomb and the
bones of thy father – I conjure thee to say, are these things
true?"

"Answer her, brother," said the Grand Master, "if the Enemy
with whom thou dost wrestle will give thee power."

In fact, Bois-Guilbert seemed agitated by contending passions, which almost convulsed his features, and it was with

a constrained voice that at last he replied, looking to Rebecca, "The scroll!–the scroll!"

"Aye," said the Beaumanoir, "this is indeed testimony! The victim of her witcheries can only name the fatal scroll, the spell inscribed on which is, doubtless, the cause of his silence."

But Rebecca put another interpretation on the words extorted as it were from Bois-Guilbert, and glancing her eye upon the slip of parchment which she continued to hold in her hand, she read written thereupon in the Arabian characters, *Demand a Champion!* The murmuring commentary which ran through the assembly at the strange reply of Bois-Guilbert, gave Rebecca leisure to examine and instantly to destroy the scroll unobserved. When the whisper had ceased, the Grand Master spoke.

"Rebecca, thou canst derive no benefit from the evidence of this unhappy knight, for whom, as we well perceive, the Enemy is yet too powerful. Hast thou aught else to say?"

"There is yet one chance of life left to me," said Rebecca, "even by your own fierce laws. Life has been miserable –miserable, at least, of late –but I will not cast away the gift of God while He affords me the means of defending it. I deny this charge; I maintain my innocence, and I declare the falsehood of this accusation; I challenge the privilege of trial by combat, and will appear by my champion."

"And who, Rebecca," replied the Grand Master, "will lay lance in rest for a sorceress? who will be the champion of a Jewess?"

"God will raise me up a champion," said Rebecca. "It cannot be that in merry England, the hospitable, the generous, the free, where so many are ready to peril their lives for honour, there will not be found one to fight for justice. But it is enough that I challenge the trial by combat –there lies my gage."

She took her embroidered glove from her hand, and flung it down before the Grand Master with an air of mingled simplicity and dignity which excited universal surprise and admiration.

CHAPTER 27

Even Lucas Beaumanoir himself was affected by the mien and appearance of Rebecca. He was not originally a cruel or even a severe man; but with passions by nature cold, and with a high though mistaken sense of duty, his heart had been gradually hardened by the ascetic life which he pursued, the supreme power which he enjoyed, and the supposed necessity of subduing infidelity and eradicating heresy, which he conceived peculiarly incumbent on him. His features relaxed in their usual severity as he gazed upon the beautiful creature before him, alone, unfriended, and defending herself with so much spirit and courage. He crossed himself twice, as doubting whence arose the unwonted softening of a heart which, on such occasions, used to resemble in hardness the steel of his sword. At length he spoke.

"Brethren," said Beaumanoir, "you are aware that we might well have refused to this woman the benefit of the trial by combat; but though a Jewess, and an unbeliever, she is also a stranger and defenceless, and God forbid that she should ask the benefit of our mild laws, and that it should be refused to her. Moreover, we are knights and soldiers as well as men of religion, and shame it were to us upon any pretence to refuse proffered combat. Thus, therefore, stands the case. Rebecca, the daughter of Isaac of York, is, by many frequent and suspicious circumstances, defamed of sorcery practised on the person of a noble knight of our holy Order and hath challenged the combat in proof of her innocence. To whom, reverend brethren, is it your opinion that we should deliver the gage of battle, naming him, at the same time, to be our champion on the field?"

"To Brian de Bois-Guilbert, whom it chiefly concerns," said the Preceptor of Goodalricke, "and who, moreover, best knows how the truth stands in this matter."

"But if," said the Grand Master, "our brother Brian be under the influence of a charm or a spell? —we speak but for the sake of precaution, for to the arm of none of our holy Order would we more willingly confide this or a more weighty cause."

"Reverend father," answered the Preceptor of Goodalricke, "no spell can affect the champion who comes forward to fight for the judgment of God."

"Thou sayest right, brother," said the Grand Master. "Albert Molvoisin, give this gage of battle to Brian de Bois-Guilbert. —It is our charge to thee, brother," he continued, addressing himself to Bois-Guilbert, "that thou do thy battle manfully, nothing doubting that the good cause shall triumph. — And do thou, Rebecca, attend, that we assign thee the third day from the present to find a champion."

"That is but brief space," answered Rebecca, "for a stranger, who is also of another faith, to find one who will do battle, wagering life and honour for her cause, against a knight who is called an approved soldier."

"We may not extend it," answered the Grand Master; "the field must be foughten in our own presence, and divers weighty causes call us on the fourth day from hence."

"God's will be done!" said Rebecca. "I put my trust in Him, to whom an instant is as effectual to save as a whole age."

"Thou hast spoken well, damsel," said the Grand Master; "but well know we who can array himself like an angel of light. It remains but to name a fitting place of combat, and, if it so hap, also of execution. Where is the Preceptor of this house?"

Albert Malvoisin, still holding Rebecca's glove in his hand, was speaking to Bois-Guilbert very earnestly, but in a low voice.

"How!" said the Grand Master "will he not receive the gage?"

"He will—he doth, most reverend father," said Malvoisin, slipping the glove under his own mantle. "And for the place of combat, I hold the fittest to be the lists of Saint George belonging to this Preceptory, and used by us for military exercise."

"It is well," said the Grand Master.—"Rebecca, in those lists shalt thou produce thy champion; and if thou failest to do so or if thy champion shall be discomfited by the judgment of God, thou shalt then die the death of a sorceress according to doom."

Rebecca spoke not, but she looked up to heaven, and folding her hands, remained for a minute without change of attitude. She then modestly reminded the Grand Master that she ought to be permitted some opportunity of free communication with her friends, for the purpose of making her condition known to them, and procuring, if possible, some champion to fight in her behalf.

"It is just and lawful," said the Grand Master. "Choose what messenger thou shalt trust, and he shall have free communication with thee in thy prison chamber."

"Is there," said Rebecca, "any one here who, either for love of a good cause or for ample hire, will do the errand of a distressed being?"

All were silent; for none thought it safe, in the presence of the Grand Master, to avow any interest in the calumniated prisoner, lest he should be suspected of leaning towards Judaism. Not even the prospect of reward, far less any feelings of compassion alone, could surmount this apprehension.

Rebecca stood for a few moments in indescribable anxiety, and then exclaimed, "Is it really thus? And, in English land, am I to be deprived of the poor chance of safety which remains to me, for want of an act of charity which would not be refused to the worst criminal?"

Higg, the son of Snell, at length, replied, "I am but a maimed man, but that I can at all stir or move was owing to her charitable assistance. –I will do thine errand," he added, addressing Rebecca, "as well as a crippled object can, and happy were my limbs fleet enough to repair the mischief done by my tongue. Alas! when I boasted of thy charity, I little thought I was leading thee into danger!"

"God," said Rebecca, "is the disposer of all. He can turn back the captivity of Judah, even by the weakest instrument. To execute His message the snail is as sure a messenger as the falcon. Seek out Isaac of York –here is that will pay for horse and man –let him have this scroll. I know not if it be of Heaven the spirit which inspires me, but most truly do I judge that I am not to die this death, and that a champion will be raised up for me. Farewell! Life and death are in thy haste."

The peasant took the scroll, which contained only a few lines in Hebrew. Many of the crowd would have dissuaded him from touching a document so suspicious; but Higg was resolute in the service of his benefactress. She had saved his body, he said, and he was confident she did not mean to peril his soul.

"I will get me," he said, "my neighbour Bothan's good horse and I will be at York within as brief space as man and beast may."

But as it fortuned, he had no occasion to go so far; for within a quarter of a mile from the gate of the Preceptory he met with two riders, whom, by their dress and their huge yellow caps, he knew to be Jews, and, on approaching more nearly, discovered that one of them was his ancient employer, Isaac of York. The other was the Rabbi Ben Samuel; and both had approached as near to the Preceptory as they dared, on hearing that the Grand Master had summoned a chapter for the trial of a sorceress.

"Brother Ben Samuel," said Isaac, "my soul is disquieted, and I wot not why: This charge of necromancy is right often used for cloaking evil practices on our people."

"Be of good comfort, brother," said the physician; "thou canst deal with the Nazarenes as one possessing the mammon of unrighteousness, and canst therefore purchase immunity at their hands; it rules the savage minds of those ungodly men, even as the signet of the mighty Solomon was said to command the evil genii. But what poor wretch comes hither upon his crutches, desiring, as I think, some speech of me? — Friend," continued the physician, addressing Higg, the son of Snell, "I refuse thee not the aid of mine art, but I relieve not with one asper those who beg for alms upon the highway. Out upon thee! Hast thou the palsy in thy legs? Then let thy hands work for thy livelihood; for, albeit thou be'st unfit for a speedy post, or for a careful shepherd, or for the warfare, or for the service of a hasty master, yet there be occupations — How now, brother?" said he, interrupting his harangue to look towards Isaac, who had but glanced at the scroll which Higg offered, when, uttering a deep groan, he fell from his mule like a dying man, and lay for a minute insensible.

The Rabbi now dismounted in great alarm, and hastily applied the remedies which his art suggested for the recovery of his companion. He had even taken from his pocket a cupping apparatus, and was about to proceed to phlebotomy, when the object of his anxious solicitude suddenly revived; but it was to dash his cap from his head, and to throw dust on his grey hairs. The physician was at first inclined to ascribe this sudden and violent emotion to the effects of insanity, and, adhering to his original purpose, began once again to handle his implements. But Isaac soon convinced him of his error.

"Child of my sorrow," he said, "well shouldst thou be called Bdnoni, instead of Rebecca! Why should thy death bring down my grey hairs to the grave, till, in the bitterness of my heart, I curse God and die!"

"Brother," said the Rabbi, in great surprise, "art thou a father in Israel, and dost thou utter words like unto these? I trust that the child of thy house yet liveth?"

"She liveth," answered Issac; "but it is as Daniel, who was called Belteshazzar, even when within the den of the lions. She is captive unto these men of Belial, and they will wreak their cruelty upon her, sparing neither for her youth nor her comely favour. Oh! she was as a crown of green palms to my grey locks; and she must wither in a night, like the gourd of Jonah!–Child of my love!–child of my old age!–O Rebecca, daughter of Rachel! the darkness of the shadow of death hath encompassed thee."

"Yet read the scroll," said the Rabbi; "peradventure it may be that we may yet find out a way of deliverance."

"Do thou read, brother," answered Isaac, "for mine eyes are as a fountain of water."

The physician read, but in their native language, the following words:–

"To Isaac, the son of Adonikam, whom the Gentiles call Isaac of York, peace and the blessing of the promise be multiplied unto thee! My Father, I am as one doomed to die for that which my soul knoweth not –even for the crime of witchcraft. My father, if a strong man can be found to do battle for my cause with sword and spear, according to the custom of the Nazarenes, and that within the lists of Templestowe, on the third day from this time, peradventure our fathers' God will give him strength to defend the innocent, and her who hath none to help her. But if this may not be, let the virgins of our people mourn for me as for one cast off, and for the hart that is stricken by the hunter, and for the flower which is cut down by the scythe of the mower. Wherefore look now what thou doest, and whether there be any rescue. One Nazarene warrior might indeed bear arms in my behalf, even Wilfred, son of Cedric, whom the Gentiles call Ivanhoe. But he may not yet endure the weight of his armour. Nevertheless, send the tidings unto him, my father; for he hath favour among the strong men of this people and as he was our companion in the house of bondage, he may find someone to do battle for my sake. And say unto him, even unto him, even unto Wilfred, the son of Cedric, that if Rebecca live, or if Rebecca die, she liveth or dieth wholly free of the guilt she is charged withal. And if it be the will of God that thou shalt be deprived of thy daughter, do not thou tarry, old man, in this land of bloodshed and cruelty; but betake thyself to Cordova, where thy brother liveth in safety, under the shadow of the throne, even of the throne of Boabdil the Saracen; for less cruel are the cruelties of the Moors unto the race of Jacob, than the cruelties of the Nazarenes of England."

Isaac listened with tolerable composure while Ben Samuel read the letter, and then again resumed the gestures and exclamations of Oriental sorrow, tearing his garments, besprinkling his head with dust, and ejaculating, "My daughter! my daughter! flesh of my blood, and bone of my bone!"

"Yet," said the Rabbi, "take courage, for this grief availeth nothing. Gird up thy loins, and seek out this Wilfred, the son of Cedric. It may be he will help thee with counsel or with strength; for the youth hath favour in the eyes of Richard, called of the Nazarenes Cœur-de-Lion, and the tidings that he hath returned are constant in the land. It may be that he may obtain his letter, and his signet, commanding these men of blood, who take their name from the Temple to the dishonour thereof, that they proceed not in their purposed wickedness."

"I will seek him out," said Isaac, "for he is a good youth, and hath compassion for the exile of Jacob. But he cannot bear his armour, and what other Christian shall do battle for the oppressed of Zion?"

"Nay, but," said the Rabbi, "thou speakest as one that knoweth not the Gentiles. With gold shalt thou buy their valour, even as with gold thou buyest thine own safety. Be of good courage, and do thou set forward to find out this Wilfred of Ivanhoe. I will also up and be doing, for great sin it were to leave thee in thy calamity. I will hie me to the City of York, where many warriors and strong men are assembled, and doubt not I will find among them someone who will do battle for thy daughter; for gold is their god, and for riches will they pawn their lives as well as their lands. Thou wilt fulfil, my brother, such promise as I may make unto them in thy name?"

"Assuredly, brother," said Issac; "and Heaven be praised that raised me up a comforter in my misery. Howbeit, grant them not their full demand at once; fort thou shalt find it the quality of this accursed people that they will ask pounds, and peradventure accept of ounces. Nevertheless, be it as thou willest; for I am distracted in this thing, and what would my gold avail me if the child of my love should perish!"

"Farewell," said the physician; "and may it be to thee as thy heart desireth!"

They embraced accordingly, and departed on their several roads. The crippled peasant remained for some time looking after them.

CHAPTER 28

OUR scene now returns to the exterior of the Castle, or Preceptory, of Templestowe, about the hour when the bloody die was to be cast for the life or death of Rebecca. It was a scene of bustle and life, as if the whole vicinity had poured forth its inhabitants to a village wake or rural feast. But the earnest desire to look on blood and death is not peculiar to those dark ages, though in the gladiatorial exercise of single combat and general tourney, they were habituated to the bloody spectacle of brave men falling by each other's hands. Even in our own days, when morals are better understood, and execution, a bruising match, a riot, or a meeting of radical reformers, collects, at considerable hazard to themselves, immense crowds of spectators, otherwise little interested, except to see how matters are to be conducted, or whether the heroes of the day are, in the heroic language of insurgent tailors, flints or dunghills.

The eyes, therefore, of a very considerable multitude were bent on the gate of the Preceptory of Templestowe with the purpose of witnessing the procession; while still greater numbers had already surrounded the tiltyard belonging to that establisament. This enclosure was formed on a piece of level ground adjoining to the Preceptory, which had been levelled with care, for the exercise of military and chivalrous sports. It occupied the brow of a soft and gentle eminence, was carefully palisaded around, and, as the Templars willingly invited spectators to be witnesses of their skill in feats of chivalry, was amply supplied with galleries and benches for their use.

On the present occasion a throne was erected for the Grand Master at the east end, surrounded with seats of distinction for the Preceptors and Knights of the Order. Over these floated the sacred standard, called *Le Beau-séant*, which was the ensign, as its name was the battlecry, of the Templars.

At the opposite end of the lists was a pile of fagots, so arranged around a stake, deeply fixed in the ground, as to leave a space for the victim whom they were destined to consume, to enter within the fatal circle, in order to be chained to the stake by the fetters which hung ready for that purpose. Beside this deadly apparatus stood four black slaves, whose colour and African features, then so little known in England, appalled the multitude, who gazed on them as on demons employed about their own diabolical exercises. These men stirred not, excepting now and then, under the direction of one who seemed their chief, to shift and replace the ready fuel. They looked not on the multitude. In fact, they seemed insensible of their presence, and of everything save the discharge of their own horrible duty. And when, in speech with each other, they expanded their blubber lips and showed their white fangs, as if they grinned at the thoughts of the expected tragedy, the startled commons could scarcely help believing that they were actually the familiar spirits with whom the witch had communed, and who, her time being out, stood ready to assist in her dreadful punishment. They whispered to each other, and communicated all the feats which Satan had performed during that busy unhappy period, not failing, of course, to give the devil rather more than his due.

"Have you not heard, Father Dennet," quoth one boor to another advanced in years, "that the devil has carried away bodily the great Saxon Thane, Athelstane of Coningsburgh?"

"Ay; but he brought him back though, by the blessing of God and Saint Dunstan."

"How's that?" said a brisk young fellow, dressed in a green cassock embroidered with gold, and having at his heels a stout lad bearing a harp upon his back, which betrayed his vocation. The Minstrel seemed of no vulgar rank; for, besides the splendour of his gaily-broidered doublet, he wore around his neck a silver chain, by which hung the *wrest*, or key, with which he tuned his harp. On the right arm was a silver plate, which, instead of bearing, as usual, the cognizance or badge, of the baron to whose family he belonged, had barely the word SHERWOOD engraved upon it. —"How mean you by that?" said the gay Minstrel, mingling in the conversation of the peasants. "I came to seek one subject for my rhyme, and, by'r Lady, I were glad to find two."

"It is well avouched," said the elder peasant, "that after Athelstane of Coningsburgh had been dead four weeks –"

"That is impossible," said the Minstrel; "I saw him in life at the Passage of Arms at Ashby-de-la-Zouche."

"Dead, however, he was, or else translated," said the younger peasant; "for I heard the monks of Saint Edmund's singing the death's hymn for him; and, moreover, there was a rich death-meal and dole at the Castle of Coningsburgh, as right was. And thither had I gone, but for Mabel Parkins, who –"

"Ay, dead was Athelstane," said the old man, shaking his head; "and the more pity it was, for the old Saxon blood –"

"But, your story, my masters –your story," said the Minstrel, somewhat impatiently.

"Ay, ay –construe us the story," said a burly Friar, who stood beside them, leaning on a pole that exhibited an appearance between a pilgrim's staff and a quarter-staff, and probably acted as either when occasion served,—"your story," said the stalwart churchman; "burn not daylight about it –we have short time to spare."

"An please your reverence," said Dennet, "a drunken priest came to visit the sacristan at Saint Edmund's—"

"It does not please my reverence," answered the churchman, "that there should be such an animal as a drunken priest, or, if there were, that a layman should so speak him. Be mannerly, my friend, and conclude the holy man only wrapt in meditation, which makes the head dizzy and foot unsteady, as if the stomach were filled with new wine –I have felt it myself."

"Well, then," answered Father Dennet, "a holy brother came to visit the sacristan at Saint Edmund's –a sort of hedge-priest is the visitor, and kills half the deer that are stolen in the forest, who loves the tinkling of a pint-pot better than the sacring-bell, and deems a flitch of bacon worth ten of his breviary; for the rest, a good fellow and a merry, who will flourish a quarter-staff, draw a bow, and dance a Cheshire round, with e'er a man in Yorkshire."

"That last part of thy speech, Dennet," said the Minstrel, "has saved thee a rib or twain."

"Tush, man, I fear him not," said Dennet. "I am somewhat old and stiff, but when I fought for the bell and ram at Doncaster—"

"But the story –the story, my friend," again said the Minstrel.

"Why, the tale is but this –Athelstane of Coningsburgh was buried at Saint Edmund's."

"That's a lie, and a loud one," said the Friar, "for I saw him borne to his own Castle of Coningsburgh."

"Nay, then, e'en tell the story yourself, my masters," said Dennet, turning sulky at these repeated contradictions; and it was with some difficulty that the boor could be prevailed on, by the request of his comrade and the Minstrel, to renew his tale. "These two *sober* friars," said he at length, "since this reverend man will needs have them such, had continued drinking good ale, and wine, and what not, for the best part of summer's day, when they were aroused by a deep groan and a clanking of chains, and the figure of the deceased Athelstane entered the apartment, saying. 'Ye evil shepherds!—'"

"It is false," said the Friar hastily, "he never spoke a word."

"So ho! Friar Tuck," said the Minstrel, drawing him apart from the rustics, "we have started a new hare, I find."

"I tell thee, Allan-a-Dale," said the Hermit, "I saw Athelstane of Coningsburgh as much as bodily eyes ever saw a living man. He had his shroud on, and all about him smelt of sepulchre –a butt of sack will not wash it out of my memory."

"Pshaw!" answered the Minstrel; "thou dost but jest with me!"

"Never believe me," said the Friar, "an I fetched not a knock at him with my quarter-staff that would have felled an ox, and it glided through his body as it might through a pillar of smoke!"

"By Saint Hubert," said the Minstrel, "but it is a wondrous tale, and fit to be put in metre to the ancient tune, 'Sorrow came to the old Friar.'"

"Laugh, if ye list," said Friar Tuck; "but an ye catch me singing on such a theme, may the next ghost or devil carry me off with him headlong! No, no; I instantly formed the purpose of assisting at some good work, such as the burning of a witch, a judicial combat, or the like matter of godly service, and therefore am I here."

As they thus conversed, the heavy bell of the church of Saint Michael of Templestowe, a venerable building, situated in a hamlet at some distance from the Preceptory, broke short their argument. One by one the sullen sounds fell successively on the ear, leaving but sufficient space for each to die away in distant echo ere the air was again filled by repetition of the iron knell. These sounds, the signal of the approaching ceremony, chilled with awe the hearts of the assembled multitude, whose eyes were now turned to the Preceptory, expecting the approach of the Grand Master, the champion, and the criminal.

At length the drawbridge fell, the gates opened, and a knight, bearing the great standard of the Order, sallied from the castle, preceded by six trumpets, and followed by the Knights Preceptors, two and two, the Grand Master coming last, mounted on a stately horse, whose furniture was of the simplest kind. Behind him came Brian de Bois-Guilbert, armed cap-a-pie in bright armour, but without his lance, shield, and sword, which were borne by his two esquires behind him. His face, though partly hidden by a long plume which floated down from his barret-cap, bore a strong and mingled expression of passion, in which pride seemed to contend with irresolution. He looked ghastly pale, as if he had not slept for several nights; yet reined his pawing war-horse with the habitual ease and grace proper to the best lance of the Order of the Temple. His general appearance was grand and commanding; but, looking at him with attention, men read that in his dark features from which they willingly withdrew their eyes.

On either side rode Conrade of Mont-Fitchet, and Albert de Malvoisin, who acted as godfather to the champion. They were in their robes of peace, the white dress of the Order. Behind them followed other Companions of the Temple, with a long train of esquires and pages clad in black, aspirants to the honour of being one day Knights of the Order. After these neophytes came a guard of warders on foot, in the same sable livery, amidst whose partisans might be seen the pale form of the accused, moving with a slow but undismayed step towards the scene of her fate. She was stripped of all her ornaments, lest perchance there should be among them some of those amulets which Satan was supposed to bestow upon his victims, to deprive them of the power of confession even when under the torture. A coarse white dress, of the simplest form, had been substituted for her Oriental garments; yet there was such an exquisite mixture of courage and resig-nation in her look, that even in this garb, and with no other ornament than her long black tresses, each eye wept that looked upon her, and the most hardened bigot regretted the fate that had converted a creature so goodly into a vessel of wrath and a waged slave of the devil.

A crowd of inferior personages belonging to the Preceptory followed the victim, all moving with the utmost order, with arms folded, and looks bent upon the ground.

This slow procession moved up the gentle eminence, on the summit of which was the tiltyard, and, entering the lists, marched once around them from right to left, and when they had completed the circle, made a halt. There was then a mo-mentary bustle, while the Grand Master and all his attendants, excepting the champion and his godfathers, dismounted from their horses, which were immediately removed out of the lists by the esquires, who were in attendance for that purpose.

The unfortunate Rebecca was conducted to the black chair placed near the pile. On her first glance at the terrible spot where preparations were making for a death alike dismaying to the mind and painful to the body, she was observed to shudder, and shut her eyes, praying internally doubtless, for her lips moved though no speech was heard. In the space of a minute she opened her eyes, looked fixedly on the pile as if to familiarize her mind with the object, and then slowly and naturally turned away her head.

Meanwhile, the Grand Master had assumed his seat; and when the chivalry of his Order was placed around and behind him, each in his due rank, a loud and long flourish of the trumpets announced that the Court was seated for judgment. Malvoisin, then, acting as godfather of the champion, stepped forward, and laid the glove of the Jewess, which was the pledge of battle, at the feet of the Grand Master.

"Valorous Lord, and reverend Father," said he, "here standeth the good Knight, Brian de Bois-Guilbert, Knight Preceptor of the Order of the Temple, who, by accepting the pledge of battle, which I now lay at your reverence's feet, hath become bound to do his *devoir* in combat this day, to maintain that this Jewish maiden, by name Rebecca, hath justly deserved the doom passed upon her in a Chapter of this most Holy Order of the Temple of Zion, condemning her to die as a sorceress;–here, I say, he standeth, such battle to do, knightly and honourably, if such be your noble and sanctified pleasure."

"Hath he made oath," said the Grand Master, "that this quarrel is just and honourable? Bring forward the crucifix and the *Te igitur*."

"Sir, and most reverend father," answered Malvoisin readily, "our brother here present hath already sworn to the truth of his accusation in the hand of the good Knight Conrade de Mont-Fitchet; and otherwise he ought not to be sworn, seeing that his adversary is an unbeliever, and may take no oath."

This explanation was satisfactory, to Albert's great joy; for the wily knight had foreseen the great difficulty, or rather impossibility, of prevailing upon Brian de Bois-Guilbert to take such an oath before the assembly, and had invented this excuse to escape the necessity of his doing so.

The Grand Master, having allowed the apology of Albert Malvoisin, commanded the herald to stand forth and do his *devoir*. The trumpets then again flourished, and a herald, stepping forward, proclaimed aloud, "Oyez, oyez, oyez.—Here standeth the good Knight, Sir Brian de Bois-Guilbert, ready to do battle with any knight of free blood, who will sustain the quarrel allowed and allotted to the Jewess Rebecca, to try by champion, in respect of lawful *essoine* of her own body; and to such champion the reverend and valorous Grand Master here present allows a fair field, and equal partition of sun and wind, and whatever else appertains to a fair combat." The trumpets again sounded, and there was a dead pause for many minutes.

"No champion appears for the appellant," said the Grand Master. "Go, herald, and ask her whether she expects any one to do battle for her in this her cause." The herald went to the chair in which Rebecca was seated, and Bois-Guilbert suddenly turning his horse's head toward that end of the lists, in spite of hints on either side from Malvoisin and Mont-Fitchet, was by the side of Rebecca's chair as soon as the herald.

"Is this regular, and according to the law of combat?" said Malvoisin, looking to the Grand Master.

"Albert de Malvoisin, it is," answered Beaumanoir; "for in this appeal to the judgment of God, we may not prohibit parties from having that communication with each other which may best tend to bring forth the truth of the quarrel."

In the meantime, the herald spoke to Rebecca in these terms:—"Damsel, the Honourable and Reverend the Grand Master demands of thee, if thou art prepared with a champion to do battle this day in thy behalf, or if thou dost yield thee as one justly condemned to a deserved doom?"

"Say to the Grand Master," replied Rebecca, "that I maintain my innocence, and do not yield me as justly condemned, lest I become guilty of mine own blood. Say to him, that I challenge such delay as his forms will permit, to see if God, whose opportunity is in man's extremity, will raise me up a deliverer; and when such uttermost space is passed, may His holy will be done!" The herald retired to carry this answer to the Grand Master.

"God forbid," said Lucas Beaumanoir, "that Jew or Pagan should impeach us of injustice! Until the shadows be cast from the west to the eastward, will we wait to see if a champion shall appear for this unfortunate woman. When the day is so far passed, let her prepare for death."

The herald communicated the words of the Grand Master to Rebecca, who bowed her head submissively, folded her arms, and, looking up towards heaven, seemed to expect that aid from above which she could scarce promise herself from man. During this awful pause, the voice of Bois-Guilbert broke upon her ear; it was but a whisper, yet it startled her more than the summons of the herald had appeared to do.

"Rebecca," said the Templar, "dost thou hear me?"

"I have no portion in thee, cruel, hard-hearted man," said the unfortunate maiden.

"Ay, but dost thou understand my words?" said the Templar; "for the sound of my voice is frightful in mine own ears.

I scarce know on what ground we stand, or for what purpose
they have brought us hither. This listed space –that chair –
these fagots –I know their purpose; and yet it appears to me
like something unreal –the fearful picture of a vision, which
appals my sense with hideous fantasies, but convinces not
my reason."

"My mind and senses keep touch and time," answered Rebecca,
"and tell me alike that these fagots are destined to consume
my earthly body, and open a painful but a brief passage to
a better world."

"Dreams, Rebecca –dreams," answered the Templar – "idle
visions, rejected by the wisdom of your own wiser Sadducees.
Hear me, Rebecca," he said, proceeding with animation;
"a better chance hast thou for life and liberty than yonder
knaves and dotard dream of. Mount thee behind me on my
steed –on Zamor, the gallant horse that never failed his rider.
I won him in single fight from the Soldan of Trebizond.
Mount, I say, behind me. In one short hour is pursuit and
inquiry far behind; a new world of pleasure open to thee –
to me a new career of fame. Let them speak the doom which
I despise, and erase the name of Bois-Guilbert from their
list of monastic slaves! I will wash out with blood whatever
blot they may dare to cast on my scutcheon."

"Tempter," said Rebecca, "begone! Not in this last extremity canst thou move me one hair's-breadth from my resting-
place. Surrounded as I am by foes, I hold thee as my worst
and most deadly enemy. Avoid thee, in the name of God!"

Albert Malvoisin, alarmed and impatient at the duration
of their conference, now advanced to interrupt it.

"Hath the maiden acknowledged her guilt?" he demanded
of Bois-Guilbert; "or is she resolute in her denial?"

"She is indeed *resolute*," said Bois-Guilbert.

"Then," said Malvoisin, "must thou, noble brother, resume
thy place to attend the issue. The shades are changing on the

circle of the dial. Come, brave Bois-Guilbert—come, thou hope of our holy Order, and soon to be its head."

As he spoke in this soothing tone, he laid his hand on the knight's bridle, as if to lead him back to his station.

"False villain! what meanest thou by thy hand on my rein?" said Sir Brian angrily. And shaking off his companion's grasp, he rode back to the upper end of the lists.

"There is yet spirit in him," said Malvoisin apart to Mont-Fitchet, "were it well directed; but, like the Greek fire, it burns whatever approaches it."

The judges had now been two hours in the lists, awaiting in vain the appearance of a champion.

"And reason good," said Friar Tuck, "seeing she is a Jewess; and yet, by mine Order, it is hard that so young and beautiful a creature should perish without one blow being struck in her behalf. Were she ten times a witch, provided she were but the least bit of a Christian, my quarter-staff should ring noon on the steel cap of yonder fierce Templar, ere he carried the matter off thus."

It was, however, the general belief that no one could or would appear for a Jewess, accused of sorcery; and the knights, instigated by Malvoisin, whispered to each other that it was time to declare the pledge of Rebecca forfeited. At this instant a knight, urging his horse to speed, appeared on the plain advancing towards the lists. A hundred voices exclaimed, "A champion! a champion!" and despite the prepossessions and prejudices of the multitude, they shouted unanimously as the knight rode into the tiltyard. The second glance, however, served to destroy the hope that his timely arrival had excited. His horse, urged for many miles to its utmost speed, appeared to reel from fatigue; and the rider, however undauntedly he presented himself in the lists, either from weakness, weariness, or both, seemed scarce able to support himself in the saddle.

To the summons of the herald, who demanded his rank, his name, and purpose, the stranger knight answered readily and boldly, "I am a good knight and noble, come hither to sustain with lance and sword the just and lawful quarrel of this damsel, Rebecca, daughter of Isaac of York; to uphold the doom pronounced against her to be false and truthless, and to defy Sir Brian de Bois-Guilbert as a traitor, murderer, and liar; as I will prove in this field with my body against his, by the aid of God, of Our Lady, and of Monsigneur Saint George, the good knight."

"The stranger must first show," said Malvoisin, "that he is a good knight, and of honourable lineage. The Temple sendeth not forth her champions against nameless men."

"My name," said the knight, raising his helmet, "is better known, my lineage more pure, Malvoisin, than thine own. I am Wilfred of Ivanhoe."

"I will not fight with thee at present," said the Templar in a changed and hollow voice. "Get thy wounds healed, purvey thee a better horse, and it may be I will hold it worth my while to scourge out of thee this boyish spirit of bravade."

"Ha! proud Templar," said Ivanhoe, "hast thou forgotten that twice didst thou fall before this lance? Remember the list at Acre—remember the Passage of Arms at Ashby—remember thy proud vaunt in the halls of Rotherwood, and the gage of your gold chain against my reliquary, that thou wouldst do battle with Wilfred of Ivanhoe, and recover the honour thou hadst lost! By that reliquary, and the holy relic it contains, I will proclaim thee, Templar, a coward in every court in Europe, in every Preceptory of thine Order, unless thou do battle without further delay."

Bois-Guilbert turned his countenance irresolutely towards Rebecca, and then exclaimed, looking fiercely at Ivanhoe, "Dog of a Saxon! take thy lance, and prepare for the death thou hast drawn upon thee!"

"Does the Grand Master allow me the combat?" said Ivanhoe.

"I may not deny what thou hast challenged," said the Grand Master, "provided the maiden accepts thee as her champion. Yet I would thou wert in better plight to do battle. An enemy of our Order hast thou ever been, yet would I have thee honourably met with."

"Thus –thus as I am, and not otherwise," said Ivanhoe; "it is the judgment of God –to His keeping I commend myself. – Rebecca," said he, riding up to the fatal chair, "dost thou accept of me for thy champion ?"

"I do," she said –"I do," fluttered by an emotion which the fear of death had been unable to produce, "I do accept thee as the champion whom Heaven hath sent me. Yet, no – no –thy wounds are uncured. Meet not that proud man –why shouldst thou perish also?"

But Ivanhoe was already at his post, and had closed his visor and assumed his lance. Bois-Guilbert did the same; and his esquire remarked, as he clasped his visor, that his face, which had, notwithstanding the variety of emotions by which he had been agitated, continued during the whole morning of an ashy paleness, was now become suddenly very much flushed.

The herald,.then, seeing each champion in his place, uplifted his voice, repeating thrice, *Faites vos devoirs, preux chevaliers!* After the third cry, he withdrew to one side of the lists, and again proclaimed that none, on peril of instant death, should dare, by word, cry, or action, to interfere with or disturb this fair field of combat. The Grand Master, who held in his hand the gage of battle, Rebecca's glove, now threw it into the lists, and pronounced the fatal signal words, *Laissez aller.*

The trumpets sounded, and the knights charged each other in full career. The wearied horse of Ivanhoe, and its no less exhausted rider, went down, as all had expected, before the well-aimed lance and vigorous steed of the Templar. This issue of the combat all had foreseen; but although the spear of Ivanhoe did but, in comparison, touch the shield of Bois-Guilbert, that champion, to the astonishment of all who beheld it, reeled in his saddle, lost his stirrups, and fell in the lists.

Ivanhoe, extricating himself from his fallen horse, was soon on foot, hastening to mend his fortune with his sword; but his antagonist arose not. Wilfred, placing his foot on his breast, and the sword's point to his throat, commanded him to yield him, or die on the spot. Bois-Guilbert returned no answer.

"Slay him not, Sir Knight," cried the Grand Master, "unshriven and unabsolved –kill not body and soul! We allow him vanquished."

He descended into the lists, and commanded them to unhelm the conquered champion. His eyes were closed; the dark red flush was still on his brow. As they looked on him in astonishment, the eyes opened; but they were fixed and glazed. The flush passed from his brow, and gave way to the pallid hue of death. Unscathed by the lance of his enemy, he had died a victim to the violence of his own contending passions.

"This is indeed the judgment of God," said the Grand Master, looking upwards –"*Fiat voluntas tua!*"

CHAPTER 29

WHEN the first moments of surprise were over, Wilfred of Ivanhoe demanded of the Grand Master, as judge of the field, if he had manfully and rightfully done his duty in the combat?

"Manfully and rightfully hath it been done," said the Grand Master; "I pronounce the maiden free and guiltless. The arms and the body of the deceased knight are at the will of the victor."

"I will not despoil him of his weapons," said the Knight of Ivanhoe, "nor condemn his corpse to shame –he hath fought

for Christendom. God's arm, no human hand, hath this day
struck him down. But let his obsequies be private, as becomes
those of a man who died in an unjust quarrel. And for the
maiden—"

He was interrupted by a clattering of horses' feet, advancing
in such numbers, and so rapidly, as to shake the ground
before them; and the Black Knight galloped into the lists.
He was followed by a numerous band of men-at-arms, and
several knights in complete armour.

"I am too late," he said, looking around him. "I had doomed
Bois-Guilbert for mine own property. –Ivanhoe, was this well
to take on thee such a venture, and thou scarce able to keep
thy saddle?"

"Heaven, my Liege," answered Ivanhoe, "hath taken this
proud man for its victim. He hath not to be honoured in
dying as your will had designed."

"Peace be with him," said Richard, looking steadfastly on
the corpse, "if it may be so; he was a gallant knight, and
has died in his steel harness full knightly. But we must waste
no time. –Bohun, do thine office!"

A knight stepped forward from the King's attendants, and,
laying his hand on the shoulder of Albert de Malvoisin, said,
"I arrest thee of high treason."

The Grand Master had hitherto stood astonished at the
appearance of so many warriors. He now spoke.

"Who dares to arrest a Knight of the Temple of Zion within
the girth of his own Preceptory, and in the presence of the
Grand Master? and by whose authority is this bold outrage
offered?"

"I make the arrest," replied the knight –"I, Henry Bohun,
Earl of Essex, Lord High Constable of England."

"And he arrests Malvoisin," said the King, raising his visor,
"by the order of Richard Plantagenet, here present. –Conrade
Mont-Fitchet, it is well for thee thou art born no subject

of mine. –But for thee, Malvoisin, thou diest with thy brother
Philip, ere the world be a week older."

"I will resist thy doom," said the Grand Master.

"Proud Templar," said the King, "thou canst not. Look
up, and behold the Royal Standard of England floats over
thy towers instead of thy Temple banner! Be wise, Beaumanoir, and make no bootless opposition –thy hand is in the
lion's mouth."

"I will appeal to Rome against thee," said the Grand Master,
"for usurpation on the immunities and privileges of our Order."

"Be it so," said the King; "but for thine own sake tax
me not with usurpation now. Dissolve thy Chapter, and depart
with thy followers to thy next Preceptory (if thou canst find
one), which has not been made the scene of treasonable conspiracy against the King of England. Or, if thou wilt, remain,
to share our hospitality, and behold our justice."

"To be a guest in the house where I should command?"
said the Templar; "never!–Chaplains, raise the Psalm, *Quare
fremuerunt gentes?*–Knights, squires, and followers of the Holy
Temple, prepare to follow the banner of *Beau-séant!*"

The Grand Master spoke with a dignity which confronted
even that of England's king himself, and inspired courage into
his surprised and dismayed followers. They gathered around
him like the sheep around the watch-dog, when they hear the
baying of the wolf. But they evinced not the timidity of the
scared flock; there were dark brows of defiance, and looks
which menaced the hostility they dared not to proffer in words.
They drew together in a dark line of spears, from which the
white cloaks of the knights were visible among the dusky
garments of their retainers, like the lighter-coloured edges of
a sable cloud. The multitude, who had raised a clamorous
shout of reprobation, paused and gazed in silence on the formidable and experienced body to which they had unwarily
bade defiance, and shrunk back from their front.

The Earl of Essex, when he beheld them pause in their assembled force, dashed the rowels into his charger's sides, and galloped backwards and forwards to array his followers, in opposition to a band so formidable, Richard alone, as if he loved the danger his presence had provoked, rode slowly along the front of the Templars, calling aloud, "What, sirs! Among so many gallant knights, will none dare splinter a spear with Richard? Sirs of the Temple! your ladies are but sunburned, if they are not worth the shiver of a broken lance!"

"The Brethren of the Temple," said the Grand Master, riding forward in advance of their body, "fight not on such idle and profane quarrel; and not with thee, Richard of England, shall a Templar cross lance in my presence. The Pope and Princes of Europe shall judge our quarrel, and whether a Christian prince has done well in bucklering the cause which thou hast to-day adopted. If unassailed, we depart assailing no one. To thine honour we refer the armour and household goods of the Order which we leave behind us, and on thy conscience we lay the scandal and offence thou hast this day given to Christendom."

With these words, and without waiting a reply, the Grand Master gave the signal of departure. Their trumpets sounded a wild march, of an Oriental character, which formed the usual signal for the Templars to advance. They changed their array from a line to a column of march, and moved off as slowly as their horses could step, as if to show it was only the will of their Grand Master, and no fear of the opposing and superior force, which compelled them to withdraw.

"By the splendour of Our Lady's brow!" said King Richard, "it is pity of their lives that these Templars are not so trusty as they are disciplined and valiant."

The multitude, like a timid cur which waits to bark till the object of its challenge has turned his back, raised a feeble shout as the rear of the squadron left the ground.

During the tumult which attended the retreat of the Templars, Rebecca saw and heard nothing; she was locked in the arms of her aged father, giddy, and almost senseless, with the rapid change of circumstances around her. But one word from Isaac at length recalled her scattered feelings.

"Let us go," he said, "my dear daughter, my recovered treasure –let us go to throw ourselves at the feet of the good youth."

"Not so," said Rebecca, "oh, no –no –no –I must not at this moment dare to speak to him. Alas! I should say more than – No, my father, let us instantly leave this evil place."

"But, my daughter," said Isaac, "to leave him who hath come forth like a strong man with his spear and shield, holding his life as nothing, so he might redeem thy captivity – and thou, too, the daughter of a people strange unto him and his –this is service to be thankfully acknowledged."

"It is –it is –most thankfully –most devoutly acknowledged," said Rebecca –"it shall be still more so –but not now –for the sake of thy beloved Rachel, father, grant my request –not now!"

"Nay, but," said Isaac, insisting, "they will deem us more thankless than mere dogs!"

"But thou seest, my dear father, that King Richard is in presence, and that—"

"True, my best, my wisest Rebecca! Let us hence –let us hence! Money he will lack, for he has just returned from Palestine, and, as they say, from prison; and pretext for exacting it, should he need any, may arise out of my simple traffic with his brother John. Away, away, let us hence!"

And hurrying his daughter in his turn, he conducted her from the lists, and by means of conveyance which he had provided, transported her safely to the house of the Rabbi Nathan.

The Jewess, whose fortunes had formed the principal interest of the day, having now retired unobserved, the attention of the populace was transferred to the Black Knight. They now filled the air with. "Long life to Richard with the Lion's Heart, and down with the usurping Templars!"

"Notwithstanding all this lip-loyalty," said Ivanhoe to the Earl of Essex, "it was well the King took the precaution to bring thee with him, noble Earl, and so many of thy trusty followers."

The Earl smiled and shook his head.

"Gallant Ivanhoe," said Essex, "dost thou know our Master so well, and yet suspect him of taking so wise a precaution? I was drawing towards York, having heard that Prince John was making head there, when I met King Richard, like a true knight-errant, galloping hither to achieve in his own person this adventure of the Templar and the Jewess, with his own single arm. I accompanied him with my hand, almost maugre his consent."

"And what news from York, brave Earl?" said Ivanhoe; "will the rebels bide us there?"

"No more than December's snow will bide July's sun," said the Earl; "they are dispersing, and who should come posting to bring us the news but John himself!"

"The traitor! the ungrateful insolent traitor!" said Ivanhoe. "Did not Richard order him into confinement?"

"Oh! he received him," answered the Earl, "as if they had met after a hunting-party; and, pointing to me and our men-at-arms, said, "Thou seest, brother, I have some angry men with me. Thou wert best go to our mother, carry her my duteous affection, and abide with her until men's minds are pacified.""

"And this was all he said?" inquired Ivanhoe. "Would not any one say that this Prince invites men to treason by his clemency?"

"Just," replied the Earl, "as the man may be said to invite death, who undertakes to fight a combat, having a dangerous wound unhealed."

"I forgive thee the jest, Lord Earl," said Ivanhoe; "but, remember, I hazarded but my own life - Richard, the welfare of his kingdom."

"Those," replied Essex, "who are specially careless of their own welfare, are seldom remarkably attentive to that of others. But let us haste to the castle, for Richard meditates punishing some of the subordinate members of the conspiracy, though he has pardoned their principal."

From the judicial investigations which followed on this occasion, and which are given at length in the Wardour Manuscript, it appears that Maurice de Bracy escaped beyond seas, and went into the service of Philip of France; while Philip de Malvoisin, and his brother Albert, the Preceptor of Templestowe, were executed, although Waldemar Fitzurse, the soul of the conspiracy, escaped with banishment; and Prince John, for whose behoof it was undertaken, was not even censured by his good-natured brother. No one, however, pitied the fate of the two Malvoisins, who only suffered the death which they had both well deserved by many acts of falsehood, cruelty, and oppression.

It seems that, after all his deadly menaces against the Abbot of Saint Edmund's, Athelstane's spirit of revenge, what between the natural indolent kindness of his own disposition, what through the prayers of his mother Edith, attached, like most ladies (of the period), to the clerical order, had terminated in his keeping the Abbot and his monks in the dungeons of Coningsburgh for three days on a meagre diet. For this atrocity the Abbot menaced him with excommunication and made out a dreadful list of complaints in the bowels and stomach, suffered by himself and his monks, in consequence of the tyrannical and unjust imprisonment they had sustained. With this controversy, and with the means he had adopted to counteract this clerical persecution, Cedric found the mind of his friend Athelstane so fully occupied that it had no room for another idea. And when Rowena's name was mentioned, the noble Athelstane prayed leave to quaff a full goblet to her health, and that she might soon be the bride of his kinsman Wilfred. It was a desperate case therefore. There was obviously no more to be made of Athelstane; or, as Wamba expressed it, in a phrase which has descended from Saxon time to ours, he was a cock that would not fight.

The nuptials of our hero, thus formally approved by his father, were celebrated in the most august of temples, the noble Minster of York. The King himself attended, and from the countenance which he afforded on this and other occasions to the distressed and hitherto degraded Saxons, gave them a safer and more certain prospect of attaining their just rights, than they could reasonably hope from the precarious chance of a civil war. The Church gave her full solemnities, graced with all the splendour which she of Rome knows how to apply with such brilliant effect.

Gurth, gallantly apparelled, attended as esquire upon his young master, whom he had served so faithfully, and the magnanimous Wamba, decorated with a new cap and a most gorgeous set of silver bells. Sharers of Wilfred's dangers and adversity, they remained, as they had a right to expect, the partakers of his more prosperous career.

But besides this domestic retinue, these distinguished nuptials were celebrated by the attendance of the high-born Normans, as well as Saxons, joined with the universal jubilee of the lower orders, that marked the marriage of two individuals as a pledge of the future peace and harmony betwixt two races, which, since that period, have been so completely mingled, that the distinction has become wholly invisible. Cedric lived to see this union approximate towards its completion; for as the two nations mixed in society and formed intermarriages with each other, the Normans abated their scorn, and the Saxons were refined from their rusticity. But it was not until the reign of Edward the Third that the mixed language, now termed English, was spoken at the court of London, and that the hostile distinction of Norman and Saxon seems entirely to have disappeared.

It was upon the second morning after this happy bridal, that the Lady Rowena was made acquainted by her handmaid Elgitha, that a damsel desired admission to her presence, and solicited that their parley might be without witness. Rowena wondered, hesitated, became curious, and ended by commanding the damsel to be admitted, and her attendants to withdraw.

She entered –a noble and commanding figure, the long white veil in which she was shrouded overshadowing rather than concealing the elegance and majesty of her shape. Her demeanour was that of respect, unmingled by the least shade either of fear or of a wish to propitiate favour. Rowena was ever ready to acknowledge the claims, and attend to the feelings of others. She arose, and would have conducted her lovely visitor to a seat; but the stranger looked at Elgitha, and again intimated a wish to discourse with the Lady Rowena alone. Elgitha had no sooner retired with unwilling steps, than, to the surprise of the Lady of Ivanhoe, her fair visitant kneeled on one knee, pressed her hands to her forehead, and bending her head to the ground, in spite of Rowena's resistance, kissed the embroidered hem of ther tunic.

"What means this, lady?" said the surprised bride, "or why do you offer to me a deference so unusual?"

"Because to you, Lady of Ivanhoe," said Rebecca, rising up and resuming the usual quiet dignity of her manner, "I may lawfully, and without rebuke, pay the debt of gratitude whic I owe to Wilfred of Ivanhoe. I am –forgive the boldness which has offered to you the homage of my country –I am the unhappy Jewess for whom your husband hazarded his life against such fearful odds in the tiltyard of Templestowe."

"Damsel," said Rowena, "Wilfred of Ivanhoe on that day rendered back but in slight measure your unceasing charity towards him in his wounds and misfortunes. Speak, is there aught remains in which he or I can serve thee?"

"Nothing," said Rebecca calmly, "unless you will transmit to him my grateful farewell."

"You leave England then?" said Rowena, scarce recovering the surprise of this extraordinary visit.

"I leave it, lady, ere this moon again changes. My father hath a brother high in favour with Mohammed Boabdil, King of Grenada–thither we go, secure of peace and protection, for the payment of such ransom as the Moslem exact from our people."

"And are you not then as well protected in England?" said Rowena. "My husband has favour with the King–the King himself is just and generous."

"Lady," said Rebecca, "I doubt it not; but the people of England are a fierce race, quarrelling ever with their neighbours or among themselves, and ready to plunge the sword into the bowels of each other. Such is no safe abode for the children of my people. Ephraim is an heartless dove–Issachar an over-laboured drudge, which stoops between two burdens. Not in a land of war and blood, surrounded by hostile neighbours, and distracted by internal factions, can Israel hope to rest during her wanderings."

"But you, maiden," said Rowena–"you surely can have nothing to fear. She who nursed the sick-bed of Ivanhoe," she continued, rising with enthusiasm–"she can have nothing to fear in England, where Saxon and Norman will contend who shall most do her honour."

"Thy speech is fair, lady," said Rebecca, "and thy purpose fairer; but it may not be–there is a gulf betwixt us. Our breeding, our faith, alike forbid either to pass over it. Farewell! Yet, ere I go, indulge me one request. The bridal-veil hangs

over thy face; deign to raise it, and let me see the features
of which fame speaks so highly."

"They are scarce worthy of being looked upon," said Rowena;
"but, expecting the same from my visitant, I remove the
veil."

She took it off accordingly; and, partly from the concious-
ness of beauty, partly from bashfulness, she blushed so intense-
ly that cheek, brow, neck, and bosom were suffused with
crimson. Rebecca blushed also, but it was a momentary feeling,
and, mastered by higher emotions, passed slowly from her
features like the crimson cloud, which changes colour when
the sun sinks beneath the horizon.

"Lady," she said, "the countenance you have deigned to
show me will long dwell in my remembrance. There reigns
in it gentleness and goodness; and if a tinge of the world's
price or vanities may mix with an expression so lovely, how
should we chide that which is of earth for bearing some colour
of its original? Long, long will I remember your features, and
bless God that I leave my noble deliverer united with –"

She stopped short – her eyes filled with tears. She hastily
wiped them, and answered to the anxiou inquiries of Rowena
–"I am well, lady –well. But my heart swells when I think of
Torquilstone and the lists of Templestowe –Farewell! One, the
most trifling part of my duty, remains undischarged. Accept
this casket –startle not at its contents."

Rowena opened the small silver-chased casket, and perceived
a carcanet, or necklace, with ear-jewels, of diamonds, which
were obviously of immense value.

"It is impossible," she said, tendering back the casket. "I
dare not accept a gift of such consequence."

"Yet keep it, lady," returned Rebecca. "You have power,
rank, command, influence; we have wealth, the source both
of our strength and weakness; the value of these toys, ten
times multiplied, would not influence half so much as your

slightest wish. To you, therefore, the gift is of little value,—and to me, what I part with is of much less. Let me not think you deem so wretchedly ill of my nation as your commons believe. Think ye that I prize these sparkling fragments of stone above my liberty? or that my father values them in comparison to the honour of his only child? Accept them lady—to me they are valueless. I will never wear jewels more."

"You are then unhappy?" said Rowena, struck with the manner in which Rebecca uttered the last words. "Oh, remain with us—the counsel of holy men will wean you from your erring law, and I will be a sister to you."

"No, lady," answered Rebecca, the same calm melancholy reigning in her soft voice and beautiful features—"that may not be. I may not change the faith of my fathers, like a garment unsuited to the climate in which I seek to dwell; and unhappy, lady, I will not be. He to whom I dedicate my future life will be my comforter, if I do His will."

"Have you then convents, to one of which you mean to retire?" asked Rowena.

"No, lady," said the Jewess; "but among our people, since the time of Abraham downwards, have been women who have devoted their thoughts to Heaven, and their actions to works of kindness to men, tending the sick, feeding the hungry, and relieving the distressed. Among these will Rebecca be numbered. Say this to thy lord, should he chance to inquire after the fate of her whose life he saved."

There was an involuntary tremor on Rebecca's voice, and a tenderness of accent, which perhaps betrayed more than she would willingly have expressed. She hastened to bid Rowena adieu.

"Farewell!" she said. "May He who made both Jew and Christian shower down on you His choicest blessings! The bark that wafts us hence will be under weigh ere we can reach the port."

She glided from the apartment, leaving Rowena surprised as if a vision had passed before her. The fair Saxon related the singular conference to her husband, on whose mind it made a deep impression. He lived long and happily with Rowena, for they were attached to each other by the bonds of early affection, and they loved each other the more from the recollection of the obstacles which had impeded their union. Yet it would be inquiring too curiously to ask, whether the recollection of Rebecca's beauty and magnanimity did not recur to his mind more frequently than the fair descendant of Alfred might altogether have approved.

Ivanhoe distinguished himself in the service of Richard, and was graced with further marks of the royal favour. He might have risen still higher, but for the premature death of the heroic Coeur-de-Lion, before the Castle of Chaluz, near Limoges. With the life of a generous but rash and romantic monarch, perished all the projects which his ambition and his generosity had formed; to whom may be applied, with a slight alteration, the lines composed by Dr. Johnson for Charles of Sweden, –

> His fate was destined to a foreign strand,
> A petty fortress, and an "humble" hand;
> He left the name at which the world grew pale,
> To point a moral, or adorn a TALE.

THE END

OTHER TITLES IN THIS SERIES

Printed in Hungary